The CEO

The Game Changers Series
Book One

Shealy James

The CEO

Limitless Publishing, LLC
Kailua, HI 96734
www.limitlesspublishing.com

Formatting: Limitless Publishing

ISBN-13: 978-1-68058-253-6
ISBN-10: 1-68058-253-4

Dedication

To Sarah:

I hope you get everything you ever wanted, because anyone with a heart as kind as yours deserves a game changer of her own. Love, laughter, sunshine, rainbows, and butterflies, my friend.

Prologue

"Eve!" His voice boomed through the house as if he were the Great and Powerful Oz. "Eve. Where are you?" I could hear the anger oozing from him but felt nothing. No fear. No regret. No satisfaction. I was completely numb. Once upon a time, the yelling would have frightened me. I would have cowered in response to the threat in his tone. But now, there was nothing.

His stomping up the stairs preceded the bedroom door flying open. My husband found me there in our bedroom, packing my suitcase with clothes that had recently become too loose on my once pudgy body.

"What in the hell do you think you're doing?"

I didn't bother answering him. It was clear what I was doing. Besides, interacting with him would only make this worse. I didn't even have to look up to know his shirt was wrinkled, his hair was a mess, and his blue eyes were clearer because his cheeks were flushed from the amount of alcohol he consumed. This was all too familiar to me now.

"What the fuck is this?" I still didn't turn, but I did wonder what he was referring to this time. It could have been anything.

"Eve, what the fuck is this?" He moved around the room as he spoke, and now I could see he was waving a stack of papers around. Ah, the papers were delivered.

"You think you're divorcing me? You will lose everything if you divorce me. I will find the best lawyer in town, and he will bury your family's senile attorney in seconds. I hope you don't think you're getting the house, Eve. I built this place. It's mine. You want to leave? Fine. You're a stupid bitch, anyway. I found girls ten times better than you, and none of them just lie there like you do."

He thought he was insulting me, but I had heard it all before. I didn't really even register his words, because I was numb to his voice now. Instead of responding, I zipped up my suitcase and dropped it to the floor. I could get the rest later, or not. Who cared?

Two steps from the door, he grabbed me from behind and pulled me against his much larger body. His arms wrapped tightly around my waist, and still I felt nothing. "Evie, don't go." He only called me Evie when he was trying to be sweet these days. He called me the nickname my family had given me as long as I had known him, but for the past couple of years, it had just been Eve, harsh and to the point.

"I love you. I know things are bad, but we can fix it. We can go to counseling. I could talk to you if we went to see a counselor."

I still didn't acknowledge him, didn't move,

didn't flinch.

"Please, Evie," he begged, then placed a gentle kiss on my neck. "Please."

When he realized I still wasn't responding, he let me go and began his rant over again. "Fuck off, Eve. Good luck in court. You're going to waste thousands of dollars to get rid of me? I'm going to make your life hell."

I almost laughed.

Too late.

Chapter 1

"You can do this," I told myself in the mirror. This morning my brown eyes appeared big and bright, and I complimented myself on my makeup application, light and natural with the exception of my red lips. Somehow, putting on my red lips made me feel complete, and I needed that extra something since I realized just how much I had stopped caring about my looks before. Now I cared and dressed to impress. My grandmother used to always tell me that when she felt down, she only followed one piece of advice—Elizabeth Taylor said to pour a drink, put on some lipstick, and pull it together. My grandmother probably wanted an excuse to drink. I was only going for the lipstick at eight in the morning. To each her own, I guess.

Dressed in my black pencil skirt, a green silk blouse, and my favorite Mary Jane heels, I was ready for my first day on the job. I didn't know why I thought I could do this event-planning job when I didn't even plan my own wedding, but there I was. It was a far cry from teaching middle school, which may have been the sole reason I accepted it. My purpose for being there was to change everything about my life, and the job and location were the first step.

I drove the twelve minutes to work because I didn't want to be lost, sweaty, or late on my first day. It was a warm and sunny day, reminiscent of a pleasant spring day in the south. I had been sure to find an apartment close enough if I ever wanted to walk to work, but I knew that Seattle weather was unpredictable. I could walk to work in a half-hour or so as long as it wasn't raining, but clear days are supposedly few and far between. I would find out soon enough.

When I parked and checked my makeup and hair one final time, I found I was still fifteen minutes early for my first day. Being early was the only thing that kept my nerves in check. Starting over wasn't easy. Last year I was trying to poke my head above water, now I was alone in a new city on the opposite side of the country, still trying to finalize my divorce. Divorced. Not single, divorced. Divorced! Well…almost divorced. Separated was really no better. It was the month before I went back to school last year that I filed for divorce. Now, a mere ten months later, I was finally getting my life back together—as together as I could, anyway, when one's husband was chronically making life as difficult as possible. I was getting away from the darkness and hopefully moving toward some light. Step one was to remove myself from the situation.

I took in my surroundings as I climbed out of my car. The parking deck was nothing impressive, but I did note I was on the second floor so I could find my car easily later. As I navigated my path to the building at the small private college housing my new office or cubicle or desk, I smiled at the manicured lawn, complete with modern benches and a fountain. The trees were immaculately trimmed, and not a single piece of trash or cigarette butt littered the ground. It was picture-perfect.

My sorority sister Tara was always such a great friend that when she heard about my divorce, she helped me by offering me a job with her. She coordinated the special events at Mitchell College, a small private institution in downtown Seattle. When her Event Manager decided to stay home to raise her baby that was due any day, Tara had an opening at the right time for me to uproot my life. Her loss was my gain, I hoped.

I entered the stone grey building that resembled a church more than an office building and made my way through the lobby up to the second floor. There was no one at the front desk, so I waited in the lobby. When no one showed up ten minutes later, I started to wonder if I was in the right place. My fingernails were just about to enter my mouth for a good chewing when the elevator dinged. Out stepped Tara in a floral dress and her trademark platform high heels. She looked exactly the same, maybe a few years older like me, but this was the same girl I graduated college with eight years ago. She was petite and curvy, but with the help of her shoes, her five-foot-one inch height became a consistent five-foot-five inches. Her small size didn't detract from her beauty. She had long brown hair with golden highlights and big, bright eyes that drove guys crazy in college.

"Eve! It's so good to see you." Tara dropped her bag and files on the reception desk and opened her arms for a hug, which I willingly returned. "I'm so glad you're finally here. Sorry about the lack of reception. Our student worker has class in the morning, so she doesn't come in until ten on Mondays."

"It's fine. I'm happy to be here. You look great."

"Thanks, hun. I quit drinking so much beer. I would look like I was a hundred if I had kept that up." She laughed cheerfully. "You aren't so bad yourself. I expected you to be starving yourself and crying your eyes out, but not our Eve. Same ol' hot tamale!" I smiled, despite how close she was to speaking the truth. Fortunately, I had moved past that stage months ago with the help of my family.

"I passed the wanting to jump off a bridge stage the day I filed for divorced. I couldn't be happier now." It was an almost truth. I would be happier if I was actually divorced. I would be happier if I had never married such an asshole, but that wasn't what your friend wanted to hear after helping you find a job, so the almost truth was better than the truth in this case.

"Well, I'm so excited to have you here. You'll love this job. It's just the two of us working full-time, so it can be a lot of work, but I've met so many great people. Seattle will feel like home in no time." She picked up everything she had set down on the reception desk and nodded her head toward a set of double doors. "Follow me. I'll show you the digs."

She led me down a hallway decorated with generic paintings with three doors on either side. "This office area was originally for administration, but they grew out of it, so here we are." We then peeked in the second door on the left. It was a simple office with a desk and two chairs in front of it. Behind the desk was a large window that overlooked the grassy quad of the small urban campus. On the desk sat a relatively new desktop computer and a black phone. I wrinkled my nose. Technology and I were permanently at odds with each other.

Tara waved her free hand around before stepping back in the hallway. "This will be your office, but follow me back to mine for a few. I want to catch up now that I have you here."

I followed her to the end of the hall into her larger corner office. Her office was at least double the size of mine, which made sense since she was the director. A small conference table was in the corner by the window, with three chairs, and piles of boxes covering the table. She nodded toward the table. "That'll be one of our first assignments once you get settled. They are invitations to the anniversary party next month." I nodded. I can do invitations. No problem.

She sat behind her desk and gestured for me to sit in one of the chairs on the other side of it. "So, did you get moved into your new apartment? I hope you found something good. This city has some doozies."

"Yes, I found one in Capitol Hill like you

suggested. My mom drove out here with me and helped me get everything in and decorated. You know she had those curtains hung and the kitchen unpacked before I drove her to the airport."

"I bet Ellen wasn't thrilled with you moving out here. How many times did she try to get you to change your mind?"

"Once the U-Haul was packed, she gave it a rest. I don't think she wanted to have to help unpack it. She and Dad are being very understanding considering the situation. They surprisingly encouraged me to come out here once I told them I would be working with you. It was just the week before I left when my mom started coming up with alternatives to me moving across the country, but I'm not the one with four kids, so she'll be all right."

"Jane has four kids? Whew! Does she work?"

"Yeah. Her husband is a corporate lawyer, and she does something in finance, so they have enough money to send their kids to the best private pre-schools and elementary schools. She also has a nanny in the afternoons and my parents on the weekend. Enough about them. Tell me about you. I don't get on Facebook anymore, so I've had to keep up with everyone through the old-school gossip mill."

"After college, it was either find a job or move back to Birmingham and live with Mama and Daddy until I got married." She grimaced. Her parents were very traditional, and the Tara I knew was a wild party girl. I couldn't imagine her mama and daddy would like that. "I took the first job I found in my field, which happened to be all the way out here with these outdoorsy health nuts. The city has grown on me though, and I couldn't imagine being anywhere else unless it was sunny and seventy-five degrees every day."

"You're doing well for yourself. I can see why you like it. Now, tell me everything I need to know. This is a far cry from teaching, so I want to make sure I learn everything I can from you." I tried to appear enthusiastic, but I think my high-pitched excitement probably gave away how nervous I was about the job.

"Your job is a lot like when you were our rush chairwoman, which is exactly why you were the woman for the job. You have to secure vendors and schedule volunteers all within a budget, a big budget. You're going to keep our online calendar and do some advertising through email and social media. We primarily conduct events for the alumni, but we also handle building dedications, community outreach, lecture series, and stuff like that. Sabrina already handled our lecture series for the summer, which occurs every Wednesday evening at seven. You will need to attend with me, so I can show you what we do for the reception. Once you get the hang of it, I'll have you take over because I have other meetings on Wednesdays with the college administration."

"Sounds good. I can handle that, and I have already looked at the calendar and files you sent me regarding the upcoming events."

"Good. It sounds like you have an idea of what we are up to. Next Friday the alumni association is hosting a cocktail event at Bistro 79. You're coming as my plus one. We technically don't run the events, but our presence helps us get to know who we are serving and gives us contact with the key players. Our goal is to keep them happy so they keep donating to the university. You know the drill."

I typed what she was telling me into the calendar on my phone. "Sounds good to me."

She clapped excitedly. "Do we need to buy you a dress?"

"My mother made sure I packed every stitch of clothing I own. She wants to turn my bedroom into a craft room. She's into monogramming for the grandkids on her new embroidery machine." I grinned knowing she would be able to picture my mother, considering she spent every year at rush in our sorority house with me. Every girl in my pledge class was well acquainted with Mrs. Ellen Barton Bryant.

"Just checking. I didn't know if Mark ever took you anywhere where you would need a dress. He was such a classy guy." Like many of my friends, Mark did not rank high on her list of likable people. My friends just never thought he was good enough for me, and, at the time, I thought they were being sweet. I truly believed they would have thought that no matter who I dated, but now I realized that probably wasn't the case.

I laughed. "Other than friends' weddings, definitely not, but that doesn't mean Mom and Dad didn't. And do you know how many weddings I have been to in the past five years for high school friends? He insisted we go to every wedding for 'the free booze.' If I never see another sparkly white ball gown or hot pink bridesmaid's dress, I'll be a happy girl."

"You'd think our sorority sisters had you sick of weddings, but it was the high school friends who did you in, huh? Well, you don't have to worry about me. I already planned to elope. Mama and Daddy want me to get married in their Southern Baptist church that holds three thousand people, and they want to invite everyone they know to fill the balcony. No way in hell I'm doing that. I think my parents want to outdo William and Kate, southern style. Can you imagine?" She laughed at the outlandish thought while I realized I felt like I might have just found my way back into my own skin.

Chapter 2

My life in numbers:

12. *The number of days I have lived in Seattle.*
11. *The number of times my mother has called since she left Seattle.*
10. *The number of months Mark has refused to sign the divorce papers.*
9. *The number of days I have been completely on my own...ever.*
8. *The number of days I have worked at Mitchell College.*
7. *The number of times my best friend has asked if I met any "hot men."*
6. *The number of new people I have met and remembered their names.*
5. *The number of minutes it took me to put on my makeup this morning.*
4. *The number of days it has rained since I have been here.*
3. *The number of glasses of wine I had at dinner last night with Tara.*

2. The number of times I have worked out since living here.

1. The number of actual events I have attended as an "Event Manager."

I was pleased that it seemingly rained less in Seattle than it did in Georgia, despite the rumors, so I decided to brave the walk to work once I believed I finally understood the fickle weather. After pinning up my wild brown hair in a loose bun to keep it from going crazy on my walk over, I headed on my way. I would do almost anything to avoid getting behind the wheel of a car, and the twenty-five minute walk was nothing. I could have even stopped for coffee if I wanted.

It also was not my intention to bring my car to Seattle, but my dad was worried about me walking at night. My parents thought danger lurked beyond every corner. To be fair, I wasn't exactly known for paying attention to my surroundings. Even if I carried mace or some sort of weapon, it would probably take me more time to find it in my purse than it would for the killer to murder me. Note to self—be more responsible. I was an adult after all...well, sort of. Did anyone ever really feel like an adult?

As soon as I had settled in my office for the day, Tara marched in my door and sat in front of me. She looked a little disheveled this morning, which wasn't unusual for her. She was cool as a cucumber from about ten o'clock on, but before then all bets were off. "You okay?" I asked, trying not to laugh at her apparent frustration with mornings.

"I was doing fine until Sabrina called. Apparently she scheduled a dinner with a couple of corporate donors for tonight and forgot to put it on the calendar. She just put it on her calendar because she was going to go while I attended the lecture series. I'll be honest, though—I don't feel comfortable sending you to the dinner without you having met these people first. They can be difficult, and we can't risk losing their generous donations by being represented by someone who hasn't had the time to learn the ropes. The son of the Mitchells who founded the college will be at the dinner, and he and his wife can cause problems for us if we don't tread carefully."

"That's fine. I went to the lecture last week. I think I can handle hosting the event alone. Dr. Clarke will be there to introduce the speaker from his department, and I can handle the reception. I brought red velvet cupcakes," I told her proudly. My cupcakes were a thing of beauty. They were more of a winter treat, but since when were delicious cupcakes not welcome at a party?

She sagged with relief. "Oh good! I was afraid you were going to think I was bailing on you. Don't worry. Every lecture runs the same. There will be between thirty and fifty people there, but no one stays past nine. You can either come in late tomorrow or take off early on Friday, but remember we have that cocktail reception at Bistro 79 on Friday."

I smiled easily at her. She seemed so grateful I was doing my job I began to wonder how Sabrina used to handle things. "Sounds perfect. I'll see how it goes. Anything else I can help you with?"

"Nope. Just call those vendors and the volunteers for the Fun Run in September to confirm the date. We want to make sure no one backs out. Oh, and check the RSVP list for the anniversary party. I need to start making phone calls to make sure the important people received their invitations if their assistants haven't called yet."

"Sounds good." I immediately turned to my computer to pull up the list of vendors she had sent me earlier in the week.

Before she left my office, she turned back to me. "You know, I could kiss that stupid Mark Stevens for letting you go. You have been the best thing to happen to me since low calorie margaritas."

I laughed and then gave her a pointed look. "I thought Ryan was the best thing to happen to you."

"He was until he tried to give me a key to his place." She wrinkled her face, clearly expressing her distaste. "I don't want or need that kind of relationship. I thought we were just casually dating. He thought we were moving on to the next level. Stupid man." She rolled her big brown eyes.

"So, did you break it off?"

"No. I just told him I needed space. I'm hoping I meet someone new on Friday who would be into a monogamous, casual relationship that's going nowhere. I mean, is that really too much to ask?"

I wasn't considering dating again, but maybe I could try what she did. Meet new guys and see if someone caught my attention. No commitments of any kind. It would have to be exactly what Tara described though, casual and monogamous. I was a lady after all. "I think it sounds perfect."

"Too bad, girl. You aren't my type." She winked at me as she walked out.

"You're too crazy for me anyway!" I yelled after her.

Time passed quickly, and before I knew it the clock said five. I ran into Tara's office and told her I was headed home to get my car and change. I was sticky from rushing home in the heat of a Seattle summer, which was really nothing compared to the Deep South, but I still wanted a shower before I threw on a different outfit.

After drying my hair and curling it into soft curls, I threw on fitted black pants with a loose black blouse and black pumps. I figured I needed to be comfortable since I would be cleaning up after the reception. With a quick swipe of red lipstick, I was out the door.

I arrived at the lecture at six fifteen and started setting up. When Dr. Clarke arrived a half hour later, a few of the guests were already seated. I had met Dr. Clarke at the lecture the week prior, so he came over and spoke to me briefly before he moved on to greet other faculty members and guests. I tried to be friendly to guests who came over to get a beverage or had questions about the lecture, but for the most part I tried to remain out of the way, seeing as I was just there to manage the event. I stood in the back of the lecture hall where I would take my seat as soon as Dr. Clarke took the stage, but I kept getting the feeling I was being watched. When I glanced around the room where professors, students, and community guests stood around talking, I saw no one looking my way.

Waving it off as paranoia from running my first event alone, I signaled to Dr. Clarke to begin. He took the stage, and I took my seat in the back row near the exits. As I tried to listen to Dr. Clarke while he listed the credentials of the guest speaker, a Mrs. Daphne Pearce, I felt my skin prickle with awareness again. This time my paranoia turned into discomfort. When I felt a presence behind me, a shiver trailed up my spine and every nerve in my body was on high alert.

I started to turn, but the man came around to the side and leaned down. "Is this seat taken?" he asked quietly. His deep voice was incredibly sexy, but it was the sight of him that left me unable to speak. I was forced to shake my head to answer his question, even though my ingrained southern etiquette dictated speaking when spoken to. It would've been easy to blame my inability to verbally respond on that same southern etiquette, because my upbringing also dictated it was rude to speak during a lecture or presentation—and rudeness was intolerable—but that wasn't the case. What made me unable to function, let alone form words, was the stunning man who was now sitting next to me, smelling delightfully sinful. He was tall—really tall—and wearing a three-piece suit. I had never seen a man in a three-piece suit outside of a rented tuxedo at weddings, if those even count, but the difference the vest made was really unbelievable. This man was sexy with a capital S-E-X. If I could have formed a coherent sentence right then, I would have come up with a better word than sexy, but words just weren't happening.

I imagined reacting similarly if Henry Cavill sat next to me, and while he wasn't wearing a cape like Superman, he rivaled Clark Kent for his good looks, minus the awkward geek thing and the glasses. He would probably look hot in glasses, though. This guy would look hot in a paper bag. In fact, it might have been easier to get through the lecture if he had stuck a paper bag over his head. That face could distract the panties off a dead woman.

My heart was pounding against my ribs, and I found myself sitting up straighter and discreetly wiping my sweaty palms on my pants, then folding them primly in my lap. I was divorced, not dead for goodness' sake. Mother Teresa would have noticed how attractive this man was. I tried to avert my eyes while silently begging the good Lord not to let me embarrass myself, but through the corner of my eye I saw the man's impeccably combed brown hair and flawless profile. He sat casually with one ankle crossed over the other knee, so the knee of his top leg was close, too close, to my leg. I crossed my legs to the opposite side to gain some distance, because I was having a hard time not "accidently" touching him.

Mr. Sex-on-a-stick had a strong jaw with a straight nose—very manly. His cologne and long eyelashes, combined with his light eyes of some indiscernible color and his grin when he asked if the seat was taken would be enough to give a girl an orgasm. If I had ever had orgasms—which sadly I hadn't—I would have combusted. As it was, I could feel my body's reaction to him down there. I guess it was good that he just rendered me speechless. An unexpected orgasm on top of a sudden onset of mutism would have been rather humiliating. Damn Tara for leaving me here by myself.

Still making a conscious effort not to stare, I turned to face the front, trying to play off my shock and awe as interest in what the speaker was talking about. The lovely woman, whose name I had now forgotten even though I looked at it every day for the last eight days, was now speaking. She sounded like the teacher from Charlie Brown because the man next to me was flooding my senses. I glanced over at him again and noticed his hands rested lazily over his leg. No wedding ring, no tan line, and no indentation like the one that had misshapen my ring finger. I crossed my arms over my stomach to keep my hands out of sight, more for me than him. There are just some things you don't want to think about while you are imagining ripping the clothes off the man sitting next to you.

For the next forty-minutes I sat stick-straight in that chair, with my legs and arms crossed and heart racing, breathing in the gorgeous man's air. I missed the entire lecture, and it wasn't until he stood to leave our aisle that I realized the lecture was over.

"Where are Tara and Sabrina?" he asked. His deep voice spoke clearly and almost caressed the words as they escaped his mouth. That could have been my imagination running away with my libido, though.

Mentally shaking off the reaction my body was having to the man, I managed to tell him Tara was at a dinner with the corporate donors, and Sabrina had decided to be a stay-at-home mom. Then I introduced myself. "I'm Eve, Sabrina's replacement," I said and held out my trembling, yes trembling—how embarrassing—hand to him. He looked at my hand, then back at my face without ever removing his hands from his pockets. With a naughty grin, he nodded and turned down the aisle to speak to the other guests. Strange man. Strange, sexy man.

I realized my hand was still outstretched, so I immediately pulled it back and headed to the lobby where a dessert reception was to be served. Mentally kicking my ass for behaving like a giddy schoolgirl, I checked that everything was set up properly for the guests, then opened the doors so guests could flow in and out of the rooms.

Guests drank wine or coffee and ate everything from cannoli to baklava to my homemade red velvet cupcakes. They were standing around the high-top tables in groups, chatting pleasantly. I smiled at the fact that my first event went off without a hitch. Granted, it was a weekly event that practically ran itself, but either way it was a success.

Laughter filled the lobby and echoed in the small but open space. I scanned the room to watch as guests were starting to leave when I caught sight of the sexy stranger. He was passing a glass of wine to the woman who had been the guest lecturer. She took the glass and gave him a grateful look. In return he wrapped an arm around her shoulder and pulled her closer to him, catching my gaze when he did. I quickly turned and busied myself with cleaning up the empty plates and glasses. I knew the lecturer was a "Mrs.," so the sexy man must be her husband. Lucky her. I bet she had orgasms. I almost gasped at my wayward thoughts. Mind out of the gutter, Eve!

My mind went back to his bare fingers. Well, one finger in particular. Some men chose not to wear a wedding band. If I married a man like that, I would insist upon it, even though I had never been a jealous person before. I would even consider handcuffing myself to that gorgeous man, so everyone would know he was mine. It was a good thing I was never getting married again. It was those kinds of crazy ideas that ended up causing women to snap.

Dr. Clarke came over to me as I was cleaning up empty dessert trays. He was a kind, older man who looked like a stereotypical college professor. His navy blazer had seen better days, but he probably only wore it when he did events like this. He placed his hand on my shoulder to get my attention. "Thank you, Eve. You did a nice job tonight. Tara should leave you in charge more often. That red velvet you brought was delicious."

I smiled at his compliment of my cakes. "Thank you, Dr. Clarke. Have a good evening."

"Do you need any help cleaning up?" he asked as he picked up his brief case and pulled out his umbrella, obviously ready to leave.

"No, sir. You go on home. Tara is letting me come in late tomorrow, so I'll make sure to take care of all this." He smiled and nodded before he slid his little old man hat on his balding head and headed out the door.

The last few people left shortly after him, leaving me alone in the lobby to clean up what remained of the reception. As I boxed up the last of the cannoli, I heard the lobby door slam shut. I jumped when it startled me and looked up, thinking I would see Tara at the door coming to check on me. Never did I expect the sexy stranger standing at the door, with that naughty grin on his face and his hands comfortably in his pockets as he watched me from across the room. The tingling in my spine was back, and my hands were back to sweating. What was with this man?

"You alone here?" he asked nonchalantly, his deep voice stirring something inside of me. Ignoring my visceral reaction, I focused on the question. My brain immediately went haywire and wondered why the sexy man would corner me alone in the lobby. Great. Less than two weeks into my new job, and I am going to get murdered. Murdered! To make things worse, I wanted to bed the man who was going to murder me. What the hell?

I started taking inventory of my surroundings. In my purse I had my cell phone and my keys. I could get out my cell phone and call 9-1-1, but I would either be dead or kidnapped by the time they showed up. My car was too far away to set off the alarm. I could try and stab him in the eye with the corkscrew I had just put in the wine box, but then what? Run? I couldn't run fast in these shoes. Maybe I should go ahead and take them off just in case, but if I kicked him I would have a better chance of inflicting pain with my shoes on. Okay, shoes stay on.

"Eve?" His deep voice saying my name weakened my knees. He wasn't coming any closer. Why was he biding his time? He looked like a lion waiting to pounce. Didn't anyone tell him not to play with his food?

At least he would have been in the guest book. Someone here knew him. His wife. Surely she wouldn't cover for him since he didn't go home with her. Wouldn't she be wondering where he was? I was suddenly hoping she would come looking for him.

My mom and dad were going to be so upset if I wound up murdered. First, I failed at marriage, and then I failed at surviving. I could see my tombstone now. Evelyn Elaine Bryant, Failure at Life.

"You okay?" His deep voice pulled me out of my morbid thoughts, because he was now standing right in front of me. "You look pale."

I blinked rapidly. "If you're gonna murder me, could you hurry it up?" I blurted out. Shame! That is what I felt in that moment. I wasn't even a good victim. I didn't try to get away. What was wrong with me?

He let out a surprised laugh. "You think I want to kill you?"

"Why else would you be here asking if I was alone?" I took a step back. Maybe he was giving me a chance to escape.

"I asked if you were alone, because, like you, I don't think it's safe for you to be here by yourself. I'm not going to hurt you." His confused expression transformed into a naughty grin. I glanced up to see his green eyes glittering. "I came back to walk you out and invite you to a late dinner."

There was no way I could eat around this man. I wasn't sure I could handle being alone with him. "I appreciate your concern, but I'm fine. Thank you." I tried to dismiss him. I really couldn't look at him anymore. He was male perfection. Strong jaw, check. Sexy grin, check. Broad shoulders and trim waist, check, check, check.

"See…" He started to move around the table with the grace of a panther. "I don't think you are fine. I think you need someone here to watch over you, just in case any actual murderers try to get you. Gorgeous girls like you need to be more careful in a city like Seattle." He looked right in my eyes as he assessed me mere inches from where I stood with my arms crossed protectively over my stomach.

I took a step back and turned to the table so he was at my side. "Thanks, but I'm good. No need to watch over me. You should go on home to your wife." I turned to grab my purse and the box of leftover desserts to take home for later. I had a feeling I was going to need something sugary after this evening, or maybe a bottle of wine or a bottle of Xanax. One or all of those should do the trick.

His brows furrowed. "My wife? I'm not married."

"Wow. I bet she really appreciates you saying that." I rolled my eyes at him and moved past him toward the doors.

He followed right behind me. "I'm not married. I'm not in a relationship at all if you would like to go ahead and get that conversation out of the way."

He grabbed my arm before I could push on the door. I stared at where his hand rested and could feel his touch throughout my whole body. Butterflies burst apart in my belly, and a deep need formed even lower. I wanted his hands on me…or at least my body wanted his hands on me. "What about you, Eve?"

I pulled loose of his grasp but remained standing in front of him. His smug grin and demeanor screamed sex, but his eyes, his hazel or green or bluish eyes, gave away the man beneath. "What about me?"

He leaned in closer, and I could smell his sinful cologne again. This time he spoke quietly while his eyes trapped mine in their gaze. "Is someone waiting for you to come home to them?" Technically yes, but it was wishful thinking seeing as I had been trying to divorce the asshole for ten months.

I shook my head because my mouth was suddenly very dry.

"Why don't you come join me for a drink?" he suggested.

I cleared my throat and stepped away. I desperately wanted his lips on mine when he was that close. Distance was necessary. This was not the man to start dating again. With how I was feeling right now, there was no way anything with him would have been casual. "I don't think so. I need to go. It was nice to meet you…um…" I realized I didn't even know his name. "Yeah. Have a good evening." I stepped out into the night and quickly walked to my car. I could feel his eyes on me, but I kept walking without turning back. It was drizzling out, but I didn't bother with my cute red umbrella. I just wanted to get to my car. It was in the safety of my familiar little car that I finally felt like I could breathe again.

Chapter 3

I slept in the day after the lecture because I hadn't fallen asleep until the wee hours of the morning. The sexy stranger's face and words kept playing through my mind. I called my best friend, Holly, when I woke up in the morning. It had been way too late to call when I arrived home last night, and I needed the kind of pep talk that only an old friend could provide. I had never been more irritated with the time difference between Seattle and Georgia than I had been last night. She was my person who always made me feel better, and had I talked to her last night, I probably would have slept instead of obsessively replaying the evening's events over and over in my head.

I didn't even get his name, but I knew I couldn't let this go in hopes of never seeing him again. Considering I saw him at a work event, there was a really good chance I would see him again very soon. Realizing this could create an awkward situation at work, I agreed with Holly that I needed to tell Tara all about it over lunch to see what she thought.

Unsurprisingly, Tara ate it up like my discomfort was the best gossip she had heard in years. When I finished telling the whole story, she was in hysterics. I mean laughing so hard tears were running down her face and people were staring at us.

"I'm so glad my distress makes you so happy," I grumbled.

"Oh, it isn't that. You have never been good at handling uncomfortable situations. I can only imagine what you were thinking. I hope this guy turns up tomorrow night. If he's as hot as you described, I might give him a whirl on the Tara Tanner train."

"Please don't. Then I'd have to face him over and over, and I think I've been humiliated enough for one lifetime." I took a sip of my lemon water. "Let's move on. How was your dinner?"

She shrugged and placed her fork and knife on her plate in a 'Q', indicating she was finished, before primly wiping her mouth with her napkin. Tara's manners were impeccable. "It was dinner with a bunch of pompous assholes who we have to wine and dine because they donate a fuck ton of money to the university, ensuring our elite status among the private schools." Well, her table manners were impeccable. She still cursed like a sailor.

"Mr. Mitchell, the son of the founders, was there. He's a generally nice guy, but I heard he's a shark when it comes to business. The president of the college was interested in the events we're holding for recruitment during campus visits. He suggested we up the ante, so to speak."

"What does that mean?" I knew the college primarily recruited from wealthy private schools across the country, but the small number of students was more of a reflection of the high expectations of the students than the number of applications.

"It means we need to show parents the responsible side and show the students the fun side. We need to come up with a way to give both the applicants and their parents what they want. Campus tours start in September, so start thinking of some ideas."

"I'm on it." We paid the waiter and walked back to the office while bouncing ideas off each other.

I continued to brainstorm and researched other college recruitment activities for the rest of the day Thursday before heading to the gym to burn a few calories. I always came up with my best ideas when I lost myself in a run.

It happened to be sunny when I left the office, so I hurried home to change then headed over to Volunteer Park. I decided to wander around the park and see what I could before the sun went down. As I ran past the tennis courts, I heard my name called out. I kept my pace assuming I was mistaken since I only knew one person in Seattle and had my ear buds in, blocking the noise around me. However, when a man ran up next to me and tugged my ear bud out of my ear—scaring the shit out of me—I realized someone was indeed calling my name.

I couldn't tell you if it was a nice surprise or not, because my body was too busy trying to recover from the fright of having someone approach me like that. To make things more interesting, it was the sexy stranger who delivered the scare. He was a little sweaty and in workout clothes that showed off his lean muscles, but he still looked and smelled amazing. I, on the other hand, probably stunk and looked like a hot mess. Typical.

"Jesus! You scared me," I snapped as my other ear bud fell from my ear.

"Come here often?" he said with a playful smirk as he crossed his arms over his large chest.

I wasn't even sure how to respond to him. "Uhh…no. I just moved here." His eyebrows lowered as his eyes unashamedly wandered the length of my body. Payback for all the times I stood speechless staring at him, I suppose. I met the man last night, and here he was today flirting with me in the park while I was covered with sweat. This was not my ideal way to see someone I may or may not have a slight crush on. Still, my body responded to him as if we were both standing there naked, daring the other to touch first.

After an agonizing moment of silent awkwardness, he spoke. "You shouldn't run alone with music in your ears. You never know who will try to murder you." That annoying grin spread across his face again.

"I'll take my chances," I told him dryly.

"How about you let me take you to dinner instead?"

"No thanks. I thought I made it clear I wasn't interested." That lie was getting really pathetic at this point. A girl didn't need an erection for her body to show when she was attracted to a man. My body was reacting so strongly that if this man didn't notice, he would have to be blind, deaf, and gay.

He stepped closer to me, his eyes focusing on mine before flicking down to my lips. The expression on his face made me involuntarily stick my tongue out to wet them. My breathing and heart rate picked up again at his proximity. I had to take a step back to gain control over my body, but he stopped me when his hand gently ran down my arm, leaving fire and chills in its wake.

"I think you're interested but won't allow yourself to say yes, Eve."

I composed myself and actually moved away this time. "Think what you want. I'm still not going to dinner with you tonight."

He was completely unfazed by my retreat. "Fine. How about tomorrow then?"

I needed to get away from this man before I let him ravage me right there on the grass of Volunteer Park in front of everybody and their mother. "Sorry. Busy. Look, I have to go." I knew he didn't have my number or know where I'd be the next day, so I just hoped there would be some time between then and the next sexy stranger sighting. I wasn't sure my libido could handle another sighting so soon.

It didn't seem like it would be that simple, though. As I started again on my path away from the man who was too good-looking for his own good, I heard him shout, "See you soon, Eve." The thought made me shiver even though I was pouring sweat from my run. That man was quickly taking over my brain.

That night, I dreamt of the stranger whose name I still didn't know. I was running and let him catch me. He lifted me from the ground and pressed his lips to mine. He walked over to a bright red blanket that rested in a field of green, green grass. He lay me down before settling on top of me. There, in the middle of the park lawn, the sexy stranger had his way with me. When I woke up, I was drenched in sweat and uncomfortably turned on. Fortunately, it was almost time to get up, so I went ahead and crawled into the shower. There was no way I was going back to sleep after that dream. I needed a distraction pronto.

Work was a distraction, but more than anything I was thinking about the cocktail party that evening. I was looking forward to it, because Tara had said it was mostly young professionals who lived and worked in Seattle. It would be nice to meet some new people who I would see often for parties like this.

At four o'clock, I was heading to Tara's office to tell her I was leaving for the day to get my nails done before the party, when my cell phone buzzed and stopped me in my tracks. My attorney was calling at his dinnertime, so I immediately crossed my fingers, hoping for the news that Mark had finally accepted the terms and was ready to sign the divorce papers.

I slid my finger across the screen to answer the call. "Martin. I hope you have good news for me," I said cheerfully. Positive thoughts. Only think positive thoughts.

"Hello there, Evie. I'm sorry to call on a Friday

afternoon like this, but I just finished going through the revisions that Mark's lawyer sent over. There are a few things I want to discuss with you."

"This doesn't sound good, Martin. What does he want now?" I had already given him the house and all the furniture, his truck that had been in my name, and our dog. What more could he want?

"Well, he doesn't want to give you the inheritance back. He said the thirty thousand you invested in the house is part of the house, and since you were willing to concede on the property, he doesn't want to give you the money."

"The house is worth well over two-hundred grand. Why isn't he selling it to pay off the debt he owes to the credit card companies?" I was thinking out loud and meant to say that more to myself, but keeping my thoughts to myself had never been my strong suit.

Martin knew the answer though. "He's a little over sixty-thousand dollars in debt between the car and the credit cards. One would hope he plans to use the money for that."

"This is so frustrating, Martin. This should have been finalized months ago. He's only doing this to drag it out further. He keeps finding something new to delay this as soon as I give in to something else. What do I do? Do I give up my grandmother's inheritance, which was supposed to be part of my nest egg, because he can't manage money?"

I heard Martin sigh. "Evie, I have known you and your family a long time, and I hate to see you give up anything else to him. Typically we divide assets in half in divorce proceedings, and you have given him much more than half. Let me see what negotiations I can do for you. Are you sure you want to stay out of court? I know it's expensive, and you'd have to fly home and face him, but we could get you half of what the house is worth at the very least."

"No, Martin. I appreciate it, but taking it to court could take months, and I'm really ready to move on with my life. See what you can do for me and keep me posted."

"Will do. How's Seattle? Rain much?" He chuckled. The rain was all he would talk about when I told him I was moving here.

"Everything's great here. I love my job and my apartment. How's Fran?"

"She's doing well. She's been teaching the grandkids to bake, so I came home to blue icing all over the fridge yesterday and no dinner on the stove. That was fine by me. We had to go to the Outback for a steak."

"It sounds like she's enjoying her summer then. Tell her I said hello. I have to head on now. Call me if you find out anything else."

"Sure thing, darlin'. Have a great weekend."

After I hung up with him, I sagged into my chair. Why couldn't Mark just move on? He had no problem finding a new girl, but he couldn't let go of the money? I didn't understand. Like usual he wanted to make everything as difficult as possible. He probably said to his lawyer, "How can I make this more miserable for her? What else can I do to make her as miserable as I am?"

It occurred to me that if I had just agreed to go to

court months ago, I might already be divorced. I also thought about the fact that I could have manned up and asked him to sign the papers myself. Maybe if he actually had to face me once, he might have finally given in to the divorce. It was doubtful considering Mark hadn't been sober a single day in the last three years. Rational thinking was a thing of the past with him, but at this point the what-ifs were killing me. I desperately wanted to be divorced, but I wanted—no, needed to do this without having to ever see my husband again. If anyone could break my resolve to move on, it was Mark. He had done it so many times before. He would beg and plead, which never worked. Then something would happen that would remind me of our high school days. It would give me hope we could get back to that happy place. After the millionth disappointment, you'd think I'd be immune to his manipulations, but no. He knew every weak spot I had.

"You all right?" Tara's voice came through my doorway and snapped me out of my reverie. She was leaning against the door with her arms crossed.

"Yeah. I just talked to my attorney. Mark wants every penny we ever had even if it didn't belong to him. Pretty soon he's going to tell me he wants my kidney and a piece of my liver before he'll sign the damn papers." I slammed my pen down on the desk then slumped back in my chair.

"That jackass. He didn't even have a job for part of the time you were married. What right does he have to claim all of your assets? Take him to court, Eve!" Tara was being a good friend. Just the mention of Mark rubbed her the wrong way because she was protective of me. She was like this with all of our friends when the topic of ex-boyfriends came up. It was easy for her to write off people who had broken her trust. I, on the other hand, was stuck with remembering all of the good times and caring about people I wished were out of my life. Damn compassion.

"I knew that if I ever wanted out, I would have to forfeit some things. I just didn't realize he would drag it out for this long to make his point."

She came in and sat in the chair I had come to think of as hers since she was the only one who ever sat in it. "Why aren't you getting angry? I want to ring his neck, and I think I only met him once or twice."

"I don't know. I guess it has always been easier to give in than get angry. It's easier to not deal with it."

"That divorce and your inheritance must not be very important to you. I know you, Eve. I may not have spent the last eight years living in a dorm with you like before, but I know you. When you care about something, you don't stop until you get your way. You aren't fighting him. You need to get angry if you want him to sign the papers. Get forceful!" She stopped, and a slow smile spread across her face. "You know what you need?"

"What?" I asked, tuning out her rampage and taking a sip of water.

"An orgasm!"

I spit my water everywhere. "What?" I grabbed some napkins to clean up the mess. Tara continued to sit in her chair comfortably as if she were telling me how to knit a sweater. She completely ignored the fact that I had spit water all over my desk in surprise.

"Yeah. You need an orgasm. That'll help you get fired up. One good orgasm can motivate you to do a lot of things."

"That may be true, but I don't think it will help in this particular situation," I said dryly while trying to keep my cheeks from turning a bright shade of red.

"When is the last time you had one? Maybe it's been too long."

"Uhh…" There was no stopping the red staining my cheeks this time. "Well, it's been a while."

"How long?"

"A long time."

"Days? Weeks? Months? Years?"

"Never," I said as quietly as possible and cringed while I waited for her outburst that was sure to follow.

"No…I…no…I didn't hear that correctly. Did you say never?" Her high-pitched squeal at the end gave away her disbelief.

"Yes, okay. Never. Can we not talk about this at work?" Or ever.

"Oh. We are talking about this right now." She tapped her red fingernail on my desk to emphasize her point. "What about when you do it yourself?"

"Please stop," I begged.

"Well?"

"I can't believe I'm talking about this." She kept staring me down, so I gave in. "Nothing really happens when I do it myself. It seems to be going somewhere, then it's just gone, and I'm done. Not everyone can orgasm, you know. Only, like, a third of women do, or some statistic like that."

"No. I think it's about a third of women have trouble having one during sex. You're saying that you never have one. What was Mark doing down there?"

"We just got it done and moved on. He tried in the beginning, but nothing was happening, so he stopped trying."

"Are you saying that he essentially used your body to masturbate?" Her shock was palpable.

"Well, I wouldn't say that. Sometimes it felt good, but I just never had an ending…a moment."

"I'm so…I don't even know what to say. I…never? Holy shit! That's it! Tonight, we are getting you an orgasm."

"Uhh…Tara, I love you and all, but I don't want you anywhere near my downtown."

She threw a pen at me. "Not from me, you idiot. We're finding you a new man!"

"No, no, no. My divorce isn't final, and I'm not finding anyone new until I'm free from the last disastrous relationship." I didn't want her hooking me up. If I was going to date again, it would have to be on my terms.

"I didn't say you had to marry him. You're going to have sex. Good sex. I'll help you find someone who knows what they're doing."

"I don't want anyone. Please," I implored, knowing that it would go unheard. Her head was already elsewhere.

She looked at me with a serious expression. "One last thing, E, why won't you fight him? Are they really not important to you, or are you afraid of him?"

"I don't think it's either, Dr. Phil. I think I'm tired of fighting. I've been fighting for the last five years, and now my top priority is to get out. The only hang up is that I want my nest egg back."

She smiled and leaned forward to pat my hand. "Then fight. I'll help you in any way I can. I was just afraid that he…never mind. Ooh! We can have him followed and look for deviant behavior that will indicate he's using the money illegally. Oh! We can set him up with a woman who will want to marry him? If he wants to marry someone else, he'll hurry it along. Now, where can we find a stripper slut who will want to date a married man who is refusing to divorce his wife?" She tapped her finger against her chin as if she was really pondering this.

I laughed. "All right. All right. No James Bond tactics, and no hooking him up with strippers. It probably wouldn't help me anyway, and I don't want to be the one to hook him up with his next wife."

"Too bad," she shrugged then checked her watch. "It's almost five. You missed your nail appointment, you know?"

"Damn. I'll go tomorrow and just do a clear polish and closed-toe pumps tonight. No one will be looking at my hands anyway."

Chapter 4

By the time I was dressed in my coral lace cocktail dress and tan pumps, Tara was supposed to be arriving to pick me up any minute. I was still putting the final touches on my makeup when my cell buzzed with a text letting me know she was there. Feeling rushed only added to my anxiety about the night. If it hadn't been for my afternoon phone call and subsequent girl talk, I would have had plenty of time to get ready. That phone call was what started all of the stress that was now threatening to bubble over. Now the idea of being in a room full of strangers was making me feel a little nauseated.

Tara probably caught on to my nerves the second I climbed in her car, so it didn't surprise me that she talked non-stop on the way to the restaurant. It also didn't surprise me when she shoved a glass of white wine in my hand mere seconds after arriving there. Once we had our drinks, she led me around and introduced me like a mingling pro. As she introduced me to the alumni, she told me their names and something about each person that would help us start a conversation. Tara was a born socializer, which I was grateful for considering I didn't really have to say anything as long as she was around. That helped keep my nerves and the nausea under control.

The constant flow of wine wasn't hurting either. Waiters were everywhere, and it seemed that the second my glass was empty another was delivered. I hadn't eaten anything by the time the third glass was delivered, and I was starting to feel the effects. I knew I needed to slow down, but I was using the wine as a way of staying busy while standing around listening to Tara speak.

Finally, tapas were brought around, so I was able to snag a crab cake here and passed on some kind of egg roll there. There was a vegetable tempura one that I liked, and just as I was about to grab a shrimp something or other, I felt eyes on me. I felt the hair rise on my neck and arms, and an uneasy feeling erupted in my stomach. I did a quick glance around the room and witnessed only small groups of people talking and grabbing from the passing trays of wine and food. No one was looking my way, but the feeling remained.

"Right, Eve?" Tara elbowed me gently, bringing me back to her conversation as she stuck a crostini in her mouth.

"What's that? I'm sorry." I apologized for paying such little attention to the conversation even though I wasn't really sorry for tuning them out.

The man standing with Tara was probably in his mid-thirties and cute. He looked like he just stepped out of a J. Crew catalog. I think his name was Jake, but honestly, I had forgotten most people's names after wine glass number two. He brought me back into the conversation. "Tara mentioned that you like to sail, so I was telling her I was planning to take my boat out this weekend."

Please don't ask me to go. Sure, he seemed nice enough, but I was totally not in the mood to be hit on right then. "Oh, you'll have such a nice time. The weather should be nice for sailing this weekend. We used to go with some friends in Charleston and down in Gulf Shores. It was rarely windy enough to actually sail, but I always had a good time on the water." There. That sounds friendly but non-committal, right?

He smiled widely at me and stepped closer. Here it comes, I thought with a mental eye roll. Sure enough, he said, "You should join me tomorrow then. I could use an experienced sailor on board." I caught Tara smiling from just behind him, nodding her head.

Oh jeez. I didn't know what to say. Obviously Tara was hoping I would take advantage of this guy's offer, but all I could think about was what excuse I could use to get as far away from this conversation as possible. "Um…I can't tomorrow. I—"

"Eve." A deep voice cut in. I felt an arm snake around my waist and breathed in a scent that could only be…Yup. I followed the three-piece suit up to the face of the sexy stranger. "You ready to go?" Go? Go where? He looked over to Jake and held out his hand. "Grant Mitchell." Jake looked as confused as I was, and I swore Tara was going to tip over in her four-inch heels.

Jake held out his hand. "Jared Loughlin. Nice to meet you." Whoops. Jared, not Jake. Good thing I didn't try to introduce them. I apparently didn't know either one of their names.

Tara seemed to snap back to reality. She stepped forward and gave him a hug and a quick kiss on the cheek. "Grant! I didn't know you knew Eve."

"Yes." He didn't elaborate before turning to me. "You ready to go?"

"Wait," Tara said. Her eyes flicked back and forth between me and Grant, who still had his arm around me, making me unable to think. Ever heard of personal space, buddy? "Is this the guy from the lecture?"

His grip tightened on my hip. "You told her about me." I wanted to slap that smug grin off that handsome face of his, but the butterflies relentlessly beating their wings in my belly kept me from doing anything but glaring at Tara.

"Just that you were—"

I interrupted Tara. "We were discussing how unsafe it is for one of us to be in the building alone so late and that perhaps we should alert campus security to be in the general area during and after the reception."

"What else did Eve say about that evening, Tara?" he asked as he pulled me closer. I felt the heat of his body throughout mine. I had never felt this kind of physical attraction before. It was palpable, like my body was desperate for his touch, the touch of a stranger, a very sexy stranger.

She looked right at me with a question in her eyes. My wide eyes told her what she needed, and she wasn't about to throw me under the bus. "Nothing much. Did you say you were going somewhere?" Nice, Tara.

"Hmm…yes. Ready to go, Eve?" He turned me so I could look in his unusually colored eyes.

"Go?" I asked aloud this time.

"I'm taking you to dinner if you're finished networking. Tara has pretty much introduced you to everyone you need to know, and some you didn't." His eyes snapped to Jared who was now turned and speaking with another woman. "Right, Tara?"

She raised her eyebrow at him. Tara wasn't the kind of girl you bossed around, and I could see his assumption displeased her. I almost giggled when Tara clenched her jaw before she said, "Sure, Grant. You can have her. Let me just speak to Eve for a moment, and then she's all yours."

They stared at each other for a moment, silently communicating or intimidating each other, which was especially funny considering the top of Tara's head only reached his chest in her highest heels. "Fine." He agreed and looked back down at me. "Eve, I'll pull the car around. Meet me at the front door." He removed his hand from my waist and walked away. My waist tingled where he had touched me.

"Uhh…what was that?" Tara asked, fanning herself.

"I have no idea." I shrugged, trying to hide my stunned reaction. "I've seen him twice and never agreed to go anywhere with him." I glanced at the door before turning and grabbing another glass of wine. I wasn't going to be told what to do. I could be a strong woman. Only one man had the privilege to boss me around, and that was only because he took part in my conception. Besides, I wouldn't even know what kind of car to look for if I went out there.

It occurred to me then that I probably should have been more concerned about the way Grant squashed Jared, but I was grateful for the interruption to the conversation. I mean, who asks someone to sail out into the ocean alone with a stranger? That sounded like a murder plot if I had ever heard one. Good gravy! When did I become so worried about being murdered?

Tara grabbed my arm and squeezed. "You need to be careful with him. He hops from one socialite to the next before he leaves them and they obsessively stalk him. Holy shit! I had forgotten about him. His sister was the speaker that night. It all makes sense." Sister? Oh! "Look, Eve, while I agree that he can give you orgasms, probably hundreds of them, maybe you should start with a guppy before you snag the great white shark."

"One, I'm not testing your orgasm theory with anyone. Two, I'm not snagging anything. Quit worrying." I pulled my arm away and waved my hand flippantly before taking another sip of wine and mentally continuing my countdown. Three, no one that good-looking should be legal.

"You aren't going?" she asked surprised.

"No. I never said I would. He just assumed. He can take his sexy three-piece suit, good looks, and arrogance and go play in the big leagues where he belongs. I'm perfectly happy hanging out with you." Tara pressed her lips together like she was trying not to laugh. "What?"

"You think my suit is sexy?" The deep voice came from behind me before his chest pressed against my back. My eyes closed, wishing away the embarrassment. For the record, it didn't work. He chose then to lean closer to my ear and whisper. "Your dress is pretty fucking sexy if you ask me. It would look great on the floor of my penthouse." The hand that snaked its way to my hip had my body reacting in the most exciting and uncomfortable way.

"Shit. Really, Tara?" I swallowed the rest of my wine in one gulp and set my glass on the bar. "Excuse me. I'm going to the ladies," I announced without turning around.

I walked away and headed to the restroom. Once inside, I finally took a deep breath to get the shaking under control. I had never met someone as intense and forward as him. Ever. Southern men may be forward in other ways, but no one had ever pressed their erection into my back moments after telling me their name. That seemed just a tad bit too forward.

After powdering my nose and reapplying my colorless lip-gloss, I faced the fact that I couldn't hide in the restroom all night. In the hall, a pair of light eyes were waiting, watching the door. "I told you to meet me out front. The valet is holding my car."

"I'm not going anywhere with you."

"Why not?" He looked truly dumbfounded, and I almost laughed out loud. Had no one ever told this guy no before?

I covered the giggle by crossing my arms over my chest, giving him my best expression of annoyance. "Well, for one, you didn't ask me to go anywhere. For another thing, I don't even know you. What I do know doesn't impress me."

He pushed off the wall and stood right in front of me looking down into my eyes. He didn't touch me, but his proximity made me want him to wrap his arms around me. My body begged for his touch. Traitor. "I did ask. You said no. I'm trying a different tactic, because, let's be honest, you want to have dinner with me. You want to do all kinds of things with me, and something has impressed you. You like my suits, and you think I'm good-looking. You shiver when I touch you, and you squirm like you are trying to give your body what it desperately needs, but that need doesn't go away as long as my hands are on you, does it, Eve? You know my name is Grant Mitchell. With that I'm sure you can put together why I'm here and who my father and grandparents are." Oh! I didn't even make the connection. He was the grandson of the founders of the college.

Not ready to give in even though I could feel my resolve weakening the more I smelled his delicious cologne, I said, "Okay. And? Why does any of that mean I should get in your car?"

"You need to give this a shot."

"No, I need to go back out there and do my job," I replied less forcefully than I would have liked.

He stood back up to his full height. "Are you always this difficult?"

"No. I'm actually very agreeable when people aren't making decisions for me and telling me what to do, or telling my boss what I'm going to be doing."

"So, that's a yes. Look, I just want to take you to dinner. Well, that's not true." He placed his hands on my neck and slowly trailed them down my arms, forcing the hairs to all rise in response. He trailed his hands down to my rear and pulled me against his hard body and waiting erection. "I want to strip you down and kiss every inch of your beautiful body. Right now, I'm going to feed you because you've had four glasses of wine and hardly any food, and I would honestly like to get to know the girl who thinks people might murder her and refuses to give in to me." Apparently intense and forward turned me on.

I stood there speechless for a moment while I looked into his challenging and incredibly sexy eyes. He grabbed my hand and started walking toward the front door. Before I could stop myself, I let him guide me out of the restaurant.

Out on the sidewalk he shooed the valet away and held the door for me. I remained on the sidewalk. "Get in," he snapped.

I crossed my arms over my chest and tapped my foot.

He strode over to me like a predator. "What now?"

I snapped back. "Just ask me to get in the car and go to dinner with you. Don't tell me. Don't command me. Ask me and see what happens."

After a deep sigh, he gritted his teeth and said, "Eve, will you please get in the car and have dinner with me?"

As seriously as I could, I teased, "I already have plans tonight but maybe another time."

He growled and then picked me up and set me in his dark grey Range Rover. Growled! He buckled my seatbelt and said, "Stay put," before slamming the door. When he climbed in the car he looked positively irate. I giggled. "What?" he snapped.

"I was just teasing you. I was going to agree, but you just couldn't ask nicely, could you? You like to be in charge, huh?"

A sly grin spread across his face. "Baby, you have no idea."

Chapter 5

The car ride was quick and silent other than the sound of a Ray LaMontagne song playing in the background. Before I knew it, Grant was holding open the passenger door for me to climb out of the car. "Where are we?" I asked.

"My favorite restaurant," Grant said as he grabbed my hand and led me from the parking lot to the pizza place. "You can't find pizza like this anywhere else in the city. It's one of the things I miss about New York."

"You lived in New York?" I asked as he held the door and then led me to a booth covered in red plastic material. Grant did not fit in this restaurant. Here we were in a casual pizza place with me in a lace cocktail dress and him in his three-piece tailored suit. Ridiculous.

"Yeah. Right after college. What do you like on your pizza?" He signaled for the waiter, a young hippie guy with shaggy brown hair and a hat turned backward on his head.

"Umm…whatever is fine."

He ordered a deluxe pizza and two waters. When the waiter had walked away, I asked, "What made you move back here?"

"Promotion. I work for the company my grandfather started, so when it was time for me to take my seat on the board, it made more sense for me to live here."

"What is it that you do?" I really knew nothing about this man except for the fact that he was unbelievably sexy.

"A little of this, a little of that. My turn." He leaned forward, pressing his elbows onto the table. "Why'd you move here?"

Nothing says sexy like telling a new man about your divorce. "Tara is one of my sorority sisters, and she offered me a job."

"So, you up and move here from Georgia?" The way he asked the question made it sound like he didn't believe me.

"Yes. It was time for a change, and she offered me an opportunity. Wait…how did you know I was from Georgia?"

He grinned mischievously. "Your accent."

I narrowed my eyes at him. "My accent says southern. How did you know I was from Georgia?"

His smug grin didn't fade. He kept his hands clasped together, showing me just how relaxed he was. "Are you always this suspicious? I thought it was my turn to find out about you."

"Apparently you already know all about me, so what is there to talk about?" I leaned back and crossed my arms defiantly. That was likely the position I would be taking whenever I was around him, which wouldn't be often after tonight. He was really too overwhelming for me. He was too attractive, too intense, too arrogant, and too controlling. The combination was just too much.

He smirked. "I don't know much about you. All Sabrina knew was that you were moving here from Georgia."

"Ah." I didn't know what else to say. Either he had asked about me or Sabrina had shared information about me. It didn't bother me either way since it didn't seem too personal. What I did find strange was that he talked to Sabrina. Were they friends? Lovers? Perhaps he was her baby daddy? Ugh. I had to stop.

The pizza was delivered while I was still trying to come up with a response to his last statement. Grant expertly served a slice onto each plate. I picked off the peppers and onions carefully with a fork. As I picked off the last pepper and checked for hidden onions he said, "Is this what you meant by being agreeable? Why didn't you just tell me that you don't like onions or peppers on your pizza? Better yet, why didn't you just tell me what you usually order?"

I looked up at him and noticed that his slice of pizza sat untouched on his plate. He was watching me. "I said 'whatever is fine,' and this is fine. I don't mind picking it off. It's better than ordering separately. This is your favorite restaurant, so I don't mind sharing what you like. Besides, this has what I usually order on it." I smirked at him in response before taking a bite of my onion and pepper-free pizza.

Once the ice was broken, we did have an enjoyable conversation. "Tara mentioned that Daphne Pearce is your sister. I assumed she was your wife the other night."

"Yeah, I figured. She's my little sister. We work together and are really close. Daphne hasn't been lecturing the last year or so, so Wednesday was a big deal for her." He spoke fondly of his sister, and I found it was hard to reconcile the arrogant man with the loving big brother.

"That was nice of you to come support her. Have you always been close?"

"Pretty much. She's only a year younger, so when we were kids we hung out a lot. She's the brave but fragile sibling. I was the kind of kid that liked climbing the tallest trees and swinging on the rope into the lake, and my parents didn't mind that I did it. Daphne was another story. She and Grace were only allowed to wear dresses and weren't really allowed to play outside. Grace didn't care. She was into dolls and tea parties. Daphne wanted to hang out with me. She was constantly in trouble for getting mud on her dress shoes or whatever. One summer we were having a party at the house, and Daph and I snuck away to climb a tree in the neighbor's yard. We both climbed all the way to the top and hid there until my grandfather came looking for us. Daph ripped her dress on a limb on the way down. Both Grandpa Mitchell and I tried to cover for her, but my mom saw it the second we walked up to the house. She sent Daphne to her room and wouldn't let her come out the entire night. Grace and I wouldn't have cared if we were sent to our rooms, but Daphne was devastated and cried the whole night."

I pictured a little brown-haired boy and a knobby-kneed girl playing in the yard of a beautiful mansion on the lake. Imagining him as a young carefree boy warmed my heart. "Why didn't your mom just have her change her dress?"

He rolled his eyes, allowing me a glimpse of the young man behind the suit. "Our outfits were coordinated. We were always the picture-perfect family, so Daphne would have looked out of place in a different outfit. Everyone would have known she wasn't perfect," he added with mock offense.

I giggled at his tone. At first glance you would think he was just as pompous and arrogant as the rest of the upper elite, but from what he had just said, I wondered if maybe he felt a little out of place in those circles as well. "I always wanted a protective big brother. My sister and I weren't close growing up, but since she became a mom, she has mellowed out big time. We fight less, but I secretly think she's nicer to me now so I'll buy her kids awesome presents and not drum sets or something equally as obnoxious."

For the first time since I met Grant, he smiled a genuinely happy smile. It wasn't a grin or a smirk; it was a full blown all-American handsome man smile. It looked good on him. "I think you should still give her kids obnoxious toys. What's the point of being an aunt? I gave my nephews marshmallow shooters a few years ago. This year I'm considering pellet guns for Christmas, maybe a Red Rider BB gun."

I smiled back at him. "Now that's a great idea. My brother-in-law is one of the few anti-gun southerners. I think I'll save that if I ever need to get back at him for something."

It was becoming harder and harder to ignore my body's reaction to him as my heart continued to thaw. I was most definitely feeling more than lust toward him, but the last thing I needed to be doing right now was feeling anything about any man.

We continued to talk about our families, and it didn't escape my notice that neither of us was really talking about ourselves. I was avoiding the topic of my divorce, but I couldn't even guess what topics he was avoiding.

After we ate half of the giant pizza, he had the waiter box it up. When we were leaving, he carried the pizza over to a table with a lone man sitting at it. He was dirty and had two large duffle bags sitting with him. Grant set the pizza on the table with a bill tucked in the edge. "Here you go, Frank."

The man who had aged beyond his years looked up at Grant with bright blue eyes. "Oh! Hey there, Grant. Thank you! Deluxe?"

"Your favorite! Enjoy your night." After saying goodbye to the man, Grant grabbed my hand and led me back out to the car. He let me climb in and buckle my own seatbelt this time before he closed the door and walked around to the other side of the car. Once he was in the car I shifted so I could watch him. "That wasn't your favorite kind of pizza either, was it?"

He shrugged. "I like it just fine."

"Do you eat there often?" I asked.

He started the car and turned to avoid my eyes. "Every Friday." I took my seatbelt off and shifted closer to him. "What are you doing?"

In a bold move that was unlike me, I put my hands on either side of his face. "Either that was a stunt to impress me, which I guess I could take as a compliment, or that was a really nice and unexpected thing you did. It turns out you may have some qualities I like after all." I leaned forward and kissed his lips gently before pulling away. I didn't miss the feeling that spread throughout my body when our lips touched. I couldn't miss it. My body reacted to his when we weren't touching, but every time our skin made contact I felt it everywhere. When our lips touched for just that moment though…

He must have felt it too, because the next thing I knew his seatbelt was off and he was pulling me onto his lap, pressing his lips to mine again as he cradled the back of my head. He opened his mouth, and our tongues met in a passionate dance. It was like we couldn't get close enough to each other, like we were trying to climb inside of each other. We were all hands everywhere, and the kissing…oh, the kissing. It was divine. I wasn't sure how much time passed before we pulled away, both breathing heavily.

He ran his thumb across my lower lip. "From the second I saw these red lips, I wanted them on me. I never imagined it would be like that. Please tell me I can take you home with me tonight."

I felt my body tense and start to panic. I'm not ready for this. "Oh. I…um…I don't think that's a good idea." I climbed off his lap, and buckled my seatbelt again. This time I buckled it to keep me from climbing back on his lap rather than keep me safe in case of an accident. "I'm sorry, but could you just take me home? I live in Capitol Hill near I-5."

He reached over and grabbed my hand. "Hey. Look at me."

I took a deep breath before turning to him.

"What just happened?" he asked with worry written all over his face.

"Nothing. I just need to get home. Thank you for dinner." I tried to smile, but even I could feel how forced it was.

"Eve, I'll take you home, but I need you to tell me what is going on in that gorgeous head of yours. You knew I wanted to sleep with you, and you were here anyway, so what just happened?"

"It isn't that. I just shouldn't...can't. Sorry." I was starting to get emotional, and that was not all right with me. I needed to get out of there. Either he was going to start driving, or I was getting out of the car and finding another way home.

"I think you may be the most frustrating woman I have ever met." He started the car and started backing out.

Anger flared inside of me. Yes, anger was good. I wouldn't cry if I could stay angry. "Because I won't sleep with you? Wow." I crossed my arms and looked out the window.

He slammed on the brakes and looked at me. "While yes, I want nothing more than to have you every way I can possibly have you, I also want to get to know you. Five seconds ago I felt certain you wanted the same thing, but for whatever reason, you're dead set on making getting to know you as difficult as possible. I can't figure you out." He was on the brink of shouting at me, and I didn't like that the pleasantness of our dinner had evaporated because I wasn't ready for this.

"I'm married," I blurted out, and his head whipped around to face me. "Well, not really. I'm in the process of getting a divorce, and my ex is fighting me on it, so it isn't final. I know it's crazy, but this is all overwhelming. You're overwhelming."

"So, you're getting a divorce? That's why you moved here?" He started driving again. "Why didn't you just tell me?"

"Because it is none of your business quite frankly," I snapped.

He stopped at a red light and glared at me. "It is my business when something I want belongs to someone else."

"There are so many things wrong with what you just said that I don't know where to begin. I'm not a thing, and I don't belong to anyone. My divorce is most certainly not your business. I don't usually share my personal business with acquaintances or one-night stands or whatever this is." He pulled in front of my building. "How did you know where I live? Sabrina didn't know that."

"You're not an acquaintance or a one-night stand. I certainly wouldn't have bothered with dinner if I only wanted you for one night."

"Then give up. Go find someone else." The

moment I said it, I wished I hadn't. I didn't like the idea of Grant pursuing someone else after spending a little time with him. It made no sense considering we had been arguing most of the time we had been around each other, but I already had dangerously strong feelings for this man.

He ran his hands through his perfectly styled hair, causing it to stick out in all directions. "I don't want someone else! How can I be any clearer? I want you, Eve."

I felt very shy all of the sudden, and the question slipped out of my mouth unintentionally. "Why?" It came out as barely a whisper. My eyes remained trained on my hands, tightly gripping my clutch.

He let out a deep breath. "Why? Because you're beautiful and elegant. You didn't start mindlessly flirting with me the moment you saw me. Your confidence didn't waver until just now. You thought I was there to murder you, not seduce you, which I found charming. You frustrate the hell out of me because I've never met anyone like you. Tonight you made me laugh and made me want to get to know you, and then you kissed me." His eyes softened, and a gentle smile appeared when he touched his thumb to my bottom lip once more. "From the second your lips touched mine, I wanted to consume you."

I was flattered and embarrassed. I didn't think anyone had ever made me feel so appealing and special. His words were like getting exactly what you wanted on Christmas morning. Of course I had to ruin it with my awkwardness. "Jeez. You could have just said that you like me."

He growled again and climbed out of the car. I was beginning to like that growl. The passenger door swung open, and he held out his hand to me. Once out of the car, he pulled me close to him and held my face in his hands. "I like you. Is that better?"

I smiled up at him. "I think I like you too."

"You think?" He smirked.

"We'll see," I said, still smiling.

"Yes, we will. Soon."

What? "Soon?" I asked, knowing that was as much as he was going to tell me. He certainly wasn't going to ask if I had plans or ask me out. He was just going to take it upon himself to make it happen. While that may work well in the business world, I wasn't sure it was going to fly with me.

Oh, who was I kidding? Of course it would. Damn him again.

"Yes. I'll see you soon. Sweet dreams, you frustrating little vixen." He pressed his lips to mine before gently kissing each cheek.

"Good night, you crazy, crazy man," I said as I walked out of his arms and into my building.

That night, I hardly slept in anticipation for what the weekend would bring.

Chapter 6

The buzzing of my phone woke me up from a dreamless sleep. I grabbed the phone off my nightstand and didn't bother opening my eyes before answering. "Mom, did you forget the three hour time difference again?"

"No, my pleasant little peanut. It's eight in the morning where you are. I figured you would be awake. How are things? Your dad and I haven't heard from you since Tuesday."

I peeled my eyes open to find a dreary day outside my windows, perfect weather for sleeping. "Everything's fine. Martin called yesterday. Mark is trying to get more money. It looks like we may have to go to mediation or court if he won't give up. I had an event on Wednesday and last night. Both went well. How are things at home?" That was a reasonable mom-worthy summary of the week's events.

"Good. Your sister and John are bringing the kids by for a barbecue today. Suzanne at work was telling me that her daughter is going through fertility treatments, you know? Well, she's going ahead with IVF. Can you believe it? I told her everything you went through, not to mention insurance doesn't cover anything. Oh! Your dad bought a new blower at the Home Depot. He wears it like a backpack. It looks ridiculous." I could hear my dad yelling in the background, and then my mother said, "Yes, it does, Bill. Anyway, Evie, how's Tara? Is she going to come back for homecoming? We already received an invitation to brunch at the sorority house. Your sister and I plan to go shopping next weekend for pink and green dresses while your dad and John keep the kids."

My mother kept going on and on and on, and I gave her the obligatory, "Uh-huh," "Yeah," "Oh, good," and "Wow," when they seemed to fit in. I stayed in bed with my eyes closed the entire time she was talking until she said, "Oh, and did I tell you that Kathy saw Mark out with that Christina girl that you guys went to high school with? Kathy said she was in a trashy dress and drinking beer with Mark. They weren't acting like strangers either if you know what I mean." Of course I knew what she meant, but it made me wonder why he was fighting our divorce tooth and nail if he was dating. What I didn't wonder was why I didn't care that he was dating anyone. It didn't bother me at all, which made me think back to what Tara said about me fighting for things I cared about. Suddenly I realized Mark just wasn't important anymore.

"Are you listening to me, Evie?"

"Yes, you're making a lasagna in the crockpot for book club? That sounds delicious." Another half-hour later I was able to get off the phone with her. By then there was no going back to sleep, so I climbed out of bet and decided to go workout. After throwing on a pair of yoga pants and a hot-pink workout top, I took the elevator down to the building's gym. There was one other girl in the gym. She was probably in her early twenties and had perfect hair and a kickin' body. She was on the elliptical and not even breaking a sweat on her made-up face. I wanted to punch the pretty girl in the face to even the playing field.

Apparently I was a little grumpy. I didn't usually notice other people at the gym, and that morning I was mentally threatening bodily harm. In an effort to elevate my mood, I climbed on the treadmill and started running. I lost myself in the David Guetta mix on my iPod. Next thing I knew, an hour had passed, and my legs felt like jelly, one of my favorite post-workout feelings ever.

With my bad mood forgotten, I hummed quietly to myself as I stepped out into the lobby where I immediately stopped short. Grant was walking in the doors of the building as someone else was walking out. He was dressed in dark jeans and a plain white V-neck t-shirt and looked good—really good. When our eyes locked and his mouth lifted on one side in a sly grin, it occurred to me how disgusting I looked…again.

"What are you doing here?" I asked, not getting any closer. I was certain I didn't smell pleasant, and maybe if I stood far enough away he wouldn't notice my bright red cheeks and sweaty forehead. Standing in place I looked him up and down.

Needless to say, I noticed everything about him. Every muscle as it moved while he stepped closer, the shift of his eyes, his long fingers as they reached for me. I noticed it all. I also noticed a shift in my breathing, and my sudden desire for the man in front of me to be the man inside of me. Oh my. When did I get so crude?

"I said I'd see you soon. Soon is now," he said as he ran his hands down my arms and wrapped them around my body. I guess he was ignoring that whole "going through a divorce" thing I told him the night before, not to mention the sweat pouring from my skin.

I tried to squirm out of his reach, away from the burn I felt throughout my body when he touched me. He kept me close and bent down to kiss my lips, sending my body into hyper drive. "I'm all sweaty," I whispered.

"You taste good," he said before he kissed my neck, and I let him, because for the first time I was willing to admit that I wanted this man to give me orgasms. Hundreds of them, like Tara said. He slowly pulled away from my neck. "You need to go get ready because you are making me want you right here in the lobby...unless you're into that sort of thing, then I'll be happy to accommodate."

I stepped away from him to find some breathing room. "What am I getting ready for?" I asked as I walked over to the elevator. I didn't ask him to come up, but it was no surprise that he would invite himself. This time I didn't mind. After last night I was already learning to pick my battles.

"Brunch," he said simply.

The elevator felt thick with tension once the doors were closed, but it only took the slight movement of the small box rising to motivate Grant to put his hands on me. As soon as the elevator was in motion, his hands were palming my ass and crushing my sweaty body against his solid, flawlessly dressed one. His lips came crashing against mine for a quick but passionate kiss, and I found myself pulling him closer. The dinging of the bell told us we had reached my floor.

He pulled away and grabbed my hand, leading me out onto my floor. I felt like I had just ridden a roller coaster. However, a perfectly unruffled Grant led me straight to my door without asking which apartment was mine, or even what direction off the elevator it was. "Should I even bother to ask how you know which apartment is mine?"

"No," he smirked as he leaned against the wall waiting for me to open my door. I unlocked the door and gestured for him to walk through, but he just said, "After you," and followed me inside.

Thankfully I hadn't brought much with me, so I didn't have a lot of clutter. I did leave my dress and shoes on the floor of my bedroom, but the living room and kitchen area were tidy and relatively unused. "Make yourself at home," I told him before stepping into my bedroom and closing the door.

I quickly showered and shaved all over knowing that my resolve to keep him away had already weakened. But, why couldn't I have a little fun? Mark was having the time of his life sticking his popsicle in every open freezer. It was my turn to be carefree and enjoy someone, and I had no doubts that some of the cobwebs might be swept away today with very little encouragement from the sex symbol who was hanging out in my living room.

Climbing out of the shower, I dried off then wrapped the towel around my head. I rubbed my favorite lotion that smelled of wild flowers all over my body before heading to my bedroom to grab a matching bra and panty set and a brunch outfit, whatever that meant on a rainy day like today.

I ended up dressing in a pair of skinny jeans and a white and navy striped shirt with a bright yellow scarf and braiding my hair over my left shoulder. I was trying to be cute and casual to match Grant's casual outfit, even though I had no idea where we were going or what we were doing.

When I stepped out into the living room, I found Grant pacing on his phone.

"Get it done," he snapped into the phone and hung up when he saw me, then directed a smile toward me. "You look beautiful," he said as he approached me.

"This okay? I wasn't sure how dressy to get."

"You look perfect," he told me before planting a sweet kiss on my lips. "Let's go before I can't be a gentleman any longer.

I giggled and pushed up on my toes to kiss him once more. He growled again and pressed his face into my neck as he tickled my sides. I squealed, pulling away from his hands. I didn't love to be tickled, but I definitely liked this playful side of Grant.

We went to brunch at a little café near Pike's Place and wandered around the area. Of course I had never been to this area of town, so I was behaving like a true tourist trying to take everything in. I walked around wide-eyed as we tasted, explored, and talked some more. When Grant held my hand, I felt the familiar tingle of excitement that only his touch brought on. It had only been a couple of days, and he had dangerously mesmerized me.

After a wonderful day exploring, talking, and people-watching, he took me to dinner at a burger place off Pine Street. It was delicious and made me long for burgers from back home. Grant took a giant bite of his cheeseburger with an onion ring on it and moaned, letting me know how good it was.

"How do you eat like that and keep a body like you do?" I wondered about his terrible eating habits. I had only taken a few tiny bites of my food, and I was already planning my run for the next day. Salads and workouts were on next week's agenda for this girl.

He swallowed and smiled. "Like my body, do you? You haven't seen anything yet."

I smirked. "Literally." He winked back at me, then I said, "Seriously, do you work out all the time?"

"Every day. I run and play tennis and golf. It helps me get out of the office, although you seem to be a better distraction."

"You work all the time, huh?"

"We've had a lot going on over the last few years, so yeah, I work a lot."

"Hmm…well, thank you for taking time out of your busy schedule to show me what a good guy you are."

"Anytime, peach," he said with a sweet kiss to my temple.

He dropped me off later and kissed me good night at my door. It was romantic that he was being a gentleman, but that didn't stop me from wanting him. Who wouldn't want this man? He was attractive and oozed sex appeal, but underneath all of his outer beauty was a man who was kind and generous in a way I had never experienced. When I fell asleep that night, I had to remind myself that all men were on their best behavior in the beginning. Even Mark was sweet and romantic to begin with, and look how well that turned out. That little reminder was enough to drag me down from cloud nine and plant my feet firmly back on the ground where they belonged.

Chapter 7

Grant had to leave town for the next week, but that didn't mean I wasn't on his mind. He called and texted daily letting me know he missed me and was thinking of me. Our daily conversations gave me a chance to get to know him without the distraction of the intense sexual chemistry I felt by being near him. Don't get me wrong. I felt the chemistry even over the phone, and we each alluded to our attraction with our witty repartee, but it was nothing like when we touched or kissed.

On Friday night, I was excited to receive the text saying he was on his way home. He said he was taking the red-eye back to Seattle and would see me in the morning.

Me: Can't wait. What time will you be here?

Grant: As soon as I can get to you. I miss you, peach.

Me: Then hurry up.

I laughed at my boldness. Blatantly flirting was a lot easier over text message.

Grant: Not the one flying the plane, but I will pass along your message to the pilot.

Me: You do that. Fly safe.

Grant: Sweet dreams, beautiful.

I was awake when the knock came, but I wasn't dressed yet. Fortunately, I had brushed my teeth and had pulled my robe on to cover my ratty pajamas. When I opened the door, Grant had me in his arms and his lips on mine before I could even say hello.

He pulled his lips away but kept his arms around my waist. "Good morning, beautiful."

I smiled. "Good morning." I led him into my small apartment. "I need to get dressed. I had just woken up when your text came through."

"It's fine," he said with a kiss. "Go get ready, and I'll take you to breakfast."

"Sounds good. Make yourself at home. I'll be quick."

"You better," he said as he placed one last kiss on my lips. I couldn't wipe the smile off my face as I hurried off to get ready.

With my wet hair wrapped in a towel, I opened the door and stepped onto the carpet of my bedroom before the scream left my body. I was quickly scrambling back in the bathroom to hide my naked body. I slipped on the tile, fell hard on my rear, and yelped again in pain as I was pulling the towel off my head to cover myself from the man who was now standing in my steamy bathroom.

"What are you doing?" I squealed. He had been sitting on my bed with his feet hanging off and ankles crossed when I opened the door. Now he was helping me and my bruised ass and ego off the floor of my bathroom.

He was obviously trying not to laugh, which did not help my embarrassment at all. "You said to make myself at home. I thought I would try out your bed. Your couch isn't terribly comfortable." He nodded to my bed that was covered in fluffy pillows and a warm down comforter. "Much better. You all right?"

"Yes! I'm fine," I snapped while still trying in vain to get the towel to cover all my bits without accidently flashing more of my self.

"You know, you can lose the towel. You really shouldn't hide that beautiful body you just flashed me." He crossed his arms over his chest and leaned against the doorframe. His grin made me notice a dimple on his left cheek. Hmm…sexy.

I gritted my teeth. "I didn't know you were in my bedroom."

He pushed off the wall and stepped up to me so our bodies were almost touching. "You have no idea how sexy you are." His strong arms wrapped around me, pulling me the rest of the way to his body so my breasts were crushed against his chest, creating a wonderful ache between my legs. His lips met mine gently at first before the spark took over like it always did. I wrapped my hands around his neck, pulling him closer to me.

With my hands on him the towel just hung between us until he tugged it loose. Suddenly, I wasn't so shy about being naked in his presence because his lips never left mine. He cupped my rear in his big hands and lifted me easily off the floor making me feel tiny and delicate. I wrapped my legs around him as he carried me the short distance to my bed, not pulling our lips apart until I was on my back and he was on top of me.

If I had been able to think clearly, I may have panicked that a guy I had only known for a little over a week was in my apartment kissing my naked body. But, right then I couldn't think beyond what my body was screaming for…him. I had only been with two men before, and one was Mark. I was the girl who lost her virginity on prom night and thought it was romantic even though the experience was horrendous. Mark became better over time, but I had never really had that hot sexual experience I read about in novels. My college boyfriend was sweet but never really made me feel wanton like I did in that moment with Grant. I had never been so desperate for a man, and fortunately my brain was so focused on what he was doing to my body that I wasn't able to second-guess it.

He pulled away just enough to look me in the eyes. "Do you want this? I really don't want to rush you, but seeing you in a towel…" He stopped talking but kept his eyes trained on mine.

"Yes," I whispered and tried to kiss him again before he pulled away slightly.

"Are you sure? Because you said you couldn't do this. You know I'm not here just for this." He was looking at me with concerned eyes, and he gently pushed hair off my forehead.

I flexed my hips, trying to find the friction I needed so badly. When he let me pull his head closer to me, I whispered again. "Yes, I'm sure I want you. Please." I flexed my hips into him again feeling his hardness between my legs.

"That's what I wanted to hear, baby." He smiled before crushing his lips back down to mine. He trailed his lips down my cheek to my neck. His path continued to my naked breasts where he kissed one while kneading the other. He kept his attention on my breasts, which didn't surprise me. The girls tended to get a lot of attention, but they never had attention that made me squirm like I was right then.

I was just about to beg for something, anything, when he continued his path down my body. As soon as his fingers touched the little bundle of nerves, my hips shot off the bed. "Hold still, beautiful. God, you're perfect. Perfect." He spoke like he was literally thanking and complimenting God.

When he kissed me and touched me, I had the urge to moan or cry out, which I was reluctant to do. I had never been a noisy bedmate, so I tried to control the urge, forcing my body to tense up. Grant must have sensed my tension because he quietly encouraged me. "Let go, baby. I know you're there. Just let go."

I couldn't do it. I didn't know how to "let go." Grant's mouth left its spot, and his thumb replaced his tongue. He kissed my inner thigh then started working back up my body, kissing a fiery path up to my breasts before finding my lips again. "Let go," he commanded me this time. He kissed me hard while continuing the wonderful torture down there that made my body shatter. I cried out involuntarily and closed my eyes while I waited for the shaking to calm. It was like nothing I had ever felt before.

When I opened my eyes again, Grant was watching me and gently running his hand up and down my body. "There she is." He kissed me just below my ear. "You're beautiful, Eve." I still didn't have words, but in the back of my mind I was thinking that Tara was right. Orgasms could motivate you to do a lot of things.

When my brain really started to function again, I noticed Grant was still watching me. He was still fully dressed, and thanks to my newfound confidence from my recent release, I made my move. I grinned and pulled his head down to mine. As we kissed, I pulled his shirt up, revealing a flat stomach and a happy trail. He sat up and pulled his shirt forward over his head like guys do. His perfectly combed hair was already a mess from my hands running through it, and the shirt didn't help. Once his shirt was on the floor, he climbed back up me, kissing his way back to my mouth.

I ran my fingers all over his bare back and chest, feeling the hard ridges of his muscles. I snaked my way down his happy trail and ran my fingers just inside the waistband of his pants until I found his belt buckle. He stood up to remove his pants, and I sat up on my elbows to watch the show. His chest was broad and strong, but not overly muscular. He had a sprinkling of brown chest hair, but he certainly wasn't hairy. I wasn't into manscaping. To me, his chest hair and happy trail were very sexy.

After his shoes and socks were off, he undid his belt and dropped his jeans to the floor, revealing his black boxer briefs first, just before a perfect erection was exposed to me. I licked my lips in response. It was the kind of equipment girls talked about during sorority sleepovers. I couldn't help but stare. He set a condom on the bed and climbed over me, making me lay back down. "You'll like feeling it even better, Eve, I promise."

I laughed at his cockiness, because I could see where it came from now, literally. "You're too much for me, you know that?" He smiled before our lips connected again. Our bodies aligned, and having him bare and on top of me felt better than I could have imagined. I opened my legs wider to allow him to settle there as I arched my back in pleasure.

I heard the rip and felt him move to put the condom on before he met my entrance. His eyes met mine again. "You sure, baby?"

"God, yes, please!" I closed my eyes and begged as I squirmed beneath him, and he assaulted my neck with perfect little kisses and licks.

He lifted up, so he could see my face. "Open your eyes, Eve. Look at me." When my eyes opened, his gaze trapped mine, and I saw his eyes had turned a green color but still showed flecks of gold and blue. They were mesmerizing, and without ever breaking eye contact, he pushed inside of me. He pressed the rest of the way in, forcing me to cry out again. He was big—bigger than I had ever had, not to mention I hadn't had sex in over a year, so my body needed a second to adjust. I grabbed his ass and held him still for just a moment.

"You okay?" he asked a little breathlessly. "Baby, you okay? Did I hurt you?"

"I'm good. You can move now. I just needed…you are…" He started to move slowly at first, and I couldn't say any more. I lifted my hips as he moved at a steady pace, forcing another build up inside of me. My hands gripped his shoulders and back. Our pace quickened as we both neared our climaxes. "Oh, god!" I think I said that out loud before crying out, "Grant!" in a second orgasm. Seconds later he stilled in his own climax, crying out my name, making it the most erotic sound I had ever heard in my life.

After our heart rates came back down to normal, he climbed out of bed and disposed of the condom in the bathroom. When he returned, he collapsed on top of me and wrapped me in his arms. "That was…you're amazing." Grant's lips found mine for a slow, sweet kiss before nuzzling my neck. We stayed there wrapped around each other for several minutes. "Am I hurting you?" he asked, because he was still partially on top of me.

I wrapped my arms and legs more tightly around him. "No. I like it." I kissed his shoulder as he buried his face in my neck and started kissing me.

"I like you." He continued kissing me. When his hands started roaming, I started squirming underneath him.

He leaned up and looked at me. "We need to get up, so I can feed you. If you keep moving like that underneath me, we'll never get out of here." He tickled my sides, and I squirmed violently and squealed. "I think I found the golden ticket, didn't I?" He tickled me again before I was able to get out from under him and run away to the bathroom. "Hurry up!" he yelled after me.

I fixed my hair and dressed quickly. I threw on a cardigan because Seattle summers have nothing on Georgia summers. Once dressed, I looked in the mirror pleased with my rushed result.

I stepped out of my room to find Grant sitting on my couch looking at one of my yearbooks from Georgia. "You ready?" I asked.

"You were a teacher?" he asked without looking up from the page.

"Yes. Sixth grade." I went over and sat next to him.

"You look different, and your name…Evelyn Stevens. Eve Stevens…Mrs. Stevens." He continued staring at the page like a secret was going to come spilling out of it, or maybe like he could change what he saw. I should tell him legally that was still my name, but I didn't think that was what he wanted to hear right then. I certainly didn't want to talk about it.

I took the book from him and placed it back on the shelf with the others. I felt his eyes on me, but I didn't look at him as I adjusted the books on the shelf. "I had a hard time the last two years." I wasn't about to tell him that I gained a bunch of weight because I was on hormones in an effort to get pregnant. The weight came off quickly after I decided to stop the hormones, and then even more came off when I decided to leave Mark. Stress and difficulties eating brought me down to a weight that was way too small for my five-and-a-half-foot frame. After filing for my divorce and moving in with my parents, I started running and eating better. The evidence of my unhappiness was still there in the yearbooks and family pictures with my nieces and nephews though.

"What happened?" he asked, moving the curtain of my long brown hair I was using as a veil to block my discomfort.

"Umm…things didn't work out. This isn't exactly what I want to talk about right after…" I turned to him knowing my cheeks were pink, but I wanted him to know that I would rather be focused on him than the past. He seemed to understand.

"I see your perfect lips are red again. Maybe we could talk about that, or maybe we could talk about how beautiful you are in the throes of passion. I would like to discuss that very much." He pulled me onto his lap and kissed down my neck and across my collarbone.

"Yes, I like this discussion much better." My stomach growled loudly. I hid my face in his shoulder to hide from yet another embarrassing moment with him. "Oh my god." I would never be one of those perfect girls who never wrinkle or whose body doesn't make random noises at inopportune times.

"Someone's hungry." He kept his arms around me and glanced at his watch behind my back. "We missed brunch, but how about I take you to lunch? I know just the place if you like seafood." He smacked my bottom gently. "Let's go."

Chapter 8

Grant took me to a small seafood restaurant overlooking the sound where I had the best clam chowder I'd ever had. We talked about anything and everything without getting too personal, which made me perfectly happy. We laughed a lot, and seeing him carefree was like watching him transform into a different person than the one I met at the lecture. While I actually think I liked both versions of this man, I found the happy-go-lucky-but-still-in-control one to be seriously tempting.

After lunch he took my hand as we walked around the city. It was still cloudy and dreary, but I honestly didn't really notice the weather.

"So, what do you think about our humble town so far?" Grant asked as I buckled my seatbelt back in his car.

"So far, I like it. Although humble town is not how I would describe it. I grew up in a town north of Atlanta where everyone knows each other. It has grown quite a bit over the years, but it still has the same small town feel. You know, one traffic light and a pharmacy with a café inside, the whole shebang."

"Sounds charming. I think I might want to see it one day," Grant said, and then grabbed my hand, bringing it to his lips.

Playing along I said, "Well, I'd be happy to give you a tour if you ever make it there. I wouldn't want you to get lost between the high school and the cemetery. It could be very dangerous for a man like you."

"A man like me?" he asked.

I turned to him to watch his reaction. Using my thickest southern accent, I told him, "A handsome devil like yourself would be in grave danger in a town where the best lookin' man around hit his peak playing high school football fifteen years ago. You, sir, would need some sort of protection against the hordes of women who would be after you."

"Good thing I'd have you to be my bodyguard. With as feisty as you are, you'd be all the protection I'd need."

"I think you'd be surprised. Apparently, I'm only feisty around you."

"How did I get so lucky?"

I rolled my eyes. "Maybe it's because you're the most arrogant man I have ever met. It's a good thing I know better now."

"What is it you think you know?"

"For one, I know that somewhere deep down is a nice guy who protects his sister and takes care of people who are less fortunate than he is. I also know where all of that cockiness comes from, and it is well earned." I gave his lower body a quick glance then winked. I was beginning to like this bold version of myself.

He laughed as he pulled the car in front of my building to drop me off. "Yes, it is a good thing you know that now." He parked and climbed out to come around on my side, letting me out.

"Thank you for a wonderful day. I had a great time," I told him honestly. He had mentioned earlier in the day that he had an event to go to with his family that night, and as much as I wanted our time together to continue, I was grateful for the reprieve. I needed time to get my thoughts together. My brain had been scrambled since this morning when I stepped out of the gym.

He wrapped his arms around me, and mine automatically went around his neck. "Me too. I'm sorry I can't take you to dinner. I promised Daphne I would be her date since her husband can't be there. I would much rather be spending the night with you." His lips went to my neck and climbed their way up to my lips.

I tilted my head, giving him better access to my neck. "I understand. I think it's sweet you're taking Daphne."

"Sweet? You think I'm sweet." He frowned. "We'll have to work on that." He cupped my face between his hands and kissed me gently. "I'll see you tomorrow, peach."

"Tomorrow?" I asked, already knowing how this would go.

"Yes, tomorrow. Since I'm having to give up my night with you, I'll be here in the morning to take you to brunch."

"What if I already have plans?" I was taunting him.

He frowned, then tersely added, "Cancel them."

"I already skipped all my plans today. I don't know if I'm willing to do it two days in a row."

He grabbed my rear and pulled me tighter against his body. "We'll see about that, gorgeous. If I didn't have to go, I would drag you upstairs and give you reasons to beg me to stay."

I could feel how hard he was against my stomach, and it was quite a turn-on. When he ran his nose up my neck, I whispered, "Hmm…promises, promises." A low growl escaped him, letting me know how turned on and frustrated he was. I laughed and pulled away. "You need to go, big guy. You have a hot date tonight, and I have phone calls to some sassy southerners to make."

I patted him on the chest where he captured my hand and held it there. "Who do you have to call?" he asked unsmiling.

Surprised by his tone, I openly explained. "I call my best friend Holly and my sister on Saturdays. I already missed both their calls, so I'm sure they think I was murdered in an alley and thrown into the sound." I had ignored their calls and texts all day knowing I wanted to call them when I was alone. I had some explaining to do.

"Are you going to tell them what you've been up to?" His face was so serious, like he was worried about something.

I stepped closer to him. "Are you asking if I'm going to tell them I bedded a very sexy man this morning? I don't kiss and tell. It's a good thing too.

Jane would tell my mom, and then my dad would be on the next flight out here with a shotgun."

"That isn't what I meant," he grumbled as he pulled me again and lightly smacked my bum. "Are you going to tell them you are seeing me?"

"Seeing you? Am I seeing you?" I didn't know what he was trying to say, but it seemed he was trying to approach it cautiously, which I knew wasn't like him, at least not as far as I was concerned.

"You want to play games, Eve?" he asked with his eyebrows raised. Then his eyebrows lowered along with his voice. "This morning when you said yes to me, you became mine. I told you this wasn't a one-time thing. I'm already trying to deal with the fact that your divorce isn't final, so don't push it."

I squirmed out of his grip and pushed him away. I was angry. I didn't know if it was what he said or how he said it, but I was actually enraged. "Are you kidding me right now? You're dealing with it? No, I'm dealing with it. I told you to leave me alone. If you had listened to me, then you wouldn't have had to deal with anything, but don't worry. You don't have to deal with anything anymore. Fuck off, Grant." I stormed inside the building and pressed the button on the elevator. He came up right behind me and didn't say a word. I could feel the heat radiating off his body and hear his angry breathing behind me. The elevator opened with a ding, and I stepped in and turned to block the doorway. "Don't follow me."

His infuriation was clear on his face. Wordlessly, he lifted me up and put me in the elevator before pressing the button for my floor. He held me there while I squirmed in an effort to get free. "What the hell do you think you're doing? Let me go."

He still didn't speak. When the elevator dinged again, he grabbed my purse and threw me over his shoulder. I was still wriggling and writhing, trying to get free, but it was futile because he was able to hold me with only one hand. Jeez, he was strong. He was able to dig in my purse for my keys and open the door to my apartment with my twisting and turning and cursing on his shoulder.

Once inside, he closed the door and took me straight to my bedroom. After he threw me on top of the bed, he leaned down over me, so we were eye-to-eye and nose-to-nose. All I could see was his eyes had turned to a brownish color. This was very different from the green I saw that morning. They were darker and menacing.

"Don't you ever tell me to 'fuck off.' I'm having a hard time with the fact that you were married, yes. I want you to be mine, completely and unreservedly mine." His tone changed and became calmer and gentler. "I didn't plan on this morning. I really did just come here to take you to brunch and spend time with you, but then you were naked and looking up at me. I couldn't stay away from you, and now I'm having a hard time leaving you even though I'm going to be terribly late."

His lips met mine, and I instantly melted into him. I felt the tension and anger leave my body. When he pulled away he added, "I don't want to think about you with another man. I don't want you to have to go back and deal with your ex. So, yeah,

Eve, I'm dealing with this, or trying to anyway."

I didn't know what to say. He was dealing with the fact he felt possessive, and while I should have thought it was crazy he had such strong feelings about me already, I couldn't, because I felt the same way. Instead of thinking too much or really thinking too much, I responded wordlessly by pulling Grant back down on top of me. My hands slid down his back and found their way under his clothes to feel the heat of his skin.

"Please tell me you're mine, Eve. I can't do this any other way." His expression was pained, and I knew I would rather see those green eyes every day for as long as I had him than ever see that hurt expression on his face again.

Chapter 9

Needless to say, Grant was late picking his sister up. She started calling as he was kissing me goodbye for the hundredth time. I felt bad for making him late, but he didn't seem to mind. In fact, he seemed downright pleased if you ask me. Unfortunately, it was only minutes after he left that my mind caught up with what was happening, and I went into a full-blown panic remembering what happened only moments ago.

"Please tell me you're mine, Eve. I can't do this any other way." His expression was pained, and I knew I would rather see those green eyes every day for as long as I had him than ever see that hurt expression on his face again.

"Yes," I breathed, knowing that I never had a choice. My body and my heart were making decisions my brain wasn't ready to make, but right then my brain wasn't in the driver's seat.

"Say it," he demanded.

"I'm yours, Grant." His lips crashed against mine, rewarding me for making the right decision.

I mean, what was I thinking? I had been here for fifteen days, and I was in the middle of a stupidly messy divorce. I had no business dating, let alone getting involved with a possessive boyfriend. Do you call a thirty-something year old man a "boyfriend?" I didn't even know what to call him.

I swore to myself I would be alone to discover myself and only just started considered casually dating. This wasn't casual. I mean, technically, I had been alone for about a year, but I just wasn't sure I was ready for all of this. I didn't have it in me to make any commitments. I mean, I couldn't even get groceries the other day because I couldn't decide if I would be home enough to drink the milk. Buying milk was too much of a commitment on Tuesday, and here I am on Saturday telling a man I met last Wednesday I was his. What was wrong with me?

Even though it was after ten on a Saturday night in Georgia, I still called my best friend Holly. She was probably out, but I needed someone to ground me. I needed her no frills, tell-it-like-it-is advice.

"Evie? Thank goodness you're alive. I was ready to call in the dogs!" she shouted into the phone when she answered.

I could hear the music in the background. "No, you weren't. You're out drinking. Where are you?" I shouted back.

The music became quieter as she was obviously walking outside. I could hear a metal door squeak open and then quiet. "Sorry! Matt's band is playing at a bar in Athens. A lot of people from school are here, including your douchebag ex and his flavor of the week."

"Yeah, Mom said he was out with Christina last weekend. Good for him. Maybe that will motivate him to sign the papers."

She laughed. "I don't know. When I saw him, I asked if he had signed them yet, and he told me to go fuck myself. We were just as happy to see each other as always." Holly and Mark always hated each other, so I was used to this. There was no chance either of them would tame their tongues when the other was around, not even when we were married. "So, what's going on with you being MIA today? Did you meet a hot guy?"

I felt the panic rising in my throat again. "Here's the thing. I didn't just meet someone. I accidentally slept with him. I'm freaking out over here!"

"You did what? You slut. Was it good? Did you finally come? I'm so excited for you. This was no accident. Penises don't accidentally find their ways into vaginas."

I think my humiliation is the theme of the week. "Holly! People can hear you. Keep your voice down. And…yes to all of those, but please don't say penis or vagina ever again.

I could hear her squealing and rattling off questions. "What does he look like? Ooh! Send me a pic. What's his name? Is he a crunchy granola hippie? I warned you about them. Does he wear socks with sandals, because that's not okay, you know."

"No. He's a suit. Brown hair, light eyes, perfect body…very sexy. He's the hottest man I think I've ever seen in real life."

"So, why are you freaking out? He sounds perfect for having fun. Just be safe."

"He doesn't want to just have fun. He wants a relationship."

"And?" she asked. I could imagine her rolling her eyes at me.

"And my divorce isn't final. Besides, you know I'm not ready for that," I reminded her.

"Oh please, Evie! Quit waiting for some neon sign that says you're ready to move on. When opportunity comes a knockin', you should answer. It sounds like you like him, so just go with the flow. I know that isn't how you usually do things, but look how well your usual method turned out." Sometimes I hated tough love. "Look, I have to go. Matt is going back on, but just enjoy yourself. Quit worrying so much."

"Yeah. Okay. Have fun and tell Matt congrats for me."

"Will do. Love you!"

After I hung up with Holly, I didn't have the energy to call my sister. Instead I made a quick dinner and changed into a pair of polka dot pajama shorts and a skimpy camisole. It was only half past eight when I climbed into bed to watch one of my beloved chick flicks, but I was exhausted. Sleep found me before Fat Amy said no to crystal meth.

A pounding noise followed by a buzzing woke me up the next morning. I sat up, still groggy from waking up when the noise started again. Someone was pounding on my door. Paying no attention to my pajamas or my hair, I walked out of my bedroom and up to the front door. I at least thought to look through the peep hole where I saw Grant there, dialing his phone. I heard mine buzzing in the bedroom, but I opened the door instead of going to get my phone.

When I opened it, Grant grinned and slid his phone back in his pocket. He looked me up and down before settling on my face. With a cocked eyebrow, he said, "You always answer the door dressed like that?"

"You're the first person who has ever knocked on my door here. Why are you here? What time is it?"

"It's eight. I told you I was coming to get you."

He walked into my apartment, and I followed him, closing the door behind me. "For brunch. Most people eat brunch around eleven-ish. I was still asleep."

"I might have missed you. I can see you are just as pleasant in the morning as you are agreeable other times. Let's see if we can do something about that." He leaned down and picked me up, pressing his lips to mine. I wrapped my legs and arms around him as he carried me back to my bed. He toed off his shoes and socks and said, "Good morning, peach."

"Good morning." I smiled sleepily back at him.

"You look sexy when you wake up. I like your pajamas," he traced a finger across the top of my exposed breasts, "but please don't answer the door dressed like this. You'll give your neighbors a show."

"And? Maybe I like being an exhibitionist."

He made his sexy growl. "Not my Georgia

Peach," he said before attacking any bare skin that was showing with kisses. Turns out that with him in my bed, I was very much a morning person.

Hours later we were showered and dressed and a few orgasms happier. I discovered the shower could be way more fun when you have a shower buddy like Grant in there with you. Watching Grant dress was almost as fun as watching him undress. He had on jeans and a button down with the sleeves expertly rolled thanks to yours truly.

I pinned my hair into a bun on my head, because Grant wouldn't leave me alone long enough to curl my hair, and I was too afraid of burning him. He even seemed to enjoy zipping my dress for me, though it took a lot longer with his help. I didn't mind. His playful mood was infectious. I couldn't help but smile as he led me to the restaurant. That smile stayed on my face right up until he said, "Good. They're already here. Come on."

He started tugging on my hand, but I froze in place. He turned and looked at me in confusion. "Who's here?" I asked nervously.

"My parents and sister. I meet them here almost every Sunday for brunch." He said it so easily, like I should be totally fine with meeting his parents after knowing him for a week. I didn't even know where he lived, and he wanted to introduce me to his parents. This relationship was moving at a speed I was definitely not comfortable with.

"You brought me here to meet your family?" I whisper screamed at him in an effort not to cause a scene. "You didn't think you should have mentioned it before now?"

"You wouldn't have come, or you would've fought me on it, and I was too busy this morning to convince you to agree. Come on. They'll adore you. They already know you're coming, so don't try to run away." He leaned closer. "Besides, you already know I would chase you and drag you back here kicking and screaming. That would give everyone something to talk about."

He was right. I didn't have a choice unless I wanted to thoroughly embarrass myself. He was staring at me with an annoying smirk on his face, waiting for me to decide what I was going to do. I sighed in defeat. "Fine, but this is in no way okay with me. You either need to slow down, or this relationship is going to be over before you know it," I said as sternly as possible.

He tugged me closer. "Hey. None of that. It's only brunch, Eve. I'm not asking you to man the space shuttle." He kissed my lips before turning and dragging me to his parents' table.

His sister lit up when she saw us approaching. She immediately stood and took Grant in a big hug and then followed suit with me. "It's nice to see you again, Eve. We didn't really get to speak at the lecture, but Dr. Clarke spoke very highly of you. I think it was the red velvet cupcakes you had there that did him in. Grant has some competition if you keep bringing Dr. Clarke's favorite desserts."

I laughed and turned on the sorority charm. "Well, red velvet is a southern favorite. I wouldn't have a reception any other way. It's nice to officially meet you, Mrs. Pearce."

"Please, call me Daphne."

"Of course."

Grant had walked over and greeted his mother, who remained in her seat assessing me coolly. She had darker hair than Grant, probably because it was dyed, and it was shoulder length and sprayed perfectly into place. Her pink Chanel suit reeked of money. Grant's dad was the older, greyer version of Grant. He even had the same peculiarly colored eyes.

Grant came back around and held my hand as he introduced everyone politely. "Mom. Dad. This is Eve Bryant. She took Sabrina Atwell's position working with Tara Tanner at the college. Eve, these are my parents, Harrison and Iris Mitchell, and you know Daphne of course." He gestured for me to sit next to his father who greeted me warmly. He was the complete opposite of his wife.

"Nice to meet you," I said politely to both his father and mother. His mother gave me an almost smile that didn't reach her eyes. In all honesty, I think she was growling at me, but I chose to ignore it. His father, on the other hand, was all smiles.

Mr. Mitchell spoke as soon as I was seated. "Grant told us all about you last night, so we're so glad you were available to join us for brunch. How are you liking Seattle so far?"

"It's been really great. I really enjoy my work at the college, and I've done a little exploring around the city when I've had time."

Daphne chimed in. "I imagine it is really different from Georgia. Wait until winter. You'll want to run back to the South as fast as you can."

Grant frowned and squeezed my thigh where his

hand was resting. "No, she won't." I felt my cheeks heat slightly at his possessiveness.

Daphne laughed at his antics and patted his shoulder affectionately. "Calm down, big brother. I was only teasing."

"What made you move to Seattle, Eve?" his mother asked, breaking the pleasant atmosphere we had all been enjoying. This was the first thing she said to me, and based on her silent assessment, I wasn't surprised at the lack of friendly greeting.

I took a sip of the mimosa that Mr. Mitchell had ordered for everyone. "It was time for a change. Tara is an old friend, so when she offered me a job, I decided to take a chance." That was the truth, and I wasn't going to give that woman any more information. I could already tell she was looking for ammunition.

"You just decided to up and leave your family on a whim?" she asked.

"Mother," Grant warned.

"It's fine," I told Grant. I turned back to his mother. "My family and I made the decision together. We live by the philosophy that you only go around once, so they are always encouraging me to try new things." I looked over at Grant, who was smiling affectionately at me.

"That sounds exciting. From the time I graduated college I was trapped in my office working, and I fear my boy has followed my tragically boring footsteps. Maybe you can teach him how to enjoy life a little," Mr. Mitchell said buoyantly.

Brunch continued on like that for the next hour and a half. Mr. Mitchell—or Harrison as he told me to call him—Daphne, Grant, and I chatted jovially, while Mrs. Mitchell observed with a stone cold expression on her face. She barely touched her food and traded her mimosa for one Bloody Mary after another. Grant had to escort her out of the restaurant while Daphne and Harrison hugged me and told me how glad they were to have met me. By the time I was back in Grant's car, I was exhausted. He climbed in the driver's seat and started the car. "That wasn't so bad, now was it?"

I simply snorted in response.

Chapter 10

The drive back from the restaurant was quiet. As I stared out the window, I wondered what I was getting into with Grant. I may have played brunch like meeting the family was as normal as drinking sweet tea on Sunday, when in reality I wanted to run from the room and avoid the man who had me captivated by his charm. I mean, really, who in the world introduces someone to his parents after one week? Ridiculous.

"Are you not talking to me now?" He was amused. I was not.

"Why should I? You probably won't listen anyway." I was sulking like a hormonal teenager. Very mature, Eve.

"That isn't true. I hear everything you say. However, I may not always agree with you." I grunted a response again. "They seemed to love you just as I predicted, so I don't know what has you fired up, but you better get over it. I'm taking you to do something fun."

"Do I need to prepare to greet the president this

time?" I replied sarcastically.

"Very funny, my grumpy little peach." He grabbed my hand and kissed my knuckles. "I think you'll like where I'm taking you. Maybe you can get out some of your frustration. If not, I can think of some other ways of handling that." He wiggled his eyebrows, and I rolled my eyes in response.

"Your mother hates me," I finally said after a few more minutes of silence. "Parents always love me, but your mother looked at me like I spilled red wine on her wedding dress before the pictures."

"My mother hates everyone, but honestly, I think you impressed her. She kept her mouth shut for most of brunch. She's usually far more unpleasant."

"That makes me feel better," I lied.

"Does it?" he asked surprised.

"No," I sighed.

"Don't worry, baby. She'll come around in no time. Although I don't think it will help that my dad will spend the next week raving about how gorgeous you are." He parked and leaned over to kiss me. "Don't worry about my mother. Come on. We're here."

Perplexed, I sat up to look out the window as he walked around the car to open the door for me. "You brought me to a golf club?"

"I figured we could hit a few balls out at the driving range. You can let your frustration out on those balls." He smirked at the mention of balls. Beneath the polished exterior, Grant was still just a boy.

"I don't know about that. I've never hit a ball beyond what is required in miniature golf."

"Come on then. Teaching you will be fun." I wasn't sure about that, but I was unenthusiastically willing to give it the old college try.

He showed me how to drive a ball, and I watched how his agile body moved. When it was my turn to try, the ball didn't go nearly as far as his did, but at least I hit it. "That was good for a first try," Grant praised before coming behind me to show me how to hold my club and help guide my swing. Now I understood better as to why he had brought me here. He was well aware of what he did to me when he was this close. I stopped listening to what he was saying. All I could focus on was his hard body against my back and his arms around me. "You aren't listening, are you, Eve?" he whispered in my ear and then kissed that spot right below my earlobe.

"Nope. I stopped right when I felt," I wiggled my bum against him, "this against me. What were you saying?" I asked playfully. It was time to take full advantage of his good mood.

He smacked my rear and growled, "Behave." He started telling me his instructions a second time. I really tried to listen. I swear. He guided me through hitting the ball before letting me try again on my own. This time the ball went a lot farther.

"Yay," I cheered and jumped into his arms while he laughed and held me tightly against him.

"That was perfect, baby. Here." He put another ball on the tee. "Try it again. Remember to keep your eye on the ball."

I was just about to swing again when a man's voice called out Grant's name. I looked up to see a tall, blond-haired man about Grant's age wearing a hot-pink polo shirt tucked tightly into dark blue chinos. Apparently Grant knew him because he was smiling wide as the man approached.

"Maddox. Hey man. How are you?" Grant said when the man made his way to us. They man-hugged and patted each other roughly on the back.

"Doing well. How about you? I heard you made an appearance at the dinner last night. That was nice of you. Was it a Mitchell family photo-op?"

"Something like that." Grant pulled me closer. "Eve, this is Maddox. We grew up together. I beat him up in first grade, and we've been friends ever since."

Maddox scoffed at the story. "Whatever, asshole. You're the one who had to get stitches." He turned to me and grabbed my hand. "Eve, it is a pleasure to meet such a beauty. Grant usually doesn't stray from his mother's harem, but I can tell you are not one of Iris's girls." He kissed my knuckles.

Grant pulled my hand away and pulled me back against his chest where he wrapped an arm tightly around my waist. "Back off, Mad."

"Your mother know about this?" Maddox flicked a finger back and forth between the two of us.

"Of course," Grant confirmed and rubbed his fingers over my hipbones. Why would it matter if his mother knew who he was dating? It wasn't like he was a teenager for goodness' sake.

"Apologies. I had no idea."

"Yeah, she met her at brunch today," Grant told him proudly and gripped me tighter against him. I looked up at him, confused by the conversation. He smiled down at me reassuringly and kissed the tip of my nose.

"Kitty's going to shit when she finds out. I might call her just so I can hear her reaction. Better yet, let her see you two together. I think she might actually show us the ugly side of her. She'll finally crack." Maddox laughed then turned serious when he noticed neither of us were laughing with him. He cleared his throat and added, "Good luck, bro." At that, Grant tensed up behind me. I looked between them confused. Kitty? Who was Kitty, and why would she "shit" when she found out about me and Grant? And who named their child Kitty? Of course, I grew up with someone named Lesley Wesley, so I shouldn't be surprised.

"Maddox," Grant's tone brought my attention back to the present. It was a warning, and his eyes were a dark color. Something told me my gut was right. "So, what are you doing here?" he asked like nothing had happened, which only made me wonder more.

"Drinks with dear old Dad. One Sunday a month I'm required to appear for drinks, or I get stuck at a family dinner with my new 'mom.'" He shivered with revulsion then looked at me to explain. "This is wife number six for my dad. He keeps getting older, and they stay the same age. This one is particularly awful about the stepmom role even though she's only a few years older than me."

I smiled at him sympathetically. "I'm sorry to hear that. I bet that makes family dinners awkward. Do you have siblings?"

"Not other than my brother from another mother,

right here. Hey! That's an idea. Why don't you come to dinner next time, Grant? Shannon will love you." Maddox wiggled his eyebrows at Grant.

"Enough, Maddox. Quit talking about your dad's wife like that before he limits your access to your trust fund."

"Yeah right. Then who would do all of his bidding? I need to run, but let's do lunch this week. I have a prototype on the specs you sent over last month."

"Sounds good, man. Call Rachel. She'll get you in when I'm free. Probably Tuesday or Wednesday."

Maddox smiled wide. "Oh, I'll call Rachel all right. Maybe I'll take her to lunch instead of meeting with you. She's way more fun than you. Although you might be the prettier one."

"Goodbye, Maddox."

"Bye, Grant. Bye, Eve. It was nice to meet you. I'm sure I'll see you again soon." I waved, and he turned and walked away.

Grant tried to jump back into my golfing lessons, and I stood behind him still reeling from Maddox's little visit. After a moment of explaining how to properly swing, he realized I wasn't paying any attention to him and turned to look at me. "Come on, babe. Try it. You're getting good."

"How about you explain what that was all about?" My feet remained frozen in their place as Grant and I stared at each other in a standoff.

"Explain what? Maddox's crazy. He was just talking out of his ass. Now come over here and try again."

"Grant."

"Eve," he mocked as we entered the mature part of our afternoon.

I stepped over to the bench and sat down with my legs and arms crossed. I knew next to nothing about this man. He said he wasn't married, but for some strange reason his mother needed to know who he was dating, and there was also the issue of Kitty, who was not a cat. There was no way I was letting him keep up this charade. "You go ahead and finish hitting. When you're done, you can drive me home." He didn't take his eyes off of me. "Go ahead," I waved him on.

He ran his hands through his perfect hair, a sign of impending doom if you asked me, but I didn't care. It was two days into this "relationship" that he insisted upon, and he was already hiding something.

He dropped the club on the ground and came to stand right in front of me. "Baby, Rachel is my assistant. He was joking about her."

I looked up at him, waiting for him to explain the rest. I didn't care about Rachel. I wanted to know what had him all riled up after Maddox mentioned Kitty. I wasn't going to ask and make myself look like a jealous harpy though. I wasn't jealous. It wasn't about that. I wanted to know whatever it was he was hiding. If he didn't want to share, we didn't have to do this. I couldn't be in a relationship with someone I didn't trust. What I could do was get over someone I had only known for a few days, even if that man was Grant Mitchell, and even if I was sure I had strong feelings for said man.

He was waiting for me to talk, and I was sure

this standoff could go on for hours. Finally I asked what I wanted to know. "What are you hiding?"

"What are you talking about? I'm not hiding anything," he groaned.

"Give me a break. I felt you tense when Maddox brought up your mother and Kitty, and if looks could kill, your mother would be in prison for manslaughter from the looks she was giving me this morning. It's fine if you don't want to tell me, but don't string me along." I stood and pulled my purse onto my arm. "Maybe you should just take me home. This wasn't a good idea," I said as I gestured between us, indicating we weren't a good idea.

He cursed under his breath before he went over and grabbed his club and the bucket of balls. He gave the bucket to a dad teaching his son how to golf before coming back to me. He grabbed my hand and led me to the car. It was a good thing I was wearing flats because I would have had a difficult time keeping up with his pace in heels.

He let me into the passenger seat and closed the door behind him. That was when I realized he was ending it. Grant was taking me home so he wouldn't have to tell me whatever it was he was hiding. Five minutes ago I felt so strong and sure of myself, but now I felt the tears stinging my eyes. I was not going to let them fall. I blinked rapidly to prevent Grant from seeing the stupid tears building up.

Grant climbed in the car jand closed the door, but he didn't start the engine. He also didn't look at me. Staring straight ahead he asked, "Why do you keep doing that?" He gripped the steering wheel so tightly his knuckles turned white. "Why do you keep fucking telling me it's over?"

"Because it is over if I can't trust you." My words were barely audible.

He turned in his seat to face me. "You can trust me."

"Then tell me whatever it is you're avoiding," I challenge him.

"Damn it, Eve. I can't right now. I promise you I'll tell you everything when I'm ready, but please just let it go for now. We had a great weekend, and Maddox has ruined it with his bullshit. Don't let him ruin it, Eve."

"Maddox isn't ruining anything, so don't blame your friend for acting like he usually does around you. Just take me home, Grant."

"Eve."

"Grant," I mocked like he had done earlier.

He exhaled noisily and then started the car. We drove silently through Seattle back to my apartment. As soon as he parked the car, I hopped out to escape the tension that built up over the half hour drive. He jumped out after me and shouted my name, but I kept walking.

"Eve, wait!" He easily caught up to me when I was waiting on the elevator. Stupid me. I should have taken the stairs. "Please."

"Grant, just go," I said, tired of all the fighting already. Been there, done that.

He was standing right behind me. "I'm not leaving. I'm going to come upstairs with you, and we're going to talk. I didn't want to tell you this today right after meeting my mother, but I'll tell you whatever you want to know if it means this isn't over," he said quietly.

I nodded. When the elevator doors opened, he followed me in and pushed the button for my floor. The elevator dinged, and he led me to my apartment where I opened the door for us. I grabbed us each a bottle of water from my fridge and signaled for him to sit on my couch. I sat down on the farthest end from him and waited.

His hair was a wreck, and he looked worried. "Well," I said.

"My mother didn't like you because of me. I've never introduced them to a girl because there has never been anyone to introduce. I have only seriously dated one girl, and that was back in college. She wanted to stay on the east coast, and I had to come home to work for my dad."

He paused for a long moment, and my frustration spiked again. "That doesn't explain why she looked like she wanted to poison my pancakes. Keep going, Grant."

"After that I only had…arrangements with women. All of them travel in social circles like my mother's. In fact, most of their mothers are friends with Iris."

"What do you mean 'arrangements?'" I asked.

"They were agreements where all parties knew the relationship wasn't going to result in marriage and kids. It wasn't going anywhere."

I didn't think I would have agreed to that even in my confused, post-marriage state. Was that what casually dating was? If so, I retracted my earlier thoughts that it could be for me. Then I had to know. "Is that what you want with me?"

He moved closer to me. "No. God no. From the moment I saw you I felt a connection to you. Remember when you offered me your hand to introduce yourself?" I nodded, remembering how instead of shaking my hand, he just walked away. "I was afraid to touch you. I thought you would see how nervous you made me."

"You seemed so sure of yourself," I told him. "I even thought you were incredibly arrogant that night."

"I was trying to seem unaffected. It doesn't matter though. Spending time with you has been everything to me. You challenge me like no woman before you, and the way you react when I touch you cuts me deep inside. I've never wanted to be with anyone like this before. I want to do everything with you, and it kills me that you are constantly trying to end this."

"I'm sorry, but this whirlwind has been really overwhelming for me. You have to think about where I'm coming from. I mean, I just moved here to start over after ending my marriage to someone I have known my whole life. I have one friend in the city, and then suddenly you're there with your three-piece suits and caveman style antics."

"Caveman? You think I'm a caveman?" he asked with a surprised laugh.

I waved him off and tried to move the conversation forward. "Finish telling me why your mother hates me."

"None of those girls ever meant anything, and my mother knew that. She was fine with it because she always thought that when I was ready to settle down, it would be with her best friend's daughter, Kitty…uh, Katherine. She's a few years younger than me, but our mothers have been planning our lives since the day Katherine was born. It's never been a secret. Both Daphne and Grace married men my mother chose for them, but I've never been one for doing what my mother says."

"Your mother is arranging marriages? Why didn't you just tell her you didn't want to marry Katherine? Or is it that you don't want to marry her right now? I mean, you're in your thirties, right? Do you want to marry Katherine one day?" I spouted off question after question as they popped into my head.

He seemed unfazed by my rapid-fire inquisition. "I'm thirty-two, almost thirty-three. No, I don't want to marry Katherine…ever. If the right girl wants to marry me, then I suppose I'll get married. If I never find her, then I won't. As far as my mother goes, she has a tendency to only see from her own point of view," he finished with a pointed look.

He was trying to put me at ease. "Sounds like someone else I know." I rolled my eyes.

"You might be asking for it, peach." He grabbed me and tickled my sides, causing me to squeal. When he stopped we were nose-to-nose, and his bright green eyes were looking into mine.

I kissed him gently. "Thank you for telling me."

"Thank you for listening. Please don't try to end this every time I screw up. I'm new to this, so give me a chance before you run." His lips touched mine gently at first, but it didn't last. This man didn't know how to be anything other than consuming.

After we ate a simple stir-fry dinner I cooked, we spent the next few hours talking—just talking—in my bed. Apparently my cute grey sofa was the most uncomfortable piece of furniture on the west coast, or at least according to my six foot something dark-haired, light-eyed boyfriend with a rock hard body and a very sexy happy trail. I didn't say I wasn't thinking about other things while lying in my bed, wrapped around this enchanting man. Unfortunately, we had used up his condom supply earlier that morning.

I had never even thought to buy such things, because I never thought I would be in this situation. Birth control was a point of discussion during our snuggle time, and we agreed that it would be best for me to get on something. I didn't tell him I couldn't get pregnant, because the doctors never found out why I couldn't, which always made me wonder if it was me. At any rate, it was always better to be safe than sorry.

Grant did suggest we could keep our physical relationship limited while I sorted the birth control situation out. I knew he was trying to slow things down in his own way after our talk, but after becoming acquainted with Lady O, waiting was not something I really wanted to do. In fact, I wanted to do him as much as possible, and I told him such. He laughed and agreed with me, and then we made out like teenagers while pretending to watch a movie. I couldn't think of a single night I enjoyed more…ever.

Chapter 11

My life in numbers:

24. The number of days I have lived in Seattle.

23. The number of hours I spent getting to know Grant this weekend.

22. The number of emails in my inbox this morning.

21. The number of emails I deleted from my inbox this morning.

20. The number of minutes it took to say goodbye to Grant this morning.

19. The number of times I told myself not to flip out about Grant today.

18. The number of times I have reminded myself of Holly's advice to go with the flow.

17. The number of times I have freaked out about my relationship with Grant.

16. The number of missed calls and messages from home this weekend.

15. The number of days I have worked at Mitchell College.

14. The number of minutes it took me to get to work once we said bye.

12. The number of minutes it took me to put on my makeup this morning.

11. The number of days it has rained since I moved to Seattle.

10. The number of months I've waited for Mark to sign the damn papers.

9. The number of orgasms Grant has given me since Saturday.

8. The number of texts about Grant from Holly since Saturday night.

7. The hour at which Grant returned with breakfast and dressed for work.

6. The hour at which I was awoken to find an empty bed and a note.

5. The number of text messages I had from Tara asking about Grant.

4. The number of times I have worked out since moving here.

3. The number of events I have attended as the "Event Manager."

2. The number of men on my mind this morning.

1. The number of men I wanted to be thinking about.

I woke up this morning to an empty bed. It was still dark outside, which meant it was way too early to be awake. I never woke up early unless something disturbed my sleep. In this case, the disruption may have been the empty space next to me. I went to bed with Grant wrapped around me only to awake very cold and alone.

I frowned and grumpily turned on the crystal lamp on my bedside table. I glanced over at Grant's empty side of the queen-size bed where I found the note.

Good morning my gorgeous Georgia Peach, I ran home to change and will grab breakfast. I took your keys, but I'll be back before you even need to get out of bed. Go back to sleep, beautiful.

– Grant

I smiled widely at his thoughtfulness. Now that we had cleared up some of the mama drama and spent some time talking, I felt like I was blissfully in this thing with Grant. If only I could get rid of the other man in my life. That thought alone ruined my happy ones, so I sunk back down into my bed and grabbed Grant's pillow. It smelled of him, and I fell back asleep, happily dreaming of dark hair and eyes that read like a mood ring.

When I was awoken an hour later, it was from kisses down my back and a handsome man in a three-piece suit. "Good morning, sunshine," he said huskily when he felt me stir beneath him.

"Good morning, handsome. I missed you when I woke up the first time."

"You were sleeping so peacefully I didn't want to wake you. I know how much you love mornings, but now you need to get up for work, peach. I have meetings to get to, but I want to have breakfast with you first."

I rolled out of bed and grumbled. "Quit calling me that. It's insulting. Peaches are fat and round."

He pulled me back to him with an amused grin on his face. "You're definitely not either of those, that's for sure." He wrapped his arms around me and kissed my nose. "It is the only thing I know about Georgia other than the capital is Atlanta, which is home to the busiest international airport in the US."

"Aren't you full of fun facts today? Should I start calling you evergreen? Or how about Washington Apple?" I smirked.

"Apple of your eye? I like it." I rolled my eyes at his cheesy joke, making him laugh before he smacked my rear. "Go get ready. I have bagels and coffee for us. I guessed that you're a cream and sugar kind of girl." He kissed my lips roughly, making me want more, but he pulled away quickly. I could think of much better ways to get me moving.

When I was out of the shower, I sauntered into my bedroom sans towel or robe only to find Grant sitting on my now made-up bed with his iPad in his lap and phone in his ear. His eyebrows raised in surprise when he noticed me. I ignored him and continued dressing in a matching light pink lace bra and panty set.

"Tom, I'll call you back when I get to the office." He threw his phone on the bed next to his iPad and prowled over to me. His lips went straight to my neck. "You're such a mean little temptress. You know neither one of us has time for that this morning."

"What?" I asked innocently. "I'm just getting dressed for work."

"Yeah, right," he whispered before he took my lips in a passionate kiss.

"I thought I had to get dressed," I said against his lips.

"Mmm…maybe we should take the day off. I can think of several things I'd rather do with my time than go meet with grumpy old business men."

"Me too, but Tara would be over here in a second. I'm sure she's dying to hear all the gossip, and we have some events coming up that need my attention."

"What events?" he asked after I pulled away, and he straightened his tie.

"One of them is the anniversary ball where all the elite, which I believe includes your parents, come and show off their money and their legacies, which I believe includes you." I tapped his nose and then stepped into my walk in closet, which conveniently was about the same size as my bathroom.

He followed me, but stood at the door, leaning against the frame with his arms crossed confidently across his chest. "Does that mean I get to take you as my date?"

I pulled on a belted floral shirtdress and tan wedges before saying, "Hmm…I don't know. I have to work the event. It isn't social for me. Some of us aren't part of Seattle's high society, Mr. Mitchell."

"You should be. It would be more respectable

with people like you in it. As it happens, I would rather be floating in your elite circle than the one my mother insists upon."

I slid past him to my bathroom to fix my makeup. "I don't have an elite circle. It's just me."

"Even better," he said as he snuck up behind me and wrapped his arms around me.

***

The rest of Monday was boring in comparison to my weekend. I followed Tara to meetings all day with professors and the college administration. We barely had a chance to talk, which I knew was driving her crazy, but I had to decline when she asked me to go to dinner. I already had a date with a very handsome man, which included pasta and him, two things I couldn't pass up.

The next thing I knew, it was a dark and rainy Tuesday, and I was sitting in my office after a long day of filling Tara in on most of my weekend. She gave me her advice about Grant and his family, and then I made phone call after phone call to confirm vendors and speakers for the next few events.

I had also spoken with my lawyer, Martin, about the divorce proceedings. He suggested we go to mediation. I told him I would think about it, which was progress, considering for the past ten months I automatically turned down the suggestion of mediation. I didn't want to face Mark. I hadn't been able to be strong in our marriage. What made me think I would suddenly grow a backbone for mediation? I didn't think having a lawyer would suddenly enable me to stand up for myself.

At just after five, I was exhausted. That could have been because I hadn't really been able to rest since before the start of my wild weekend, though. Tara had already left for the day, and I was ready to be home. As I dropped my bag on the entry table in my tiny apartment, my phone rang. Holly.

"Hey, Hols. How are you?" I answered.

"I'm great now. I just finished packing. Matt and I are headed to the beach tomorrow for some fun in the sun. Maxine let me off work for the next three days when I started cussing under my breath after spending an hour with a woman whose loan I had to deny because she thought she could use her boyfriend's assets without his permission. She was fake all over and attempting to dig for gold with a man fifteen years her senior. Nightmare."

"Sounds fun. Now I'm totally regretting never taking a job in banking. Shucks!" I said sarcastically. "How's everything else? Matt?"

"Good. Dad actually invited Matt to go fishing with him on Sunday. It was pretty funny watching my rocker fiancé fishing with my dad and brother. Mom and I giggled for hours about it when Matt caught more fish than the big boys."

I laughed knowing how much that probably drove the Benton boys crazy. "You should make Matt a trophy for his achievement. Your dad and brother would hate that. They would make him fish every Sunday until they proved it was beginner's luck."

"Probably. Enough about me. My life is boring. Tell me all about your new man. What's his name?"

"His name is Grant Mitchell, and he's the grandson of the founders of the college where I'm working. This weekend was a bit of a whirlwind." I proceeded to tell her all about my weekend. I filled her in on all of the fights and some of the fun. I did leave out some of the dirty details. She didn't need to know everything, but it felt good to share this with her. Living in Seattle was a little lonely since I was used to having friends and family just down the street. Now I was living alone for the first time ever, in a place where I had one friend—now two, I guess.

She was silent for a moment on the other end. I thought I lost her. I looked at my phone and saw it was still connected. "Hols?"

"Yeah. I'm here. I just…Evie, have you Googled this guy?" she asked timidly. Her tone had me grabbing my laptop and sitting down on my uncomfortable sofa.

"No, why?" I asked as I tapped my nails against my glass coffee table, waiting for my computer to wake up. I put her on speakerphone and set the phone next to the computer.

"Just Google his name and Seattle. I looked at the images page. I just wanted to see what he looked like since you never sent me a picture. I didn't expect to find this. He's kind of famous, or at least well-known."

I was typing. "What? What did you find?"

"You need to see it for yourself. You may already know, in which case I'm making a big deal out of nothing."

The first image that popped up was one of him

and his father in their tailored suits in a Forbes article. It was a great picture. "He's really good-looking, isn't he?"

"He definitely has good genes, but so do all of the well-bred models who grace his arm."

"Yes…I'm seeing that." What I was seeing was a nightmare. Grant had dated every daughter of every rich family in the state of Washington, maybe even some from California and Oregon as well. His beautiful sisters were in some photos, but it was really one beauty after another at one formal even after another. I wondered if these were the "arrangements" he told me about. If so, he had a lot of them.

"Did he date all of these women?" Holly asked.

"I don't…well, no. Two of them are his sisters. I don't think he had relationships with all of these women, but that doesn't mean…oh god!" I kept scanning the pictures. "He must think I'm an idiot! He told me about women, but I didn't know we were talking this many. Well, that explains why the son of a bitch is so good in bed. He has been polling women for the last fifteen or so years. He's so out of my league, Holly."

"Stop it right now, Evie. If anything, I'd say you're out of his league. Compared to him, you're practically a virgin."

"Oh jeez." I cringed. I'm probably terrible in bed compared to these girls. I was no tiger in the bedroom. These girls looked like they could make a guy hard just by walking into the room in one of their perfect dresses, with their shiny hair and bikini-ready bodies. No one ever liked having your new boyfriend's last bed buddies thrown in your face, and here I was looking at a parade of them. In the back of my mind I counted three separate girls with the name Katherine or Catherine, and it made me wonder which one was Kitty, if any of them.

"Evie, you knew he had a past. You're just freaking out about seeing it in pictures. The photos are part of the life he lives. Every one of these is at some charity event or holiday party. None of this is an indication of how he really lives his life. Look at him. He looks exactly the same in every picture. There isn't one where he is smiling candidly."

I took a couple of deep breaths. "No. You're right. The Grant I'm dating is really different than the Grant in these pictures, but the man in the pictures is the Grant I met the first night at the lecture. I'm just not so sure I can reconcile this man with the one who I might really like."

"You really like him?" I could hear the smile coming through the phone.

I smiled back. "I might. He's pretty great, smart, and funny on top of all that other stuff."

"Good on paper meets good in bed."

"To say the least." I agreed with her assessment. "He's just...different...in a good way. The way he touches me, it's like I'm precious. He's so careful yet possessive at the same time." I could gush all day about the very sexy man who spent the weekend with me, who was not the same person I was currently stalking online. The man in those images was stiff and unapproachable.

"Then don't let this get in the way. If you keep looking for reasons to end it, you're going to find them. Not all men are like Mark where the bad things outweigh the good, but everyone has things about them we wish they didn't."

"Yeah? What does perfect Matt have?" I challenged. I had never heard or seen one negative thing about Matt other than the fact he's in a band, but that's Holly's dad's issue with him, not Holly's.

"You really want to know?" she asked.

"Yeah. Does he wear your underwear or have a weird fetish? Oh, please tell me he has a fetish. That would make my day so much better."

"No, you freak. Matt doesn't have a weird fetish. He's a mama's boy and way worse than Mark. We could be in the middle of sex, and if his phone rings with her ringtone, everything stops. He has to answer it. The worst part is she calls all the time."

I paused for a moment before bursting out in laughter.

"It isn't that funny, Evie," she whined. "My fiancé would rather talk to his mom than finish giving me my happy ending."

"Oh god! Stop. Please! I can't take it." My hysterical laughter had progressed, making me clap like a seal. I had officially lost it.

"I'm going to hang up on you."

"Okay. Sorry. Seriously." One more giggle and then I was able to compose myself enough to speak. "It was just so unexpected." My phone beeped with an incoming call. Grant's name was on the screen. "Hols, Grant's calling me."

"Then you better answer. Call me if you need anything. Love you, Evie."

"Love you. Call me if you need a phone buddy. I

promise not to answer if I'm in the middle of—"

"Fuck you, Eve!" I heard her laughing as she hung up.

I was still laughing at Holly's calamity when I clicked over. "Hey there, handsome."

"Hey, babe. You sound happy."

"Just had a chat with Holly. How are you? You have a good day?"

He blew out a deep breath. "Day's not over yet. I have to go to a business dinner. Do you want to meet me at my place afterwards?"

"I might meet Tara for dinner and drinks. I blew her off last night to have dinner with you."

"Then come over after that."

"Grant, I have never been to your apartment. I don't want to just show up there and wait on you. I'll see you tomorrow if you plan to come to the lecture. Of course, your sister isn't lecturing, so you may not want to come."

"And miss your famous red velvet cupcakes? No way."

"Then I'll see you tomorrow," I said, disappointed that I wouldn't see him sooner.

"We'll see. I have to go, babe. My dad just waved me over to the table."

"Enjoy your dinner."

"You too."

After I hung up with him, I called Tara and met her at a sushi restaurant nearby. We were sitting on the patio drinking saki and laughing loudly at our girl talk when Tara saw some of her friends come in. Three guys came and joined our table. Sure enough one of them was Jake, the J. Crew guy from the other night.

"Eve, you remember Jared." Jared, not Jake. Why couldn't I remember his name? "This is Michael and Daniel."

I greeted each of them, suddenly feeling uncomfortable when Jared sat down next to me. I wanted to make friends in the city since I didn't have any of my own, but I had a feeling Grant wouldn't like this one bit. Eh, what he didn't know wouldn't hurt him.

"So, Eve, how's it working with Tara?" Michael started the "get to know you" conversation, but it wasn't long before the guys were telling embarrassing stories about each other, and I reciprocated by sharing what kind of girl Tara was in college.

We were still laughing about Tara's first keg stand when a deep voice behind me said my name. "Eve?"

I turned and found Grant standing there with an angry expression marring his exquisite face. "Grant! Hey, what are you doing here? I thought you had a business thing." I stood up to kiss him, but it was barely reciprocated.

He did wrap his arm around the nape of my neck possessively. "You've been drinking."

"Yeah. Saki. It's good. You wanna try some?" I asked, happily ignoring his foul mood, knowing it had everything to do with the company I was keeping.

"No. We need to go." He let go of my neck to grab a hundred dollar bill out of his wallet and dropped it on the table. "It's good to see you, Tara."

"You too, Grant. You coming tomorrow?" she asked him.

"Perhaps. It may be the only way I can keep my girl out of trouble." No one missed the way he emphasized my girl.

"Oh, stop," I said playfully. "Well, friends, I have some baking to do. I'll see y'all another time. Tara, drink some water."

She laughed. "Bye, Evie. Have a good night."

The guys all said goodbye, and I was sure a conversation about my new boyfriend acting like a caveman was about to ensue amongst them, but I had bigger fish to fry right then. That big fish was currently dragging me out of the restaurant at a pace my feet didn't want to carry me.

"Slow down, Grant." He ignored me. "You know you didn't have to pay for dinner? I can pay for myself, and it certainly wasn't in the hundred dollar range."

He ignored me again. He didn't even talk once I was settled in his car. In fact, Grant continued to silently fume all the way to my apartment. He pulled up in the turnaround and turned off the engine. He obviously wasn't planning to stay, but his manners were infallible, so he helped me out of the car and walked me to the door.

"You aren't coming up?" I asked.

"Not tonight."

"Do you want to tell me why you're so angry?"

"No. Go inside. I'll see you tomorrow." He wasn't touching me, and the tense expression hadn't left his face.

I didn't say anything else. I just walked inside.

As the elevator doors closed I saw his car pull away. Okay then.

It was after ten when I was back in my apartment, but I could make cupcakes in under an hour and then let them cool overnight. I would just have to get up early to ice them. No problem. I didn't think I would be sleeping much anyway with the possible demise of my new relationship bothering me.

I pulled out everything to make cupcakes and started mixing the batter. I heard my low battery signal, so I grabbed my phone from my purse only to find six missed calls and three text messages from Grant asking me where I was. Apparently he had come by my apartment. He knew I was out with Tara, so why would he come by here? Then something occurred to me. How did he know where I was? I started mixing more vigorously. At this rate, I wouldn't need to use my beautiful red Kitchenaid stand mixer I loved so much.

After I poured the batter into the cute little paper cups and put the trays in the oven, I called Grant. He didn't answer, which didn't surprise me, so I sent him a text.

Me: How did you know where I was?

Grant: Does it matter?

Me: Yes.

I sat on my couch biting my fingernails, waiting for either an explanation or the oven timer to go off.

When I had successfully chewed my entire thumbnail, I decided to go change into my pajamas. By the time the oven timer went off, I still didn't have a response. I set all the miniature cupcakes on the cooling racks and covered them with thin dishtowels. When the cupcakes were ready and my alarm was set for six in the morning to ice them, I headed to bed. I plugged my phone back in knowing I wasn't going to be getting an explanation tonight.

Unfortunately, sleep did not come easily. I tossed and turned for a little while, but I kept smelling him on my sheets. That would prompt me to check my phone just in case I missed something. Then I would lay back down, stay comfortable for a few minutes, then find the need to roll over and start the process over again. Finally I climbed out of bed and grabbed a spare pillow and blanket from the closet and moved to the couch.

I guess I fell asleep, because I woke up the next morning when my alarm started blaring from the other room. I threw the blanket off and shuffled to my bedroom to shut off my alarm. I went ahead and showered and dressed for the day. I went with my hair up because I didn't have the energy to curl it. I did have to spend some time covering up the dark circles under my eyes, which really burnt my butter. I was sick of my body wearing my emotional turmoil on the outside.

I threw on my monogrammed red and white polka dot apron and made coffee before I mixed the cream cheese icing, opting for my expensive mixer instead of attempting to mix it by hand. When I felt like it was ready, I filled a pastry bag and started piping away. Lost in the motion of swirling the icing on the tiny cupcakes, I jumped when I heard a knock on my door when I was about halfway through the batch.

When I peeked through the peephole, sure enough, there was Grant in his stupid three-piece suit with his stupid hair perfectly combed into place. I opened the door and walked back to the kitchen without even greeting him. I wasn't in the mood to talk. We could have done that last night when I wasn't so tired and grumpy.

"You're up early," he said carefully.

"Yup."

"I brought you breakfast."

"Thanks." I didn't look up from my cupcakes.

He leaned across the bar on the opposite side of sink on the opposite side of my galley kitchen, so he was speaking to my back. "I traced your phone." I froze. "I was worried when you didn't answer your phone and I couldn't find you. Then I show up, and there you were getting cozy with that guy from the other night."

"You traced my phone? Are you out of your mind?" I shouted. "How did you even do that?"

"Maddox runs a tech company specializing in security technology. My father's company owns Maddox's tech company, so I have access to all of their programs. He has an app that traces phones simply using the number. That's also how I knew you were from Georgia and where you lived."

"What do you mean that's how you knew?"

He rubbed the back of his neck before folding his hands and setting them on the counter. His face changed to reflect no emotion, just as a good business executive would do in a tense situation. "I looked into you."

I was not a business executive, on the other hand. "Why would you do that?" This time my voice came out low and was reminiscent of the tone my mother would use when Jane and I were in trouble. It was the same tone I used to discipline students when I was a teacher.

"I wanted to find a way to get to know you. I've never been interested in a woman my family didn't already know. I wasn't sure how to proceed." He spoke so blandly, as if I was annoying him by making him explain his behavior.

I was angry…really flipping angry. "This is ridiculous. What else do you know about me? Did you know I was caught speeding a week after I turned sixteen? Did your little background check tell you I had surgery when I was seventeen? Maybe you found out I bounced a check once. What were you expecting to find that you couldn't have just asked me about?"

"I don't know. You wouldn't give me the time of day, so I had to find a way to reach you. I didn't find anything before we went out. I wasn't expecting to see you on Friday. I was hoping to ask Tara about you, but then you were there and that jackass was flirting with you just like he was last night." He was raising his voice now.

"Oh, get over it! Tara was introducing me to her friends. It was unplanned, and I wasn't going to be rude to him. I couldn't even remember his name. I wasn't interested in him then, so I certainly wasn't interested in him after our weekend together."

"That little fucker needs to keep his hands to himself," he snapped.

"You need to manage your jealousy better."

"Jealousy? You think I'm jealous of that wannabe little prick? Please!" he scoffed.

"Could you be any more arrogant?" I sneered.

He ignored me because his phone rang. "What?" he snapped to the person on the phone. "No, Rachel, I told you that I would be there by eight-thirty. Set up in my conference room, and I'll be there in a half hour." He hung up his phone and set it on the bar with his keys. "Look, I have to go. I can't come to the lecture tonight, but I'll pick you up afterwards."

"Don't bother." I turned my back to him and went back to my piping.

Grant came up behind me and placed his arms on either side of the counter, effectively trapping me. "You promised you wouldn't do this anymore." He spoke quietly, but the anger still lingered in his voice. He moved the collar of my shirt and kissed me before running his nose down my neck, knowing it would be hard for me to resist him.

"Do what anymore?" I whispered.

He kept his lips against my neck, causing my body to heat in response, and this time it wasn't from anger. "You promised you wouldn't keep trying to end this."

I pulled away from his lips. "That was before I knew you were tracking my phone and performing a background check on me. Not to mention, you were the one who left last night. We could have easily talked about this then."

"Babe, we do background checks on all employees of the company and college. I was just using that information to find you. I tracked your phone because I thought something was wrong, and I'll do it again if it means I know you're safe. This city isn't safe for a girl like you. I left last night because I didn't want to say something I would regret. Don't be mad. I have to go to work, and I can't be worried about you all day while I'm negotiating a fifty million dollar merger."

He kissed up my neck to my cheek. "By the way, you look gorgeous today." He stepped away after one last kiss to my cheek. "Eat your breakfast. See you tonight."

After the door closed I started breathing again. The anger didn't disappear, but I didn't know what to think about Grant right then. What I did know was that the icing on top of every single cupcake was a perfect little swirl. I sprinkled them with red shimmer dust. Perfection.

Chapter 12

Obviously Tara knew something was up by the way she was treading lightly around me at work. We went to lunch together at one of Tara's favorite sandwich shops. It was quick and busy and distracting. She told me all about how much she liked Daniel, and she was excited about going on a date with him this weekend. I tried to be excited for her, I really did, but I just couldn't muster the enthusiasm.

Tara was kind enough not to ask. She knew if I wanted to talk, I would. I didn't want to tell anyone what was going on, which was strange for me, because I always wanted other people's advice to help guide my decisions. This time I didn't want anyone else's voice in my head, because I already knew I had forgiven Grant for invading my privacy. The only thing I wanted to discuss at this point was his behavior when he found me last night. He couldn't go around claiming me and embarrassing me. He was far too charming to be so disconcerting.

That discussion would have to wait until later,

though. I had another mundane lecture to sit through first. At least that meant I would be busy until Grant showed up, or so I thought.

Tara came into my office at four in the afternoon, right as I was shutting everything down. "You leaving to run by the bakery?"

"Yup. I also need to run by my apartment to get the cupcakes I made."

"Why don't I come with you? I'll come with you to your apartment, and then you can stay there and take the night off. I'll handle the lecture tonight."

"That's really nice of you, but I don't mind. It's my job, and I like doing it." I picked up my purse and headed toward the door that she was blocking.

"Eve, I'm not trying to be mean, because you know I love you, but you look exhausted. I know there is a lot going on with Mark, and now Grant. Just take the night off and get yourself together. You've been awesome jumping in the way you have, but you need to take a break tonight. I can't have my best employee burning out on me."

Tears started filling my eyes, but not because I was upset. I was getting emotional because I was tired. Some professional I was. Tara saw it. "Aw, see! That's it. You're going home. Come on."

"I'm sorry. I just didn't sleep well, and then I woke up early to ice the cupcakes," I tried to explain, but even I heard my voice crack.

"Not to mention you hardly ate anything at lunch," she scolded me. I rolled my eyes because that is exactly what my mother would have said.

By the time I had the cupcakes packed up and sent Tara on her way, I was thankful for the time off. I washed the makeup from my face and changed into an old sorority t-shirt that had been washed a million times and some hot-pink sweatpants—my comfort clothes I only allowed my parents to see me wearing. I climbed on my couch where the blanket and pillow were still sitting from last night. It turned out my couch actually was comfortable. I fell asleep in a matter of minutes.

Knock, knock, knock.

Silence.

Pound, pound, pound.

Silence.

Buzz, buzz.

Buzz, buzz.

The ceaseless racket woke me from a dream, leaving my muddled brain confused as to where it all was coming from until I heard one word. "Eve!"

My apartment was really dark like it was the middle of the night. Someone was at my door. Someone was at my door! I tried to climb off the couch and tripped over the blanket. My body crashed to the floor, and I fell on my arm that was still wrapped in the blanket. "Shit!" I cursed.

Knock, knock, knock.

Buzz, buzz.

Buzz, buzz.

"Ugh, I'm coming," I shouted and then whispered, "Chill out," to myself. Once I was free from the blanket, I made my way to the door. Grant. I opened the door to find a disheveled Grant pacing the hallway.

"You are here!" Grant took two large steps to me and wrapped me tightly in his arms.

"Of course I'm here. I fell asleep." Oh shit on a shingle! I just realized what I was wearing. Apparently it didn't matter, because Grant wasn't letting my body away from his. He picked me up like a child and carried me inside my dark apartment straight to my bedroom.

When we were both lying on my bed, he turned on my crystal bedside lamp and looked at me. "You all right? Tara said you weren't feeling well."

"I'm fine. Just tired. I stayed up late last night baking then woke up early to make the icing."

He gently pushed hair out of my face. "You had me worried. I couldn't get in touch with you. I have been pounding on your door for near twenty minutes."

"I'm sure my neighbors hate you."

"Don't worry about it." He shrugged it off like only men can do.

"What are you doing here?"

He seemed completely unperturbed. "I told you I would see you after my meeting. I was going to take you to a late dinner, but you weren't there. Tara said I could find you here."

"You didn't trace my phone?"

"My gorgeous girl and her sarcasm. Do they teach you that in Georgia schools?"

"Who's sarcastic now? Do they teach you how to run over people in Seattle prep schools?" I countered.

"I don't know what you're talking about."

I laughed silently. "Grant, you have two speeds. Stationary or stampede. There is no in between with you." Secretly, I thought I could like them both, but

I wasn't going to tell him that, especially not when I was still trying to get over the last stampede.

"Is that a problem?" he asked with a single brow raised.

I glanced up at him and melted at the way he was looking down at me. "No, I don't think it is," I reluctantly admitted. So much for keeping my heart firmly closed.

He pulled me closer to him and whispered, "Christ, I hope not. I don't think I could take it if you didn't feel what I feel."

I hummed in response, so he kissed me, making my body immediately surrender to him. It would have been a perfect moment had my body not decided to make one of those unpleasant noises that only happens at the most inopportune times.

My stomach growled…loudly.

When the obnoxious rumble escaped my body, Grant laughed. "Okay, my little peach needs to be fed. How else are you supposed to get round and fat-like peaches?"

"Oh, shut up and feed me."

Chapter 13

The first time I went to Grant's apartment was that weekend. Like Grant, his home was overwhelming. It was the entire top floor of his building, having been his parents' originally, which explained the décor. Everything in the giant penthouse was expensive and could belong in a museum. It was very old world and seemed strange to see in Seattle, a city known for its modernism and green movement. There was nothing modern in this place except the appliances.

I think what tripped me up the most was the fact that Grant had a staff. He had a live-in cook and a housekeeper. Now, my mom had a lady come to the house and clean every other week, but it wasn't anything like Grant's staff. Grant had someone to do his laundry and make his bed every day. How lazy must you be to pay someone to fluff your pillows? Needless to say, the introduction to the museum-like penthouse didn't go as well as he'd hoped.

I knew I was in trouble the second he punched in

a code to a private elevator. When the elevator opened to a private foyer, I felt the lead in my stomach. This was what Tara had been warning me about. When she said he was out of my league, she meant his parents' finances put him in a league all of his own. I knew Grant made his own money now, but he was old money, the kind of money that came from a well-bred, well-to-do lifestyle. We were doomed. Not only did I not fit into his world, but it was only a matter of time before Grant realized it too and found his way to Kitty or some equally worldly society girl.

When Grant opened the giant double doors leading into his penthouse, I was already biting my lip in discomfort. It was like entering Buckingham Palace, complete with expensive crystal chandeliers—yes, plural. Girls like me did not belong in Buckingham Palace. We had only entered the expansive living room before my brain started pumping out excuses for why I needed to leave. Grant had a firm grasp on my hand, so I couldn't run, but I thought about a sudden illness, period cramps, diarrhea, anything. Then I realized how disgusting all sudden illnesses are, and simply because of the fact they crossed my mind was precisely why I didn't belong in the palace. I bet Kitty and Iris never got cramps that left them bedridden for a day or two.

Grant tugged on my arm, pulling me further into the palace. "What do you think?"

I couldn't say what I thought, so I answered a question with a question. "You live here?"

He looked confused. "Yes."

"Hmm…" was all I could think of to say aloud.

"Why?"

"It looks like a museum, or a showroom. I mean, have you ever sat on that loveseat?"

"No." He paused for a moment. "I don't think I have. You're more than welcome to try it out." He gestured to the antique wood-trimmed loveseat with fluffy gold cushions. It and the matching chairs sat atop an expensive looking blue and gold oriental rug. The furniture was consistent with the other antiques skillfully placed throughout the room. Built-in shelves lined one of the walls, filled with expensive displays from all over the world. Another wall had several windows with floor to dentil moulded-ceiling silk drapes.

I shook my head. I wanted out of this ridiculous room as quickly as possible.

"Come on," he said as he pulled me along. "I hate this room. My mother decorated the whole place. I have never bothered redecorating because I know how much time and money she spent on the place. I like the kitchen though, and I promised you food." It was a relief he wasn't into the grandeur of this particular decorating scheme. "Scott," Grant shouted.

A pudgy, dark-haired man in his late fifties came out from a door in the kitchen just as we walked into the predictably huge kitchen. It was beautiful. It had all the old world charm to match the décor in the other room but top of the line appliances for modern convenience.

Maybe everything seemed bigger because I was used to my tiny apartment. I didn't think so, though, because I was sure this kitchen was larger than my parents', and they lived in a nice colonial house. This was a penthouse—a penthouse that took up an entire floor—but a penthouse nonetheless.

"Hey, Grant. Let me get your brunch out of the warming drawer. I'm headed to the store today for your parents. Iris requested only local produce this week. You want anything different?" Scott said with a hint of derision in his tone.

Grant replied with more than just a hint of contempt. "No, I'm good. Iris will probably want you to grow her a garden next week, so you might want to be prepared. Scott, this is Eve Bryant. "

Scott greeted me warmly before he started to set out platters of pancakes, bacon, eggs, and fruit on the rectangular kitchen table that Grant was leading me to. After he set the last plate down, Scott said, "Soon I'll be milking cows and pasteurizing milk for her. Enjoy your brunch. I'm off. See you both later."

After he was gone, I said, "He seems nice."

"Yeah, he prefers working here where he can make me whatever he feels like creating, and he knows I'll eat it, even if it doesn't happen often."

He dropped a kiss on my cheek before he filled my plate. "When you said you were going to make me breakfast, I thought that you would either cook or you would pour me a bowl of cereal. I didn't expect this."

He smiled like I had complimented him, but that wasn't really how I meant it. "Eat. I'll show you the rest of the penthouse afterward."

"A tour? Let me guess. The tour ends in your

bedroom," I teased, hoping that it was true and that the bedroom was a room for common-folk like me. Another room like the living room would kill my libido that had just jumped to attention at my suggestion.

"If you're good. Now, eat," he commanded.

"Yes, sir!"

After a delicious brunch and enjoyable conversation, Grant made good on his promise of a tour. He guided me from room to room, if you could call them that, and my stomach felt like another stone sunk in it with every new room. It was beautiful, but it just wasn't a place I would ever feel comfortable. By the time we were in his bedroom, I had a long list of excuses to get out of the palace where I was constantly telling myself not to touch anything.

I walked over to his floor to ceiling windows lining two walls of his corner bedroom and stared out at the city. Grant quietly padded over and wrapped his arms around me. Wrapped in his warmth felt comfortable, like home, but with every step around his meticulously decorated palace in the clouds, another seed of doubt was planted until I was about to sprout doubt. I hated this feeling.

I was a pretty confident girl. I liked who I was and what I did. Sure I had insecurities when it came to my body, but what girl didn't? I mean, I was curvy and not very tall. I had more junk in my trunk than I should, and my rear didn't get smaller no matter how many miles I ran. With that being said, only one other person made me doubt my self-worth, and it was because he reminded me daily of how boring and easily replaceable I was. To feel that way again because I didn't fit in my boyfriend's real life was leaving me unsettled.

Grant set his chin on my shoulder. "You hate it here, don't you?"

"It's beautiful."

"But…"

"I don't belong here." I left it at that.

"And you think because you feel like you don't belong here that you don't belong with me," he said, reading my thoughts.

I turned in his arms and lifted my arms around his neck and ran my fingers through his hair. "I didn't say that."

"But you thought it." He exhaled with defeat.

"But I thought it," I confirmed.

"How many reasons have you come up with so far to tell me it's over?" he asked sadly.

I smiled up at him. "None, actually. I do, however, have a long list of reasons why I needed to leave this museum right away."

He laughed. "Like what?"

"The first thirty weren't appropriate to say aloud in such a place, and the second thirty were arguable. You wouldn't have believed any of them."

He nodded his head like he was considering this. "Wow. It sounds like you have done a lot of thinking since we arrived."

"I guess." I pushed away from Grant to gather my thoughts. "This place is a little overwhelming. Your life is overwhelming. We've existed in this wonderful little bubble where it is just us in my tiny apartment with my Target bed sheets, Pottery Barn lamps, and IKEA couch you hate so much. You, on the other hand, have a staff."

"Is this the part where you tell me that we don't belong together? That you don't fit in my world? That I don't fit in your world? We're just too different, right?" He spoke quickly, and the anger in his voice rose as he paced in front of me.

"No," I said quietly.

He apparently didn't hear me, because his angry rant just continued. "Because that's ludicrous. You promised you wouldn't do this anymore. I've been doing everything I can to show you who I am, and you know what? You should know this place isn't me. My parents stopped staying in the city when I came back, so they let me live here. I didn't have any reason to get my own place, because this place would have sat empty, because they weren't willing to sell it.

"Hell, I don't even sleep in the master bedroom. That is on the other side of the penthouse. This is the guest room I always stayed in when I was in town. I like it because of the morning light, not because of the four hundred dollar sheets. I knew you were going to hate this place because you are the first girl who didn't care about who my parents were or what I had in my bank account. You scolded me for over-tipping the waiter last night because I didn't want to wait for change. I get it! You aren't interested in my money, or my parents' money in this case."

I had been quietly laughing at him throughout his whole diatribe. He stopped pacing when he noticed. "Are you laughing at me?"

I nodded.

"Why are you laughing? This isn't funny."

I walked over to him and wrapped my arms around him, sneaking my hands under his t-shirt so I could feel the warm skin of his back. "Did you hear me arguing with you?" I asked.

He frowned.

"I wasn't going to leave. I was going to continue to bite my lip until you were ready to leave your palace in the clouds and head back to reality. I may not be comfortable in your home, but how I feel in your arms is a different story. I'll try to get used to this museum if it's really important to you."

He thought to himself for a moment. "We can stay at your place anytime you want. I like it there. It's very you."

"Small and charming?" I teased.

"Exactly." He kissed me chastely. "Thank you, baby."

"For what?"

"Accepting this place. It is a little like a palace, isn't it? You should see my parents' house. It's awful. This is tame compared to what she's done there. It rivals Versailles. Iris loves her antiques." I laughed. I should have known this wasn't his reality as soon as I saw it. "We good?"

"We're good. Just don't make me ever sit in that living room with your mother. That might make excuse number two come true."

"What was excuse number two?"

Diarrhea. "Sick to my stomach."

"Got it. I would hate for you to vomit on her hand-woven Persian rug." Me too!

He bent down and lifted me off my feet before throwing me on his fancy bedding. "Ahh! My shoes."

"Quit worrying, babe." He found a way to make me forget where I was. In fact, he found several ways to help me forget. I didn't even mind waking up in his expensive bed later that day, not even with the guilt that plagued me for enjoying his luxurious four hundred dollar sheets.

Chapter 14

The next Friday night, Grant and I stopped by the pizza place so Grant could take care of Frank, then we went on our first double date with Tara and Daniel. Suddenly, Tara had found someone she "could really see herself with," whatever that meant for her. Grant was charming as always, and I fell a little deeper for him when he was so entertaining with my friend and her new boyfriend. I had never had the awesome boyfriend before, but I did that night and the many nights before.

Over the past week he guided me all over Seattle, and I showed him how to enjoy it all. We had gone back to the driving range last Sunday after we skipped the family brunch—Grant's idea, not mine—and this time Maddox wasn't there to spoil it all. Maddox did meet us on Tuesday for dinner where he brought his boyfriend, Nolan. The whole boyfriend thing was a shock considering how flirty he seemed when we first met, but seeing the guys together made perfect sense.

The best part was Nolan ended up becoming my

new best friend. I informed Holly of her impending replacement right away, and she was fine with it for as long as we were a country apart from each other.

Nolan and I had lunch every day after our first meeting, and it was Nolan who I called when I started to freak out over the Fourth of July party Grant insisted I attend with him. His parents were hosting, and it was cocktail attire. Nolan was going as well, but Maddox's father didn't know he was gay, so they weren't going as a couple. After I introduced Nolan to Tara on one of our lunch dates, he decided to take her to the party instead. She knew Daniel wouldn't mind her attending a party with a gay man, so she excitedly agreed.

Nolan had already tried to convince Grant to let him take me, but Grant wasn't having it. In fact, Nolan and I continuously taunted Grant about it because it made him growl, and we all knew what that did to me. Plus, the possessive "she's mine" sex was definitely one of my favorites.

Saturday morning after our double date, Grant and I were enjoying our alone time in bed. The weekends were the only days he stayed in bed until I woke up. It was also the first night all week I had spent the night at his penthouse. It wasn't exactly my choice, but his place was closer to the restaurant, and after hours of teasing each other, we both wanted to be in a bed as quickly as possible.

I didn't mind sleeping in his comfortable bed with his expensive sheets, and he was right about his room getting morning light. He could close the heavy drapes blocking it all out, but my man was a morning person. Lying in his bed with him running his fingers up and down my back was the most relaxed I had been in a really long time. I smiled contentedly.

"You awake, peach?" he asked when he felt me stir.

"Hmm…"

"Is that a yes or a no?"

"Hmm…" I turned my head to kiss Grant's chest but remained lying on top of him, cuddled in his arms.

"That's a yes. I need to talk to you about something while you're still half asleep." Of course that woke me right up. I set my chin on his chest so I could see his eyes. He looked down his nose at me and ran his fingers soothingly through my hair. "I know you, Nolan, and Tara are going shopping today, so I'm going to give you a credit card. Tara and Nolan both already know, so you aren't going to get away with not using it. I want to buy you a dress for the party and anything else you need or want. Tara said you needed a new handbag, so buy one. Buy whatever you want."

"She said that, did she? I don't need a bag, and I don't need your credit card. I can afford a dress."

"I know you can, but I want you to get whatever you want. Please just use the card and don't argue with me about this. You're coming to this party for me, so let me spoil you. I figure it's the least I can do. It's very possible I'll still owe you a thousand favors after dragging you to this."

I started trailing kisses up his chest. "What kind of favors?" I asked before climbing on top of him and straddling his narrow hips.

His hands trailed down my back and settled on my bum. He reached over into his nightstand and grabbed a condom, then asked, "When is your doctor's appointment again?" as he rolled it on.

He sat up and trailed kisses down my neck as I answered. "Wednesday. It was the earliest I could get and only because someone had just cancelled right before I called."

"I can't wait," he whispered as he rolled me onto my back and worshipped my body.

We were so wrapped up in each other that we didn't hear the alarm beep when the front door opened. We didn't hear the high heels pounding on the wood floors, and we certainly didn't expect Iris to open his bedroom door, only to find both Grant and me crying out in pleasure as our climaxes ripped through us simultaneously. Yes, we were seriously both moaning when she opened the door.

"This explains it then." Her voice was like pouring ice in the bed. I froze, and Grant whipped his head around. Oh god, oh god! This was not happening. This was not happening. "When you and your whore can be bothered to put some clothes on, I'll be waiting in the kitchen." This was happening.

"Mother!" Grant roared while remaining on top of me, effectively blocking Iris from my view, and hopefully me from hers considering I was naked and now a hideous shade of red from pure humiliation. By the time the door closed, my face was buried in one of Grant's stupidly expensive down pillows. "Baby?" Grant tried to take the pillow from me, but I gripped it tighter. "Come on, Eve. Move the pillow, so I can see you."

"No. Just go talk to your mother, and I'll go ahead and die from embarrassment." My words were muffled through the pillow.

"It wasn't that bad. She could only see me, although she probably heard more than just me." He laughed.

I removed the pillow so I could hit him with it. "Grant! This isn't funny. Your mom just called me a whore!"

His amusement quickly turned to anger. "Yeah. That won't happen again. Let's throw some clothes on and go face her."

"I'm not going out there!"

"Yes, you are."

"No, I'm not." I was considering jumping out the window of Grant's top floor condo. Unfortunately, the windows didn't open and the rooftop deck had glass windscreens, not to mention I would have to walk past the devil woman to get there.

Grant grabbed my chin and made me look at him. "You're my girlfriend, and we can do what we want in the privacy of my bedroom. You need to face her and show her that her bitchiness doesn't affect you."

I narrowed my eyes at him. "Not happening, Grant."

"Do it for me, Eve." He headed to the bathroom after one of his motivating ass slaps. Before I could climb out of bed, Grant was back in the bedroom zipping up a pair of jeans. "Baby, either you get up and throw on some clothes or I'll carry you out that way. I don't mind either way, but I'm sure you would prefer to be wearing clothes in front of my mother."

"I don't have any clothes, Grant. All I have is my dress from last night, and it's a wrinkled mess. I wasn't planning on staying here last night, remember?" I reminded him as I sat up in his bed and covered myself with his fancy sheets.

He marched into his giant closet and brought out a t-shirt and a pair of sweatpants. "Put these on. I'll take you to your apartment as soon as she leaves. When you're out shopping today, buy some clothes to leave here, even though I like you in my clothes. I like you naked too. Either way works for me." He threw the clothes at me before walking over and giving me a quick kiss. "I'm going to talk to her. You have two minutes before I come back and drag you out there."

I was about to have a conversation with Grant's mother in Grant's clothes. An hour ago I was the most relaxed I have ever been. Now I was trying to recover from possibly the most humiliating moment of my life. Oh, how the mighty do fall.

I threw on his clothes with my bra. I ignored the panties I wore last night and rolled the pants so they wouldn't fall off in front of Grant's momster. They were still too long, but I did the best I could. I ran into the bathroom and brushed my teeth and combed my hair. I tried splashing cold water on my face, but there was no helping the mess that was Eve Bryant on this lovely morning. I sent an emergency text message to Nolan telling him to come get me ASAP from Grant's. He replied back right away.

Nolan: Problem in paradise? On my way.

"Eve," Grant yelled.

"Coming," I called back and headed out of the bedroom to face my doom.

When I walked into the kitchen, Iris was sitting at the table with a cup of coffee. She was wearing another Chanel suit, pale blue his time, and her hair was flawlessly pinned into a sleek French twist. "Well, well, well, I was wondering if you would join us."

"Mother…" Grant warned. He seemed to do that a lot.

I was taken aback by her hostility. I thought Grant was going to talk to her. "Oh, umm…I was going to hide in the bedroom, but Grant didn't want to face the music alone. It takes two to tango, so to speak." I laughed uncomfortably. Oh my heavens! Could this be any more humiliating? No. No, I don't think it could. Thankfully, Grant laughed and wrapped his arm around me.

"Yes, it does. Maybe next time you decide to tango, you could do it with someone—"

Grant cut her off before she suggested that I find someone else, someone who wasn't her wealthy son. "Mother, that's enough. You will not insult my girlfriend. Get on board or go away."

"Don't you dare speak to me with that tone, Grant Mitchell. This has gone on long enough. You are too old to be fooling around like this. Time to grow up."

"Thanks, Mom," Grant said. "Did you come here to dish out insults and ruin everyone's morning, or did you have a real reason for stopping by?"

I didn't hear her response because the house phone rang. Grant answered and quickly hung up. He turned to me. "Nolan's here to pick you up?" he asked with a raised eyebrow. Grant was no fool. He knew what I had done. Surely he could understand how badly I wanted to escape this nightmare.

I did the only thing I could do. "Shopping," I sang then sprang into action. "Don't worry. I'll change before I go out in public." I ran back into the bedroom to grab my dress and purse.

Just as I grabbed my shoes, Grant walked in the room and leaned against the doorframe with his arms crossed over his chest. "What are you doing?"

Without looking up I shoved my panties in my purse like the cliché that I had become then explained, "Going shopping for the party. Do you not want me to go anymore?" Deflection attempt number two?

He let out a deep breath. "Of course I want you to go." Success!

"All right then. I need to get a dress. I need to make sure I look good if I'm going to be on the arm of the prince of Seattle." I smiled mockingly. "I have to go. Good luck with your mother." I kissed his lips quickly and darted toward the door.

"This isn't over, Eve. I know you called Nolan."

I laughed. "I don't know what you mean," I said as innocently as I could.

I avoided the kitchen and ran out the door barefoot, carrying my dress and my platform pumps. When I arrived in the lobby, Nolan was waiting for me looking sharp and grinning at my distress. "Not a word!" I snapped. "Car?"

"Right out front, Georgia girl." We walked outside to a blessedly empty sidewalk and he let me into the passenger seat of my car. Once we were on Alaskan Way, he said, "Spill it."

"His mom walked in."

"Walked in where? When?"

"You know when." I glared.

"His mom walked into the penthouse while you two were going at it?"

I nodded and covered my face as I relived the mortification of the morning.

"Where were you? In the kitchen? Living room? Rooftop deck?"

I shook my head to all of those. "Nope. We were in his bed."

"She walked in his bedroom?"

I closed my eyes and nodded again.

"Then she deserves what she saw. No mom should ever walk into her thirty-two-year-old son's bedroom. What was she thinking? I think the only sex uptight Iris has had was when her children were conceived. I don't know how Harrison puts up with her unless he's getting some tail on the side."

"Ew. Moving on. I think she was thinking she could humiliate me into leaving him."

"Isn't that what she did?" he asked with a raised eyebrow.

"No. I left to avoid Grant's credit card. Avoiding her insults was only the icing on the cake. I was pretty much done with the woman after she called me a whore."

"She called you a whore?" he squealed.

"I was naked in bed with her son at the time. I can see why that would be confusing for someone of her closed-mindedness."

He laughed as he parked at my apartment. We walked inside, fortunately bypassing any of my neighbors who might witness my walk of shame. I let him into my apartment. "Text Tara and tell her to meet us here, and then we can all go. I'll be ready in a half hour. Make yourself at home." I didn't think I had to worry about Nolan coming in my room when I was showering. He wasn't interested in what I had to offer.

After I showered, I was ready for dress shopping. Once I had my wedges buckled, I stepped out of my bedroom expecting both Tara and Nolan in my living room. Needless to say I was surprised when neither of them were there, but Grant was in the kitchen rifling through my refrigerator.

"Can I help you?" I asked.

He looked up from his search. "I was hungry. I didn't get to eat breakfast because I was explaining to my mother why my girlfriend ran away dressed in my clothes."

I ignored his outburst. "Where's Nolan?"

"He's going to pick up Tara. I told him that I would drive you to Barney's where you will be meeting him and Tara and a personal shopper."

"What? No!"

"Yes, Eve."

"No, Grant." Here we go again.

"Eve, you agreed. I'm giving you my credit card in case you don't find anything there, but Leila has an account set up for you at Barney's. She's already pulling dresses and a few other things for you. You'll pick out whatever you want. Tara and Nolan will help. If you don't buy anything, I'll take you back tomorrow." He was in his alpha mode again. While I agreed it was hot when he took charge, I did not want him buying me clothes. It was a little too Pretty Woman for me. His job was even similar to Richard Gere's in the movie too. To top it off, I would probably send the snails flying across the restaurant if he tried to feed me escargot. If only I were a hooker, we could recreate the whole movie. Lovely.

That thought just pushed me over the edge. I was completely aware of how crazy I was being. However, knowing I was being loony and stopping the train wreck that was about to occur were two very different things. To be fair, no one ever said I was rational when I was upset.

"You know what, Grant? You can take your credit card and your personal shopper and shove it up your ass. I like my clothes, thank you very much, and I don't need some rich playboy, whose mother already thinks I'm a whore, buying me clothes. Go to the party alone, because there is not a chance in hell I'm going. Better yet, take one of your mother's girls. That should get her off my back." I followed up my tirade with an angry stomp to my bedroom where I dramatically slammed the door and locked it.

As soon as Grant cursed and started trying to talk to me through the door, I stripped off my dress and threw on my hideous hot-pink sweat pants and another old sorority shirt. I climbed into my bed with my cheap Target sheets and turned on my small television and one of my rom-coms that I had on DVD. All the while Grant remained on the other side of the door. I knew it wouldn't be long before he unlocked the door, so I hunkered down in my little fortress to wait for his assault.

He was fuming by the time the door flew open, but I didn't care. How many times could members of the Mitchell family insult me today? Whore. Tramp. Hooker. Whatever. I decided I was going back to bed to start my day over.

"What the fuck was that?" he asked breathing heavily, his tone menacing.

"That was me hitting my limit of the number of times I can handle being called or implied that I'm a prostitute."

"What are you talking about?" His hair was a wreck from him running his hands through it. For some reason, that made me smile.

"You're sending me to a personal shopper to buy new clothes. What's wrong with my clothes? Too cheap for you and your mom? Too slutty? What?"

"Stop it! You know that was not what I was implying. I want to buy you things because I want you to have everything you need or want. I want you to have clothes at my place, so when you wake up in the morning, you can just get dressed. How does that make me the bad guy?"

I sighed disappointedly. "I don't want your money or your personal shopper, Grant. I thought I made that quite clear. Look, I'm tired now. I have only been awake for a few hours, and already this day has been hell. You have work to do, so just go.

I need to call Nolan and Tara anyway."

"No. Stop fucking pushing me away! Why are you this upset about the damn money?" he roared as he stepped closer to my bed.

Finally I sat up and looked at him. "I'm not upset about the money. I'm humiliated your mother walked in on us this morning, and you forced me to listen to her treat me like I'm nothing but the scum beneath her feet. I'm pissed that you want to buy my clothes so I can look like all your little playthings. It makes me a little unhappy that you sent Nolan away just to fight with me about money I don't want, and I'm really sick of the uncertainty that comes along with being your girlfriend. I have enough shit going on in my life. I don't need all of this." I was out of breath by the end of my little rant. I didn't mean to express all of the madness inside my head to him, because some of it I was still unwilling to acknowledge myself. Once I started, though, the words just came pouring out of me.

He sat down on my bed and rested his elbows on his knees. When he spoke, his voice was deep and regretful. "I'm sorry about my mother. I know she was horrible to you. I told her to either find a way to be civil and kind toward you or find a way to stay away from me."

I gasped. That wasn't at all what I wanted. She probably hated me more now. Now I was the whore who was trying to take her son away.

"I don't know why you're so upset about the shopping thing. I really don't get it, but I'll let it go if you buy something for the party on the fourth. I have to go to the party for work. I'd like for you to be there with me."

"I don't want to cause problems between you and your mother," I told him.

He turned to look at me. "Eve, baby, you aren't causing problems between me and my mother. My mother is causing problems between me and my mother."

Just then his phone started ringing. "Nolan," he greeted brusquely. "Yeah. She'll be there in a half hour." He hung up and looked at me. "Get dressed. They're waiting on you."

I was tired of fighting for the time being, and I knew he was still in stampede mode, so I did what I was told. I was only getting a dress for the dreaded Independence Day party, no matter what Tara, Nolan, or the personal shopper said.

Chapter 15

Grant led me to where Nolan and Tara were trying on party outfits before leaving for work. He barely said a word, which was fine with me. I had said everything I needed to say.

Nolan, Tara, and I had a blast picking out our red, white, and blue ensembles. Those two were the perfect distraction to make me forget about my troubles with Grant, but I didn't forget about him completely. I made sure to get him a red tie for his navy blue suit for the party. He bought my dress, and only my dress, so I felt like I owed him a little something. It was not an apology in any way.

By the time we were all squared away with our purchases, I still hadn't heard from Grant. I tried calling him to see what his plans were for the evening, but naturally he didn't answer. I wasn't deterred, though. It wasn't like we had to hang out every night together anyway. With that in mind, I asked Tara and Nolan if they wanted to get cocktails somewhere. They happily agreed and both called their men. Of course, Maddox and Daniel answered their phones and happily agreed to join us. I enjoyed the company, but once again I was the girl with the problem relationship. It was all a little too familiar.

We went to a Mexican cantina that Nolan loved. He was raving about their pomegranate margaritas, which was all it took for Tara and me to agree. Daniel showed up first and immediately wrapped Tara in his arms and gave her a very warm greeting. "Oh my…" Nolan said as he watched the pair kiss like they hadn't seen each other for weeks. I knew for a fact they were together last night, because I was there too, but I didn't remember them being quite so affectionate.

Was our double date only last night? After the day I'd had, the double date seemed like a lifetime ago.

By the time Maddox showed up, Nolan and Tara were already on their second margarita and telling me to hurry it up. I wasn't exactly in a party mood, and binge drinking was the last thing on the agenda. Maddox walked around the table, greeting Nolan with a quick peck on lips before hugging me and lifting me off my feet. "Where's the hotshot businessman tonight, Eve?"

"I don't know. Working, I guess."

With a quick glance, I caught the look Nolan gave Maddox that told him not to press the issue. Maddox understood Nolan's silent communication and introduced himself to Daniel and Tara, and the night moved forward. The five of us ordered, which did include another drink for me. The conversation was lively, and I was fine to sit back and listen while Maddox and Daniel discussed phone apps, and Tara and Nolan discussed local real estate. Not only did I have nothing to contribute regarding either of those topics, but I was also busy checking my phone, obsessively thinking Grant would call or text.

Before our food came out, my phone did start buzzing. Unfortunately, it was only Jane. Her calling was the perfect excuse I needed to step away from the table. I waved my phone at them and told them I would be right back. The patio was quiet because of the rain, so I stood over to the side under the overhang and answered my phone. "Jane?"

"Hey, peanut. I didn't expect you to answer. I thought you'd be hanging out with your new man."

"No. I'm out to dinner with some friends though. What's up?"

"John's sick with some stomach bug. I took the kids to Mom and Dad's anyway, but now I'm bored. Why are you answering if you're out to dinner with friends?"

"Rough day." I proceeded to give her a quick run-down of my morning and my fight with Grant. "That's the gist of it, so you can imagine how much I want to be out with friends, especially when some of them are his friends, but it's better than sitting at home sulking, right?"

"I'm sorry, Evie. It all sounds very dramatic. His mother sounds…lovely."

"Lovely is not on the list of words I'd use to describe her."

"Just remember she doesn't know you. Her judgments are based on Grant's past behavior.

Women like that don't get where they are because they're easy going. She's used to being in control, Eve, and if you want her to respect you, then you have to stand up to her. You can't just ignore the problem and pretend it doesn't exist."

"I also don't want to drive a wedge between Grant and his mother."

"No, of course not, but don't let her talk to you that way. It's really tacky that she would call you names anyway. This isn't preschool. The twins are only five, and they know better than to call people names."

"She only does it in private. When I went to brunch with his family, she sat there almost completely silent for the duration of the meal. I would rather her call me names than stare at me like that again."

"I'm sure," Jane agreed.

"Eve?" Tara called my name. I turned and found her peeking out the door. "Food's here."

"Janie, I have to go. Our food just arrived. I'll call you tomorrow."

"Hang in there, little sister. Everything will be better once you talk to Grant. He just needed time to think, like you said."

"I know. Love you, Janie."

"Love you too, Evie."

I hung up my phone and checked for any new text messages. Nada.

Back at the table, they were all still happily drinking and talking. "Was that Grant?" Nolan asked.

"No, my sister. She never calls this late, so I was

worried something was wrong."

"Is Jane all right?" This was from Tara, who looked like she had ordered another cocktail.

I laughed. "Yeah. Her date night was cancelled because John is sick. Now she's bored."

"I bet she never gets time to herself," Tara mused. "She should do something relaxing."

"She hates downtime, so she'll probably build an entire tree house or something. I'm like a sloth compared to my sister. How's the food?" I asked everyone. They were quick to tell me it was delicious.

I picked at my food even though it was as good as they described. I should have been hungry since I'd skipped breakfast and picked at my lunch, but stress was like kryptonite to my appetite. What I needed was a bath and sleep…and Grant.

Everyone else was finished eating, so I set my fork down. "Hey guys. I think I'm going to head on out. I'm really tired from today."

"Just wait a little while, and I'll take you home," Nolan offered.

"I'll get a cab." I couldn't walk. I had no idea where I was exactly.

"You'll do no such thing."

"Nolan, it's fine." He pulled me back down in my seat and firmly refused to let me leave alone. "You're acting like Grant now," I said, exasperated with yet another man bossing me around.

"Who's acting like me?" a familiar deep voice asked from behind me. As I turned to let my eyes confirm what my ears thought they heard, I saw Maddox smirking before Grant leaned down to kiss my cheek. Nolan quickly moved to the seat on the other side of Maddox at the large round table, allowing Grant to sit next to me.

"What are you doing here?"

He patted Maddox on the back. "My good buddy Maddox said you were all out enjoying margaritas and asked me to join the fun. Sorry I'm late."

Just then a waitress came by to see what Grant wanted. He ordered water and something to eat for himself and another round of margaritas for everyone. He turned to me. "You want another, babe? You hardly ate anything."

I said, "No," at the same time that Nolan and Tara shouted, "Yes."

Grant laughed and ordered me another one "just in case I changed my mind." I couldn't figure it out. He was acting like nothing ever happened.

Throughout the rest of the evening everyone seemed to have a good time, but I just felt withdrawn. Grant's arm was around me, somewhat grounding me. I was talking to everyone, and it was like I was there, but I felt more like I was watching from the outside. I knew what the problem was, but there was nothing I could do about it with all of our friends sitting around us.

After we said bye to everyone, Grant guided me to where his car was parked and held the door for me as usual. He didn't close it right away, though. Instead, he stopped me from climbing all the way in so he could stand in between my legs. He slid his hands up my thighs and asked, "Did you have fun shopping with Nolan and Tara?"

"It was fine. I have to pick up my dress on

Tuesday, though."

"No problem. I'll take you," he said as he pushed hair that had escaped from my bun out of my face. "You okay?"

"Fine."

"Shopping was fine. You're fine. Can I get another word?" he teased lightly, even though I could tell he was worried.

"Tired. I'm tired."

Grant kissed my forehead and my cheeks. "Then let's get you home and in bed."

I asked the important question. "My home?"

"Your home," he confirmed with a kiss on my lips.

"Okay." I didn't know if that meant he was staying or not, but I was glad to at least have my bed and my stuff for the night. I needed my space to deal with whatever this was.

The car ride was silent other than the music Grant had playing, but he touched me as much as one possibly could while driving. He held my hand as we walked and wrapped his arms around me in the elevator. It seemed he was as desperate as I was to get rid of the uneasy feelings that had developed between us since this morning.

Once we had both settled into my bed, he pulled me onto him so our bodies were against each other. He started tracing his fingertips up and down my back as I rested my head on his chest. This was the position I was in this morning when I woke up, before the day went to shit. I was sure it wasn't a coincidence.

"How did you know where we were tonight?" I

asked.

"Maddox. Here." He grabbed his phone from the nightstand and pulled up Maddox's text.

Maddox: Are you really the jackass that leaves his girlfriend checking her phone every five seconds? Get your ass over to the Mexican Cantina on Pine before Nolan switches teams for her.

Nice. Thanks, Maddox. I tried to explain my needy girlfriend behavior. "I called you. I figured you would call me back."

"I was going to call you back. I was talking to my dad. After my meeting, I went by my parents' house to talk to my dad about work and you. My mother apparently wanted to talk to me again. It didn't go very well, and my dad intervened. I don't think you'll have any more problems with my mother now."

I rolled off of Grant's chest and rested my head on my pillow. I wanted to be able to look him in the eye. "Let's get something straight. I don't have a problem with your mother. We have a problem. She hates me because I'm not who she chose for you, and the more you fight her in my favor, the worse the tension will become."

"Then what do you want me to do, Eve? I'll do anything to not have another day like today. I was miserable knowing how upset you were with me and with my mother. Honestly, I didn't know what to do, because I know you're waiting for a reason to end this."

"I guess we both have our insecurities then."

"What do we do about it?"

"I don't know." I felt the tears welling in my eyes.

It was then he saw my face. "Oh baby, don't cry." He pulled me to his chest and held me there. I held back a sob I was fighting.

I blinked the tears away and said, "I guess we have to learn to trust each other. I have to find a way to believe I fit in your world, and you have to trust that I'm not going to end things when we argue."

"What about the money thing? I want to be able to spend my money on you. I have plenty of money, and I have never wanted to spend it on anyone. I would buy you the world if I could, Eve, and you'd be mad at me forever." He ran his fingers through my hair after I set my chin on his chest to look up at him.

How could I explain the money thing to him without telling him how much I had given up? I slid my arm under my chin and started talking. "Here's the thing about the money. I work hard to live independently. I always have. Other than tuition, my parents haven't paid for me since I moved into the dorms at eighteen. My ex didn't have a job when we moved in together, so I paid for everything. Like you, I was more than happy to share what I had. He took advantage of my generosity, but it was fine because I had the "what's mine is yours" mentality.

"Eventually, my dad gave Mark a job working for his company. Mark started making good money, better than my teacher salary. We built the house and combined our bank accounts, but by then he was in control of the money. I had to ask permission to go to the grocery store. If I spent more money than I said I was going to, he would yell at me, even though some of the money was mine. If I wanted to go shopping, he had to be there to approve my choices. He picked out every item of clothing I had for two years. When I gained weight, he ridiculed me for needing to get a larger size. I was just disgusting and wasting his money on clothes according to him.

"In the meantime, Mark was accruing debt on credit cards and spending hundreds of dollars at bars and strip clubs. Of course, I didn't know that at the time. Now I have given him everything, every last dime, except for my inheritance from my grandmother that we used as our down payment on the house. He's fighting me on that too, though. That's supposedly why he won't sign the papers.

"So, I'm sorry if I seem a little touchy about money, but money is used to control people. I've given up every dime that I practically ever had so I could be on my own again, and I've worked hard to save up enough money to live in this tiny apartment with my cheap furniture and my inexpensive clothes." I had tears running down my cheeks by the time I finished telling Grant everything.

He wiped the tears from my cheeks with this thumbs. "Eve, I don't want to buy you things because I want to control you. I want to buy you things because I want to show you how much I care about you. As far as I'm concerned, you can wear whatever you want as long as all the essentials are covered. I don't want to have to be fighting off all of your admirers everywhere we go."

"Yeah, right," I said with a dramatic eye roll.

"Come here," Grant whispered as he tugged me up his body, so I was directly on top of him. "I do want to share everything with you, and I want us to be partners. You let me do my thing and buy you lots of extravagant crap that you don't need, and I'll shower you with affection and hang out on your uncomfortable couch as much as you want. Deal?"

I just wanted to hold on to this moment forever, because Grant seemed so content. For that reason alone, I agreed to his deal. Well, for that reason, and the fact that his very hard erection was nestled a little too close to the part of my body that was aching for him. This time I didn't have to be worried about his lunatic mother walking in, so I was able to really enjoy my generous man and his mad bedroom skills.

Chapter 16

Sunday morning I woke up before Grant. It was the first time that had ever happened, and I took full advantage of the opportunity to watch him sleep. He looked so young and relaxed. I tried to sneak out of bed, but strong arms trapped me and pulled me back. "Where do you think you're going, peach?"

I wiggled in his arms. "I was going to go to the bathroom."

He opened his arms for me. "Then by all means…" Just as I was about to set my feet on the floor, he grabbed me again. "I changed my mind. Bathroom is too far away."

"If you don't let me go, we might have another problem then." I rolled over and kissed my way up his chest to his lips. "I'll come back, you know."

"Will you?" He kept his eyes locked with mine.

I smiled at his worry. "Always." This time he let me up.

I took care of my business only to find an unpleasant surprise that was going to put a real damper on our sex life for a few days. Ugh! At least

I could use cramps as a real excuse if I needed one today. I brushed my teeth and hair before heading back into bed. Grant was already on his iPad reading the morning's news, but he set it aside as soon as he saw me. He opened his arms, and I happily climbed on top of him.

His hands started to roam, and I unfortunately had to put a stop to them. "Not a good time, handsome."

"Always a good time, beautiful."

"Not this morning or for the next three to four days." His mouth formed into an "O" as he understood what I just told him. He kept his hands firmly planted on my rear. "And I think we should join your parents for brunch."

His eyes closed and his head fell back. "Why would you want to go to brunch with my family?"

"Because, my darling prince of Seattle, I want to show your mother it isn't my intention to come between you two. And let's not forget that two out of the three of your family members adore me." I smirked. Grant tickled me in response, causing me to squeal and squirm.

"We better stop that if I can't have you for the next couple of days." He rolled me onto my back and kissed up my neck. "You know, I would say three out of four Mitchells you have met adore you. I also think you might be on to something. You'll get to meet Daphne's husband. He's back in town. He'll probably be just as charmed with you as Dad and Daph." He kissed me again before pulling me off the bed and giving me a motivating slap on my bum. "You get ready. I'm going to call my dad and let him know to save two seats at the table."

This time I pulled out all the stops on my brunch outfit. The last time the devil woman saw me, I was wearing Grant's clothes. This time I would be wearing a cream-colored wrap dress with a dusty-pink belt and matching peep toe heels. It actually had a designer label, and I had spent a lot of money on it, so there was no way I was ever getting rid of this dress.

I carefully curled my hair and meticulously applied my makeup. My pearl and gold jewelry looked traditional and classy. I applied my rose lipstick instead of my usual red.

Grant walked in as I finished putting my lipstick on. He was already dressed in a pair of khakis and a blue and white checked button down that he had left here last week. "Whoa, babe. You look gorgeous."

"You always say that."

"I always mean it too, but this dress is very sexy. Maybe you shouldn't wear it to brunch." His lips immediately found their way to my neck. "Mmm...smell good too."

"I like this dress, and it is one of the few things I have that might put your mother and me on the same planet, which is all I can hope for at this point."

"Baby, you don't have to try to impress my mom. She doesn't have a problem with how you look or dress. She's acting this way on principle because you aren't..."

He stopped before finishing that thought, but I let the cat out of the bag. Pun intended. "I'm not Kitty."

"Thank heavens for that." He kissed me. "Let's go. We don't want to keep the queen waiting."

Brunch number two was equally as tragic as brunch number one, but not nearly as humiliating as our pornographic moment in front of Iris yesterday morning. Daphne and Harrison were jovial and entertaining, as I had come to expect. Daphne seemed a little edgy with her husband Ian there. He was nice enough, but he was definitely on team Iris in the game of life.

Iris did actually speak to me during brunch, but it was mostly to get answers about the anniversary party. On the way out of the restaurant was when her claws came out. She stopped me and pulled me to the side. "I would like to speak with Eve for a moment." Grant looked suspicious, but he nodded his acceptance after seeing that I wasn't panicking about spending five seconds alone with the woman. I had to admit I was curious.

Once we were a few steps away from everyone, she leaned in and spoke quietly. "I don't care how many designer dresses you have in your wardrobe or what kind of tricks you have in the bedroom. You are not now, nor will you ever be good enough for my son. That being said, you don't appear to be a complete idiot, so let's make a deal. Since you obviously have him trapped in your sticky little web, you're going to have to leave him. How about you run away back to Georgia to your husband, and I'll pay two-years of your salary you would have earned working from the college?"

My mouth hung open for just a second, shocked at the fact she had offered me money to leave Grant, and at the fact she knew I was married. I never wondered why it didn't bother me that she insulted me and said I wasn't good enough for Grant. I happened to agree with her. Everything else was just plain rude.

I turned my lips up into a little smile and channeled my inner diva. "Look," I said firmly, "your son pursued me, not the other way around. I tried to avoid him for many reasons, but one of them was because I somewhat agree with the fact that I don't belong in his world of snobs and hypocrites. But you know what I discovered?" Her perfectly threaded eyebrow rose in question. "Grant doesn't belong in that world either. He's kind and decent and cares more about people than he does about the ridiculous amount of money he has. I care about your son, and I'm not going anywhere. You can continue to treat me like the trash you think I am, but all you'll do is drive a wedge between you and him. I don't want that for him or for you, but the ball is in your court, Mrs. Mitchell. How will you play?"

I walked away from her before she could say anything else and didn't look back. I had no interest in her words, because I was sure they would have been insulting. I was going to have to wait and see what her next move would be. For now, I was proud of myself for following Jane's advice and standing up to the devil woman.

The pride quickly wore off on the way home, though, and self-loathing spread like a stain on my mood. While Grant was on a business call on the drive back to my apartment, I stared out the window, lost in my depressing thoughts. I realized I was a sellout. I dressed up for that terrible woman against my better judgment, because I wanted to make up for the fact that she saw me at less than my best. It didn't matter, though. It only gave her more ammunition, because she knew I was doing it to impress her, and for that, I hated myself just a little.

Back in my apartment I walked quickly to my bedroom where I kicked my shoes to the back of my closet and threw my dress on the floor. I put on a pair of comfortable jeans and a plain white tank top. When I came out of my closet, Grant was sitting on my bed watching me. "You want to tell me what my mother said to you?"

"Nope." I walked over to him and wrapped my arms around him. With him sitting and me standing, it was the first time I'd ever had to look down to him.

His arms automatically wrapped around me and pulled me closer to him. His worried brownish-greenish-bluish eyes met mine. "You want to tell me why you're so upset?"

"Nope." I was smiling at his concern. I was done being angry with myself. Throwing my dress on the floor was just the release I needed, and now, standing in Grant's arms, I was perfectly content.

"How about why you kicked your shoes off and threw your dress on the floor and stomped on it?" So, maybe my closet time was a little more dramatic than I let on. Sue me.

"I just wanted to change." I tried to go with a simple explanation.

"Babe, you're doing it again." He was running

his hands up and down my waist, but the look on his face was suspicious. It must seem strange to a man to watch a women throw a silent temper tantrum and then be perfectly fine the next minute. He probably thought I was crazy, but I simply needed to let my frustration out.

"I'm not hiding anything or running or pushing you away or whatever else you say that I do. I'm not going to get in between you and your mother. If you want to know what she said, you should ask her. I told her how I feel about you and that I wasn't going away."

"Okay…" He was still suspicious.

"Everything's fine now. I was just mad at myself for a moment. Regular day in the neighborhood it seems."

Grant pulled me down on the bed and held me close to him. "Don't say that."

"I'm fine. Everything's fine. Now what do you want to do for the rest of the day?" I asked as I ran my hand down his chest and the front of his pants, deciding to give him a reward for being such a kind and caring boyfriend. Not to mention that my man was sexy as hell, and every time he wrapped me in his arms, I wanted to take his clothes off and do dirty things to him and with him. Fortunately, he didn't seem to mind.

After brunch on Sunday, my week took a turn for the good. I picked up my dress on Tuesday with Tara during our lunch. It fit like it was made for me, which I suppose it was after the alterations. Wednesday I went to my new lady doctor, and she gave me my birth control prescription that I could start right away. Now it was Thursday and time to celebrate Independence Day.

Grant and I started by enjoying our independence from work and went out to breakfast. While we were out, we watched a parade and wandered around Pike's Place Market. I figured he was trying to keep me distracted from worrying about the party at his parents' house that evening. It was my first Iris Mitchell event, and I had to admit I was more than just a little nervous about the whole ordeal. Not only did I have to get all dressed up and go to a place where all of the women used glam teams to get ready—I told Grant absolutely not when he offered to hire one for me—but I'd also be running into many of Grant's ex-whatevers, and quite possibly Kitty. As if Iris wasn't enough to deal with in one night, I would likely be in the presence of the chosen one. It wasn't like I could forget that by watching a parade of people dressed in red, white, and blue.

It was early afternoon when Grant took me home to get ready. I made him go home to his palace so I could get ready in peace. That really meant I would be getting ready listening to my favorite "get dressed for a stupid party but at least I have good taste in music" mix of Rihanna, Eminem, and Beyonce. I didn't want Grant to see me take way too long to get ready because I was shaking my booty all over my apartment. He wouldn't understand.

I did take my sweet time getting ready, though. My shower was longer than usual where I spent extra time shaving everywhere. I washed and conditioned my hair twice, hoping for some extra shine. Originally, I had planned to wear my hair up because Grant likes access to my neck, but I needed the protective shield that wearing it down offered. I curled it into soft curls and inconspicuously pinned it so it would hang artfully over the shoulder that was also covered by the dress. I was pleased with the result.

My makeup didn't take long. I put on a little black eyeliner with light eye shadow and some extra mascara, so my eyes would really pop. My lips were really the superstars, though, with my bright red lip stain and gloss. With my dress and shoes on, I felt ready for the red carpet, and this time I was dressed for me, not some old hag with control issues.

I turned off my music when Beyonce started singing about putting a ring on it. I didn't want Grant getting any ideas, and I knew he would be there soon. I wanted to be ready when he arrived, but I was too late. When I stepped out into my living room, I found Grant sitting on the uncomfortable couch on his iPad. His wide eyes took in the sight of me but said nothing.

"I didn't know you were here." He just kept staring. "What? Is it bad?" I glanced down at my dress. I thought I looked pretty darn good.

"Peach." That was it. That was all he said, but he kept his eyes on me. Finally, after spending an eternity squirming under his scrutiny, he stood up and walked over to me. He handed me a single red rose before gently kissing my neck. When he pulled away, he said, "You look stunning. I don't even have words."

I felt my cheeks turn red. He liked it. "You don't have to say anything," I managed to say with a gravelly voice. I felt too much in that moment, so I cleared my throat and changed the subject. "How long have you been here?"

"Long enough for Rihanna to love the way Eminem lies and Beyonce to sing about your halo and a ring." Three songs, not long. "I didn't want to bother you." He went for my neck again. "I can't kiss you right now, can I?"

"Nope. Not yet. You don't need to be wearing my lipstick when we see your mother."

"Fine," he grumbled, "but you owe me. Let's go. The car is waiting."

I set the rose on my counter and grabbed my clutch before following him out. In the elevator he pouted. "I really want to kiss you."

I smiled up at him. "What if I promise you limo sex on the way home? Will that make up for it?"

"Yeah?"

"We're good to go." Thank goodness! Four days without Grant was way too long.

He pulled me against him, so I could feel how hard he was already. "Then I can't wait for this night to be over."

Me either.

***

I had never dreamt of showing up naked to school or a party, but I now understood what those dreams felt like. When Grant and I walked into the large tent set up on the Mitchell's massive lawn, people stopped and stared, and then started whispering. I felt like an animal in the zoo, which then made me think about all the times I went to the zoo and stared at the poor creatures. I am sorry, zoo animals of the world. I shall not stare at you anymore, unless you are doing something entertaining like playing a guitar while walking a tightrope. I'm afraid I couldn't look away if that were the case.

People looked us up and down and blatantly stared as we walked into the party. Photographers took our picture, and people continuously greeted Grant as we walked through the crowd at the entrance. Grant, of course, didn't seem to notice all of the staring, because this was normal for him. He was busy greeting familiar faces. I, on the other hand, was having a silent mental breakdown. With the flashes going off in my face and men and women everywhere staring at us, I was tempted to run, until I saw the friendly smile on Grant's face. These were his people.

I decided to ignore the gawking and look for a bar and some liquid courage. Instead of a bar, I saw Tara and Nolan first. As more and more people surrounded Grant, he stopped introducing me. Thankfully, I was able to slip away and make my way over to Tara and Nolan. I guess Nolan saw me coming, because he had a glass of champagne ready for me when I arrived.

"How's it going, Georgia?" he asked as I downed the champagne.

"Well...I just met ten people, one of whom was

named John. I don't know which one, and I only remember because it is my brother-in-law's name. People were staring at us like we were a couple of dancing elephants. Now I'm here with you and an endless supply of alcohol. So far, so good. How are you two this evening?"

They were both laughing at my distress. "You look beautiful, though," Tara offered.

"Yeah, whatever. You both clean up nicely as well. We're the very epitome of the American dream. Expensive clothes and alcohol."

"Oh, is that what the American dream is? I thought it was for a man and woman to marry and have 2.5 kids," Nolan commented derisively. He was having a hard time with Maddox not coming out to his father, even though he and Nolan had been together for several months now.

I wrinkled my nose at him. "Who would want that? It sounds like a load of shit to me."

"And vomit and sleepless nights. No thank you," Tara added.

I felt a pair of strong arms snake around my waist, and a deep voice spoke into my neck. "You left me."

I leaned against Grant's hard chest. "Sorry. I needed safety and alcohol. You draw a lot of attention, sir."

"I don't think that was me. You look amazing, and everyone here already noticed. Don't walk away again, please. You're here with me, so you stay with me."

I leaned over to look at his eyes. Brown. He was upset with me. "I'm sorry. That was a bit uncomfortable, but I'll take my role as Grant's arm candy more seriously."

He knew I was joking in an effort to make light of the situation, so he smiled and tapped me on the nose. "Please do. How else will I be able to get a drink in this dump?" Whew! Crisis averted.

We continued to chat with our friends when Maddox joined us with his date. I felt Grant tense behind me when they walked up to us, and then he said, "Rachel?" Rachel was Grant's assistant, and apparently Maddox's date for the evening.

"Hello, Grant," the Pippa Middleton look alike said as she batted her eyelashes at my boyfriend.

Maddox attempted to make introductions as we all stared at the beauty, who was still eyeing Grant, by the way. "Ah, Rachel, this is Nolan, Tara, and Grant's better half, Eve."

I put on my friendliest smile. "It's nice to meet you. How do you like working for Grant?" How do you like spending every day staring at my man, bitch? So maybe my catty side was ready to come out in preparation for Kitty, and the other hundred or so women who wanted to bed my boyfriend.

"I love it. He's a good guy." She gave him a flirtatious wink. I had to bite my cheek to keep from rolling my eyes. Grant pinched my side knowingly.

Maddox laughed. "I think you have Grant confused with someone else, Rach."

"Oh, stop." She giggled and slapped Maddox's chest. Nolan grinned when he and I glanced up with the same expression on our faces. Grant didn't seem to notice as he took a sip of his scotch.

Tara was a whole other can of worms. "Then the

only good guy here is Nolan?" She raised her glass. "Here's to you, Nolan, my new favorite man."

"What happened to Daniel?" Maddox asked then added, "I liked that guy."

"Nothing happened to him," she responded with a nasty glare. I suddenly understood that her bad attitude was all about him. If my mind weren't already too busy keeping an eye on Rachel, I would have been totally entertained by her. I was disappointed in Maddox for being so spineless. He would be seen everywhere in Seattle with Nolan, but he encouraged Nolan to bring a date, a female date, to an event that was sure to have press and his father in attendance. Nolan acted like he didn't mind, but we knew he was hurt. The only saving grace was Tara was willing to blow off Daniel and come with him.

I was also grateful for the benefit of having Tara there. The way Rachel was still eye-fucking Grant made me want to punch her. I needed Tara's wrath to distract me from my own.

"Enough about that. Where are your parents, Grant?" Nolan asked. "Is Daphne coming?"

"I don't know about my parents. Daphne said she and Ian were coming."

"How's she doing? I hope she liked the flowers I sent," Rachel asked.

"Better. Much better."

I turned to look at him. "Was she sick?"

Grant shook his head. "No. I'll tell you later." Hmm…that didn't settle well in my brain. I didn't have time to worry about it right then, though. Tara shoved another glass of champagne in my hand, just in time for Iris and Harrison to walk up.

"Grant, darling, how are you?" She leaned over so he could kiss her cheek. Harrison greeted me first and then the rest of the circle.

"Mother. Dad," he greeted.

Iris turned to me. "Eve. You look lovely tonight. Did Grant take you shopping?" Just a minor poke. Not too bad.

Grant spoke before I could. "Actually, Nolan, Tara, and Eve went shopping while I closed the deal with the Williams Group on Saturday."

She smiled unconvinced and then turned to Maddox. "Maddox, you look charming as always. I see you brought our little Rachel. It is so nice to see you, dear. How's your father doing?"

Rachel smiled widely. "He's doing really well, even though he's traveling more. He just bought a new building in Paris. I can't wait to see it."

"I'm sure it's wonderful. He has the most impeccable taste. Tell him we said hello." Apparently Rachel has the Iris Mitchell stamp of approval.

She continued to greet the rest of our friends before grabbing Harrison's arm and floating off. Harrison turned to me and playfully rolled his eyes before giving me a wink and following behind her.

"Perfect timing," a sweet voice said. It was Daphne. "We just missed the Iris greeting show."

It wasn't long before the emcee made his welcoming announcement and then asked for everyone to be seated. Grant grabbed my hand and threaded it through his arm so he could lead me to the table. On the way I mentioned that Rachel seemed nice.

He responded, "Yeah. She's a nice girl."

I laughed. "I can see why she likes working for you."

"Why's that?" he asked.

"Who wouldn't want to look at you all day? She sure likes to mentally undress you."

He paused and glanced down at me. "Jealous, peach?"

"No, because I actually get to undress you," I said playfully. Grant tensed and looked away. I stood there confused for a moment when it hit me. "She has also gotten to undress you, hasn't she?"

"Not here, Eve," he warned, but it fell on deaf ears.

"You screwed your assistant? Could you be more of a cliché?"

He leaned down so no one would hear him. "It was a long time ago, baby. Don't make a big deal out of it." One out of the hundreds has a name to go with her pretty million-dollar face.

"Oh, I won't. I've seen the photos online. I knew what to expect."

I started walking again, but he pulled me back. "You what?"

I stepped closer to him. "Holly Googled you, so I had to see. After she talked me off the roof of the building, I decided it didn't matter as long as it was in the past. You've never given me any reason to doubt you, so I won't start now. Rachel can keep her little crush on you. I understand the appeal."

He kissed my lips, not caring if he ended up with red lipstick on his lips. My lip stain worked perfectly now that my gloss was on the edge of a few champagne glasses. "Thank you, baby. You know I only have eyes for one girl, and she's all mine."

We started walking again. "I would love to meet her. She sounds fascinating."

He pressed his lips to my ear, because his next words were just for me. "You have no idea. She's remarkable, not to mention dynamite in the sack."

I slapped his arm just as we approached the table we were sharing with his parents, Daphne and Ian, and two other board members and their wives. I, thankfully, was seated between Daphne and Grant. Grant was next to one of the board members, Mitch I think. From the moment the first course was served, the man kept Grant's attention, so I talked to Daphne while Ian was wrapped up in his own conversation with the other board member, whose name I didn't remember at all.

Dinner was a long process, and Daphne and I ran out of things to talk about because we just didn't know each other that well. By the time the crème brûlée topped with red and blue berries was served, I was a little tipsy and a lot bored. The emcee announced dancing would ensue, and the big band started to play on the far side of the dance floor. Couples flooded the dance floor, but Grant continued to chat it up with Mitch.

I saw Nolan and Tara laughing and having a good time dancing, and that thought made me smile. Of all of us, it seemed they were having the most fun. I tapped Grant's shoulder, and he excused himself to turn to me. "I need to use the restroom.

I'll be right back," I told him.

"You want me to go with you?"

"No. Finish your conversation. I'll be back in a few."

He stood when I did because Grant's manners were impeccable. After he gave me a chaste kiss, I headed to the luxury bathrooms. I fixed my makeup and started back to the table but didn't make it far before Iris stopped me. I immediately looked for help, but of course Grant's back was conveniently turned to me.

"Eve. I would like to introduce you to some of Grant's friends." I stepped over and plastered on a smile. It helped I was a little drunk, but I still grabbed another glass of champagne from a passing waiter as I approached Iris and the cast of Gossip Girl ten years later. "Eve, these lovely ladies went to school with Grant. This is Victoria Templeton, Penelope Allen, and the wonderful Miss Katherine Peters." Ah. Kitty, I presume. Game on, Iris.

Kitty had bright blonde hair pinned up into a sleek side chignon. Her red dress made her look like a siren, dangerous and threatening, but even I couldn't deny she was gorgeous. I hated her immediately, but I slapped on a smile and did my Georgia girl thing. "Nice to meet you. I haven't heard much about Grant's friends from school, but it's great to meet some of them." Iris thought she had me judging by the way her eyes widened at my friendly greeting. Silly old coot.

Katherine smiled sweetly, too sweetly. "I'm not surprised. Grant didn't tell me he had a girlfriend when we had lunch last weekend. He isn't really into sharing personal information sometimes." Lunch?

"Hmm…I guess not." Nolan caught my eye and waved at me from the dance floor. Tonight, he was my favorite for sure. "If you'll excuse me, I'm being summoned."

I walked right past Grant and joined Nolan on the dance floor. "What was that all about?" he asked when I arrived.

"Introductions."

He nodded and then started leading me in some semblance of a swing dance that was more fun than impressive. Once Tara was back, I left her with her dance partner and wandered back to Grant. I ran my fingers across his shoulders before I took my seat next to him. He excused himself from his conversation again and turned back to me. "Did you have fun dancing with Nolan?"

"Yeah," I said simply.

He leaned over and wrapped his arm around the back of my chair. "I thought you were going to the restroom."

"I did, and your mother stopped me on the way back to introduce me to some of your friends from school. Nolan called me over while Tara was in the restroom."

"I see. Do I have my girl back then?"

"She's been waiting all night for you."

He leaned over so his lips were against my ear. "I'm sorry about dinner. I should have warned you that Mitch would talk my ear off. I promise I'll make it up to you…in the limo on the way home, perhaps?"

I kept my head close to his and whispered. "How about you start paying your debt by dancing with me?"

"Nothing would make me happier. Well, nothing that we can do here at the party." He winked before giving me a sweet kiss. He stood and held out his hand. "Dance with me, gorgeous."

"I would love to dance with you, sir." I took his hand, and he escorted me to the dance floor.

We danced near Tara and Nolan, and Maddox and Rachel joined us shortly after. I caught Maddox eyeing Nolan every now and then, and a part of me felt bad for him. Anyone who knew what was going on could tell he was really struggling, but I hated that Nolan had to pay for Maddox's choices.

"Where are you, Eve?" Grant asked, bringing my attention back to him.

"I was just thinking about Maddox and Nolan."

"Not our business, babe. Maddox's dad is difficult and his only living family member. Nolan understands."

"Still sad." I shrugged.

"Yeah. I'd be going crazy if I couldn't be dancing with you, or if you came here with someone else. Do you know how many men have been watching you tonight? I can't imagine not being able to touch you or hold you or kiss you all night."

"You just want to claim me, caveman."

"Damn right."

I laughed. "Don't worry. If it weren't for you, I wouldn't be here."

He pulled me closer to him, so close that if my

middle school teachers were there, they would have been sticking a yardstick in between us to separate us. "If you weren't here, I wouldn't either. I want to be wherever you are."

His bright green eyes were shining down at me, with something akin to…love? God, I hoped so. "You know I feel the same way." His kiss this time was a prelude, and I felt it in my core and everywhere else.

"My, my Grant. What happened to no PDA with your arrangements?" A woman's snide voice broke our perfect moment.

He pulled away and turned both of us toward her. "Virginia," he greeted apprehensively.

She stepped over and gave him a kiss on the cheek, but he held on tightly to me. "Oh, Grant. Why so cold? I've missed you."

Grant was obviously uncomfortable, but he couldn't even imagine how awkward I felt. The girl didn't even have the decency to come on to him in private. "Virginia, this is my girlfriend, Eve."

"Girlfriend? Since when do you have girlfriends?" she asked with a surprised laugh.

"Since Eve." He turned to dance with me again. "Have a nice night, Virginia. Tell my mother I said to keep it up." Thank you, Grant. Point for Eve. One to one, Iris. One to one.

We danced for a couple of songs before heading over to the bar to join Tara, Nolan, and Maddox, who was now missing a date. "Where's Rachel?" I asked when we were standing in our little pack.

"She's hanging out with the bitch brigade of Brantley High," Maddox said with a mindless shrug.

"Rachel went to high school with you guys?" That was news to me.

"No. She wishes. She went to public school." Not public school! How dare she? "Only Pen and Kitty went to school with us. Victoria went to college with them, and Rachel is their project."

"I see."

"Here you go, baby." Grant handed me a bottle of water before his lips found my cheek. He was really the most affectionate man I had ever met. I wouldn't need to pee on his leg to mark my territory, because he was always too busy marking his.

"Thank you."

"Of course. You need to make it a little while longer before the fireworks show here."

"Can't wait. I love fireworks," I said as he wrapped me in his arms.

"Then you'll love Iris's show." Kitty. I turned my head to find Kitty and her pretty little friends standing next to our group. Sure enough, Rachel had also joined Maddox, who was standing close to Nolan. "Grant, it's nice to see you as always," she said too sweetly again. Maybe that was her 'I'm about to be a bitch' tone. "Iris introduced me to Eve earlier this evening. Why didn't you tell me you had a girlfriend? I would have loved to hear all about it last weekend at your parents' house." Rawr!

"I don't share my personal business with my mother's minions, Kitty. You should know that by now." I looked up at Grant's brownish-colored eyes. My man was not a happy camper. I was pulled so tightly against his chest that air wouldn't be able to come between our bodies right then.

"You should know by now that your relationships meant to piss off your mother only cause problems for everyone. Isn't it time you grew up and stopped screwing around? When you decide to become the man you are supposed to be, you know where I'll be." She turned to walk away.

"Don't hold your breath, Kitty," Maddox muttered.

She turned and glared at him. "What did you say, Maddox?"

"I said 'don't hold your breath.' Grant isn't coming for you anytime soon, so you might want to move on, princess." Thank you, Maddox. Point two for Eve.

"Really, Maddox? Maybe I should hold my breath for you. Oh wait, you would rather sleep with—"

"Katherine, that's enough!" Grant roared and moved me out of his way to get in her face. "You will not behave this way here. You will only embarrass yourself. Take your friends, and step away. I am not now, nor have I ever been interested in what you have to offer. You will not insult Eve or Maddox like that again."

She opened her mouth to speak, but the emcee interrupted her. "Fireworks will begin in five minutes. Mr. and Mrs. Harrison Mitchell are grateful you chose to spend your holiday with them and hope you enjoyed your evening. Now, please follow the path to the viewing area."

Grant took my hand and led me to the path. He

patted Maddox's back to lead him away from Kitty and her loyal subjects. Maddox looked over at him once we were a few steps away and gave a grateful head nod.

Grant just nodded his head in response and kept walking with his buddy. In the viewing area, our little crew of Tara, Nolan, Maddox, Grant, and myself huddled close together. Grant stood behind me and wrapped me tightly in my arms. "I'm sorry about all of that." He spoke quietly so only I could hear.

I turned in his arms and my hands wrapped around the back of his neck into his hair. "It's fine. You handled it well. I do have one question, though."

"What's that, beautiful?"

"Did you really have lunch with her last weekend when we were fighting?"

He kissed my lips quickly then explained. "No. I went to the office for my meeting. My mother must have put her up to it, because she tried to bring me lunch from my favorite deli. I let her leave the food but sent her away. Then she was at my parents' house when I arrived there to speak to my dad."

"Why didn't you tell me?"

"We'd had a rough day. I didn't want to add anything to it. It seemed unimportant since I didn't say more than five words to her. You know she doesn't matter, right?" No, I didn't know she didn't matter. I wasn't so sure Iris was going to let Kitty not matter. This problem wasn't going away. Instead of worrying, though, I kissed my man with everything I had.

The fireworks started, and I moved away to watch the show. I didn't make it far from him. He wrapped his arms around my shoulders so they rested just above my breasts. I felt safe and secure tucked against him, but I wasn't the only one looking for comfort. I watched as Maddox's hand searched blindly for Nolan's. When they connected, Nolan looked down for a moment then back up to his partner. I watched as Maddox turned and mouthed an "I'm sorry" to Nolan, and Nolan responded with an "I love you." Maddox repeated the phrase, and they turned back to watch the fireworks display hand-in-hand.

I looked up to watch it as well, after I wiped the tear from my eye. Grant leaned down and kissed my cheek. "See, I told you everything would be okay." He nodded toward his best friend and his partner. "Don't worry, baby. I'll make sure of it."

It would have been easy to believe him, but I knew all too well there were some things that were out of his control. He may have been the master of his universe, but there was some darkness in mine he couldn't stop no matter how powerful he was. Running away was only a temporary solution. Eventually I would have to put on my big girl panties and go back to Georgia. That thought was displeasing, so I swept it under the lumpy rug where I kept my problems and focused on the very handsome man holding me safe in his arms.

Chapter 17

After the extensive fireworks display, the emcee wished everyone good night. People started trickling away in small groups or couples. Our little group seemed reluctant to let the moment go. We all just kind of stood there together, hanging on to it, but unfortunately, it wasn't long before Nolan had to let go of Maddox's hand and Grant had to go say goodbye to his parents and sister.

Grant squeezed my hips and said, "I'm going to go tell my family bye. You stay here with Maddox."

"I'll come with you," I offered.

With a kiss to my forehead he said, "No, baby, I don't want my mother to ruin your night. Mad, keep an eye on her, and keep the wolves at bay." By wolves, I wondered if he meant he-wolves or she-wolves like Kitty.

Maddox wrapped an arm around my shoulder. "Sure thing, boss."

With a look of warning toward Maddox and a smile and kiss for me, Grant disappeared into the crowd. With Nolan and Tara gone, it was just me and Maddox left standing there. This was the first time I had been alone with Grant's best friend. To break the silence between us, he asked if I had a good time as he walked me back up the path away from the crowd to wait on Grant.

"Yeah, aside from the usual mama drama, it was a fun party," I told him truthfully.

He turned to me. "Look, I owe you an apology. I haven't been very nice to you because I'm always suspicious when Grant has a new girl. He was protective of you when I first met you, so I knew you were more than just one of his absurd arrangements."

"I really care about Grant."

"I know that now, but you have to understand a lot of girls want to marry into the Mitchell family or want him to buy them expensive things. He just isn't into it. Not only does he loathe the fact that people covet the Mitchell lifestyle, but he also couldn't care less about the things his parents care about. He isn't like Iris and Harrison, or even Daphne and Grace."

"He seems to respect his dad," I argued.

"He does, and that's why Grant eventually took his seat at the round table, but don't be fooled. Harrison cares about the money and their reputation as much as Iris. He's more private, though, and can be duplicitous."

"All right. So, why are you telling me this?"

"I've been with my share of women—"

I interrupted him. "What?"

He nodded. "Yeah, I tried and tried to please my dad, but I have never once felt anything more than friendly toward a woman. When Nolan came along, it was like my life made sense. Nolan is my first partner, so to speak. Of course I was attracted to guys all along, but I wasn't willing to admit it to anyone, not even Grant, until Nolan and I started dating."

"I bet he already knew. He's your best friend."

"He did. Even though I have done some pretty raunchy things with women with Grant in the room, he said he always suspected. Grant never judged me, though. It was just the way it was with him. Anyway, this isn't my sob story. My point is that Grant was the same way."

"Oh, I'm one hundred percent sure Grant isn't gay."

He tapped me on the forehead. "Not gay, Eve. He never felt anything real for a woman until you. You're his Nolan."

"You think?"

"I know."

I smiled widely. "That's the nicest thing you've ever said to me."

He held up a finger, letting me know his point was still to come. "Here's the thing. If you aren't in it for the long haul, you need to let him be. Iris is going to come in between you every chance she gets, and like I said before—don't underestimate Harrison. I don't want Grant hurt because you have your own shit to deal with, you know what I mean?" He means my divorce. My fucking divorce.

"Sure." I managed to agree, frightened by what he was implying. Then I turned and saw Grant walking toward us. Seeing him so confident and handsome, I knew he was made for me. Tonight he wore the navy blue suit with the red tie that I had bought him. His jacket was off and back at the table, but damn if he didn't look hot in that vest. His sleeves were rolled up a little, revealing his strong arms. His hair had been perfectly combed when he walked away from us because I kept my hands to myself all night, but after one conversation with his parents, it stuck out in all directions. That made me smile. When he caught sight of me watching him, he locked gazes with me and smiled widely. I returned the smile knowing all the while I was in this for the long haul. I had accidentally fallen in love with this man.

I turned and hugged Maddox. "I'm in this," I said without a shred of doubt. I pulled away and looked up into his blue eyes. "You're a good friend, Maddox. I understand that and was never offended that you didn't welcome me with open arms. If you ever decide you want to tell your dad about Nolan, you know we're all here for you. You don't just have Grant."

"Thank you, Eve. That means a lot to me." He wrapped an arm around me once more just as Grant came up behind me.

"You trying to steal my girl, Maddox?" Grant asked as he pulled me away from Maddox.

Maddox wiggled his eyebrows, and we both laughed when Grant glared at him.

"She's all yours, Grant. I have my own to hurry home to tonight."

"Yes, I better get this lady home before she turns into a pumpkin," Grant said and started to lead both us out of the party.

"I think you mixed that story up. Cinderella doesn't turn into a pumpkin," I said. "She goes back to being a servant."

"Hmm, perhaps we can test your servitude when we get home then, Cinderella."

"Get a room, you two," Maddox interjected playfully.

When we made it to the car, Grant offered Maddox a ride home while I silently begged him to decline. Thankfully, he did, leaving Grant and me alone in the back of the limo. Once the door was closed and the privacy screen was blocking the driver from our view, Grant pulled me into his lap.

"Did you have fun?" he asked as I nuzzled my head into his neck.

"Mmhmm," I responded.

"Are you drunk, babe?"

I shook my head. "No. The water helped, and I stopped drinking over an hour ago. I'm just tired now."

"You looked amazing tonight. It's like every time I see you, you knock my socks off." He kept rubbing one hand up and down my back while the other held my legs tightly to him.

"It's the dress. This ridiculously handsome and stupidly rich man bought it for me. He's very generous."

"He'd give you anything you wanted," he whispered into my hair.

"Just you, Grant. I only want you."

"You have me, Eve. You had me from the moment I walked into my sister's lecture and saw you standing there dressed in black and white with those beautiful red lips, smiling dreamily as you set cupcakes on platters."

I smiled into his neck and whispered the truth to him. "You made me so nervous I didn't hear a single word your sister said. You smelled so good and were so incredibly good-looking, my body practically shut down when you sat so close to me."

"I had to sit next to you. I thought if I could only be close to you for a moment, it would have been worth it."

"Was it worth it?"

"It wasn't enough. Nothing will ever be enough." He took a deep breath and sat me up so he could look into my eyes. "Baby, I think about you all day, every day. I dream about you even when you're right next to me. I can't stand the thought of spending a day without you, so I do everything I can to get to you each night. You're it for me, Eve."

"I know the feeling."

He sat me up, so I was looking him in the eyes when he spoke. Then he said the words that both terrified me and made me feel whole at the same time.

He whispered, "I'm so in love with you, baby, that every morning I wake up elated you are still there, and at the same time terrified I'll lose you, that my mother will finally make you give up on me, or you'll realize how undeserving I am of you. I've never felt like this before, and I don't exactly know how to handle it without smothering you. I would keep you with me all day, every day just so I knew for certain you were still there."

I smiled at him and ran my fingers through his hair. "Even though I have made some imprudent choices in my life that might lead you to believe otherwise, I have never felt this way about anyone, and I definitely didn't think it was possible to feel this way this fast. But, the truth is, I'm head over heels in love with you too, Grant. You need to know I'm not fighting against us anymore. I'm fighting for us and will continue to fight for you, for us, so that nothing will come between us, not even your mother. This is the first time I have ever thought it was worth it, that I'm worth it."

His worried eyes looked relieved, and our mouths came together in a kiss where we each poured all the words we didn't have into each other. I had never felt so loved as I did in the back of the limo, and we didn't have sex in the car like I had promised Grant. We just held each other and kissed until we arrived at his penthouse.

When I saw where we were, I frowned. "Why are we here?"

"It was closer to the party, and I want you in bed instead of in the back of a limo. I don't want to rush tonight."

"That sounds nice."

"It does, doesn't it?" He grinned and I nodded. "I also have a present for you here, and I don't want you to argue with me."

"Okay."

"Okay?" he asked surprised.

"Okay," I agreed.

When the driver opened the door, Grant climbed out with me in his arms. He didn't set me down as he strode into the lobby and right into the elevator.

"I can walk, you know," I told him, even though I didn't mind being in his arms.

"I know, but I don't want to put you down." He carried me all the way to the bedroom where he gently set me on his bed.

"Did you lock the door? I don't want any surprises in the morning."

"Don't worry, baby. I took care of it. I told you that you never needed to worry." He kneeled down and carefully took off each of my dark-blue satin shoes. His hands slid up my legs and body and pulled the few pins out of my hair. He gently pulled me to stand so he could unzip my dress. When the dress slid down my body, Grant held on to it and tapped each leg, so I could step out of it. He went into his closet where he presumably hung the dress up even though it would probably need to be cleaned.

When he came back I was lying atop his stark white sheets in my lace strapless bra and matching thong. "There's something I would like to see every day," he said as he loosened his tie and stalked toward me.

I sat up and slid to the edge of the bed. "Let me do it." He came and stood in front of me. As his hands gently roamed my body, I took my time unbuttoning his shirt and his pants. His bright green eyes stared into mine with love and affection.

Once he was completely undressed, he peeled the last layers off me and kissed a trail down my body and back up again. He worshipped every inch of my body, making only one stop to provide me with my first orgasm of the night. Once he had kissed his way back up my body, he kissed my lips and tasted faintly of me. I didn't mind. "You know I've never done this without a condom before."

"Good," I said. "Then this will be a night you'll never forget." I rolled him to his back and climbed on top of him. I kissed a similar trail down his chest before tracing my tongue over his erection.

"No, baby. I want to be inside of you."

"I know." I pressed a kiss to his tip before kissing back up his chest and neck. "We'll get there. We have all night," I whispered into his ear as I moved to straddle him.

Our lips connected as I sunk down on to him slowly. He took in a deep breath when I had taken all of him. "Hold on. I just want to feel you," he said. "This is…holy shit, babe. You feel incredible. I might not be able to last."

I kissed him. "This is all about you, Grant. What do you want?"

He took my hips and guided me, slowly at first and then faster until he couldn't take it anymore and rolled me over on to my back. He lifted my hips, and I felt him everywhere. "Open your eyes, Eve. Look at me." I stared into his green eyes with the bright gold flecks that could barely be seen in the moonlight as we came together in by far the best orgasm I'd had yet.

We lay there for a long time with him still inside me before he slid out and shifted to my side. "Baby, you still awake?" Grant spoke quietly.

"Mmhmm."

"We're never using condoms again."

I laughed. "Okay."

"Was it as good for you?"

I opened my eyes and ran my hand down his cheek. "That was the best I have ever experienced. You want to know something?"

"Of course. Anything," he said nervously, probably thinking I was going to tell him something about his performance.

I smiled. "I had never had an orgasm before the first time I was with you."

His eyes widened. "What? Never?"

"Never. I tried to give myself one, but it just never happened. Then you touched me for the first time, and I practically convulsed on the spot."

"No wonder you were so tense. You wouldn't let go. Not a problem anymore." He kissed me. "So wait, what about with…never mind. I don't want to know."

He tried to turn his head away to rid himself of the thought of me with another man. I pulled him back to me and looked into his eyes that were back to their indiscernible color. "Never, Grant. Only you." That made him smile and apparently ready for round two.

I woke up the next morning to an empty bed. It was still early, and I had the day off of work thanks to my wonderful boss who knew we would be out late after the party. Grant had to work, though. He always had to work, but he wouldn't have left without saying goodbye. I crawled out of bed and checked the bathroom, but it was empty and the shower hadn't been used. I threw on Grant's shirt from the night before, smelling it as I buttoned a few of the buttons. I didn't want to put my panties back on from the night before, so the shirt was just going to have to do. After brushing my teeth, I went in search of my favorite workaholic.

Avoiding the kitchen because I knew there was a chance Scott was there, I headed to Grant's office. On the way I passed by the laundry room just as Lana, Grant's housekeeper, came out. "Oh! Good morning, Miss Bryant. Would you like me to send your dress to the cleaners with the other things I am taking today?"

"No, thank you. I'll take care of it."

"Very well. Mr. Mitchell is in his office if you're looking for him."

"Yes, thank you." I was thanking her for the information and the fact that she didn't seem to notice I was only wearing Grant's shirt with nothing underneath. Ever the professional that Lana.

When I was closer to Grant's office, I could hear him talking. The door was open, so I leaned against the frame and watched him work. His office had floor to ceiling wooden bookshelves, complete with one of those old library ladders. He had a large wooden desk and the signature floor to ceiling windows of the penthouse. The office was very old world and even had a globe from the seventeenth century or something ridiculous.

When he noticed me he smiled widely. "Yes, sir. I'll have my assistant forward you the details of the contract by the end of the day. Thank you." When he hung up the phone, he walked over to me wearing just a pair of athletic shorts. I met him halfway and my arms immediately went around his neck. "Good morning, peach," he said as he wrapped me in his arms and kissed me like he hadn't seen me for days.

"Why are you up so early? It's only seven something."

"Seven forty-five," he said after reading the clock on the wall behind me. "East coast has been at work for a couple of hours, and the early bird gets the worm, so to speak." My mouth formed an "O." "What are you doing out of bed? You hate mornings."

"I woke up alone, so I came out in search of someone who could warm the bed for me." I smiled as I climbed my way up him to reach his lips. He lifted me easily off the ground and carried me over to his large leather desk chair then sat down with me straddling him.

"I'm so glad you found me first."

"I didn't. I found Lana first, but she's not my type," I teased him.

"Lana saw you dressed like this?" he asked, and I nodded, knowing he was going to get possessive even though it was just Lana. "Baby, you have nothing on under my shirt." His hands were roaming under his shirt. "I do like seeing you in my shirt, but this," he grabbed my ass, "and these," he cupped my breasts and ran his thumbs over my nipples, "and this," he touched my little bundle of nerves making me squirm, "are all for me."

I leaned forward and kissed him while his fingers kept playing me like Charlie Daniels plays the fiddle. As he kissed his way down my neck and I moved my hips rhythmically against his fingers, I found myself so close, and then the flipping phone in his office rang.

He moved to get it. "No, please don't stop," I begged and tried to stop him.

"I have to answer, babe. I'm waiting on a call." He kept his hands in place and answered the phone with his free hand. "Grant Mitchell."

I heard a woman's voice on the other end just before his finger left my body, leaving me frustrated and a little angry.

"Mother. It is lovely to hear from you this morning. What can I do for you?" He put the phone on speaker and then went back to kissing my neck and torturing my body. I stopped his hand and gave him a dirty look. He was not about to get me off with his mother on the phone.

"Grant, don't play games with me. I'm in the lobby. Why the hell did you change the code to the penthouse elevator?"

I pressed my face into his shoulder to contain the giggles that suddenly overcame me. I could hear a smile in his voice when he said, "Because I don't like my mother charging into my house and my bedroom anytime she pleases."

"You never used to mind. In fact, I remember escorting many of your lovely dates out of the penthouse after you were done with them."

I stiffened at her words, but Grant's hand soothingly rubbed down my back while he spoke his next words. "Eve's different, Mother. I told you that after the first day I spent with her." I leaned up and smiled at him. He looked me right in the eye. "I love her, and she'll be around for as long as she'll have me, so get used to it."

"Let me up, Grant. We need to talk. Now!" his mother snapped and then hung up the phone.

Grant rolled his eyes and lifted me up to place me on my feet. "I think it's time I showed you your surprise then. We'll finish this," he gestured to the chair, "as soon as she leaves."

I couldn't text Nolan this time, so there was no getting out of this impromptu meeting. "What about your business call?" I asked, hoping he didn't really have time for his mother.

He grabbed his cordless office phone and waved it at me. "Come on, baby. I think you'll appreciate your surprise now."

He led me back to the bedroom where we didn't pass anyone on the way this time. He closed the door behind us and let me into his closet, which was actually more like a dressing room. One of the reasons I picked my apartment was because of the large walk-in closet. My closet was tiny compared to the room where we were standing. It was practically the size of the island in the middle of his dressing room.

I looked up confused until I saw the shelves of women's shoes on the wall next to the door that we walked in. "I don't understand."

"This side is for you. When Leila took your measurements last weekend, I had her send over anything she thought you'd like. I want you to have everything you need here."

"So, you bought me a whole wardrobe?" I asked as I started opening the mirrored doors to find dresses, skirts, pants, and tops all hanging up. There were shelves with jeans, perfectly folded t-shirts, and handbags. Everything appeared to be designer, and therefore expensive.

"Everything still has the tags, so anything you don't like can go back. I just want you to have options. She didn't know what you like, and I didn't know what to tell her, because every time I see you, you're dressed in a different style. All I knew was that you seem to like dresses, so all three of those sections are dresses." He moved over to the island. "Last thing. These are all yours as well." He pulled open a drawer and revealed rows of matching bra and panty sets. "I know you like to match, and this was a little easier for me to pick out. You like lace and light colors. I like you in all of it."

"Grant," I said shaking my head.

He pulled me into him and lifted my chin so I would look at him. "Eve, you said you wouldn't argue. My mother is probably waiting in the kitchen, and now you have clothes to wear."

"Fine, but a lot of this is going back."

He kissed me. "We'll see. Now get dressed, and no texting Nolan to come get you," he commanded as he threw on some jeans and a plain red t-shirt. He went through the other door in the closet, which I already knew led to the bathroom, even though this was the first time I had ever actually been in his closet.

I quickly grabbed a simple white bra with lace trim and matching panties, then found a pair of skinny jeans that I liked. I threw those on with a black and white patterned t-shirt. I didn't look too shabby considering I hadn't showered, didn't have makeup on, and didn't want to get dressed this morning.

"Let's go, babe," Grant called from the bedroom. "She's waiting."

We walked out of the bedroom hand-in-hand. I liked that we were both barefoot in jeans and t-shirts. It felt comfortable, something I hadn't yet felt in this monstrosity of a penthouse.

We walked into the kitchen to find Scott setting out a platter of pastries and fruit, and Iris was sitting at the head of the kitchen table in her typical pastel-colored Chanel suit drinking a cup of coffee. Grant held my hand as he kissed her cheek. I twisted my hand loose and headed toward the coffee as he said, "Mother, I see you made it up here safe and sound." He sat down on the other side of the table, so his back was to the windows.

"Yes, I happened to still be in the lobby when Scott came in. He said you told him not to tell anyone, including me, the code."

"I did," Grant agreed as he smiled at me and took the cup of coffee I brought over to him, fixed just how he liked it with two sugars and no cream. "Thank you, Scott."

Scott nodded and left the room without a word, presumably to hide out. I wondered where he went and if I could hide there as well.

"Does Eve know it?" she asked.

I opened my mouth to say no, but Grant spoke too soon. "Yes. I want her to feel at home here. Of course she knows it." I just sipped my coffee in silence as I leaned against the counter away from their tête-à-tête. He winked at me when he caught my raised eyebrow.

His mother hummed. "I see. Well, I came over here to discuss your behavior last night. I spoke with Violet Peters this morning, and she said you were positively awful to Kitty. You need to call her and take her to lunch to make up for it."

Grant laughed. "Absolutely not, Mother. Kitty insulted Eve and Maddox. I simply asked her not to be so rude."

"That's not how she took it, and you know how important her family's relationship is to us. As the acting CEO of the company, surely you understand the importance of the connections the Peters bring."

"Not happening, Mother."

"We'll see about that. I'll make your apologies again and let her know how busy you are with getting the new subsidiaries started. Now, in other news," she folded her hands primly on the table, "who are you planning to bring to the anniversary party? We need to coordinate, so we all arrive together."

Grant sighed. "We've already discussed this. I'm not bringing anyone. Eve will be working there, so I'll be there for her and with her." He looked up to me, "Babe," his mother winced at the pet name, "what time do you have to be there?"

I walked over and sat in the chair next to him, and his hand was instantly on my thigh. This was the first they had acknowledged me since we walked in the room. "The event starts at seven, so I plan to get there at noon to place the flowers and finish setting everything up. I'll probably stay all day and just get dressed there."

Iris tapped her perfect manicure on the table. "Just as I told you, Grant. You can't walk into the party without a date, and you can't take Eve. Even Grace and Harvey will be in town."

"Mom, I'm not taking anyone other than my girlfriend anywhere unless one of my sisters needs me, end of discussion. Now, have you called Daphne lately?" He tried to change the subject.

"Of course. I call her every day," Iris said defiantly. This conversation was none of my business, so I started to get up from my seat, but Grant's hand tightened its grip on my leg.

He looked at me. "Where are you going?"

"I was just going to give you some privacy," I told him.

"Sit down, Eve," he said before turning back to his mother. Let the awkwardness continue. "You should spend some time with her. She's still having a hard time, and Ian doesn't want to try again right away," Grant suggested kindly.

Iris waved him off. "She's fine, Grant. Quit treating her like a baby. She'll only continue down this emotional path if you play into it."

"Mother, she lost her baby at sixteen weeks. That's traumatic. The least you could do is have some sympathy for your own daughter." So that's what Rachel was referring to last night. Poor Daphne.

Iris rolled her eyes. "I do. I took care of her when she came home from the hospital, didn't I? It has been two months. Time to move on. The world doesn't stop turning for personal tragedies. You should know that by now, Grant." She stood from her seat. "Since you obviously aren't feeling agreeable today, I'm going to leave. Your father said you are working from home today. Maybe your friend should go home so you can actually do what your father expects of you."

Grant stood and took her coffee cup to the sink. "Goodbye, Mother," he said as he kissed her cheek like he always did. I remained in my seat. It wasn't like we were going to hug it out.

"Goodbye, dear," she said sweetly and then changed her tone to say, "Eve," with a nod of her head.

"Have a nice day, Mrs. Mitchell." I tried to say it sincerely. I really did, but that was not how it sounded when the words came out of my mouth. Ah, well.

Scott returned to the kitchen as Grant was taking a bite of some kind of pastry. "She gone?" he asked.

Grant nodded. "Yeah. You're safe."

Scott's shoulders sagged with relief. "Good. She blamed me for her dress feeling too tight last night, and then she gave me hell when I wouldn't tell her the code to the elevator."

I was as grateful as Grant for Scott keeping it a secret, so I spoke for us since Grant had a mouthful of melon. I walked over to the giant island and leaned on the counter next to Grant. "Thank you for not telling her the code, Scott." Then I turned to Grant. "Why did you tell her I knew it? Don't rub salt in her wounds. She hates me enough."

Scott laughed. "Oh, honey, she hates everyone who isn't related to her or in business with them. Take it as a compliment. It means you're a real person." Grant gave him a look of mock offense. "Grant, she hates you and Daphne most of the time anyway. That's why us normal people actually like you."

"He's right, you know," I told Grant with a smile. "Everything I like about you and Daphne is what your mother despises in me."

Grant shrugged. "She doesn't hate anyone. She just acts that way so no one will know she is a lonely housewife."

Just then the phone rang. Grant answered, and after a moment of listening to the other person, he gestured that he was heading to his office. I nodded and he kissed me on the head and walked away.

"You want anything else to eat?" Scott asked.

"No thanks. I'm going to take a shower. Iris loves to interrupt my mornings."

"Iris loves to interrupt anything and everything. I'll be going to the store later if you need anything. Just let me know."

"Thanks, Scott," I said as I walked back to the bedroom.

I took a quick shower and braided my wet hair. I didn't have anything to get ready for anyway. Grant would probably be on his call for a while. I threw on a casual tank dress and some sandals then headed up to the rooftop deck with my cell phone. I made my weekly calls—Martin, Holly, Jane, and my parents. I had spoken to everyone but Martin several times during the week, but I liked to catch up as much as possible.

The rest of my family was at our lake house enjoying summer on my dad's pontoon boat, so they just passed the phone around. Even Fitz and the twins got on the line to talk to their "awesome Aunt Evie." Holly and Matt were at another lake, water skiing and wake boarding with a couple of friends, and Martin was at work. No surprise there. That man would do anything to avoid babysitting his wild grandkids his daughter constantly left at their house.

Martin said he sent the request for mediation to Mark's attorney on Monday and hadn't heard anything back, so he was going to call when we got off the phone. I told him I was ready to pull out the big guns, so I briefly shared about Mark's drinking and control issues. I told him about the financial reports my sister had on him, and about the multitude of charges on the credit card at local strip clubs. Martin warned me that if he didn't agree we would have to go to court, and that information would be helpful in my case.

"Sounds good, Martin. Thank you for everything."

"I'm proud of you, Evie. Have a nice day." I hung up and felt a sense of power run through me. The girl who never stands up for herself was finally going to do something about it.

Chapter 18

"Babe?" I heard Grant calling.

"Yeah. I'm over here." I was still sitting in the lounge chair thinking about what I was going to say at the mediation. He walked over with wet hair and clean clothes on.

"I was hoping you had waited for me to shower, but Scott said you came up here after you left him to take one." He lifted me up so he could sit behind me. Once he was settled I lay back down on his chest. It was a lot more comfortable than the lounger. "What are you doing up here?"

"Nothing. I called everyone to check in and then was sitting here thinking."

"Thinking about what?" he asked.

I wasn't sure if I wanted to tell him, but I didn't want there to be more secrets. "I decided to meet with Mark and his attorney to get the divorce settled. I have to go back to Georgia for the mediation, and if Mark won't agree to what I've asked of him, we'll have to go to court. I'm sick of giving in to him only for him to screw me over. I want my grandparents' money back and out of this joke of a marriage."

Grant stayed silent for a moment. "That could drag your divorce out for months. I thought you didn't want to do that."

"I don't want to, but I don't want to give up my nest egg either. That money was from my grandparents. He doesn't deserve it. I certainly don't think he should get to stay in that big house while I'm giving up everything just to get rid of him."

"You aren't giving up everything," he said irritated.

"You know what I mean, Grant."

"How much money is it?"

"Thirty grand."

"Babe, I'll give you thirty grand right now if that's all it takes to end this." I tried to sit up and he tightened his arms around me knowing I would try to escape. "Don't even start, Eve. You know I'm not flippantly offering you money. I want him out of your life just as much as you do. If money is what is keeping you from being completely mine, then that's something I can handle. Hell, I'd pay him off just to get him to sign the damn papers. I love you, baby, and I want you to be happy. Now, if something else is keeping you from finalizing your divorce—" I cut him off before he could even voice that thought.

"No, and I appreciate your willingness to help. I know that kind of money is pocket change for you and your family, but that money meant something to me. I don't want to leave it in the hands of the man who helped turn me into someone I couldn't stand to see in the mirror. I feel like I'm finally getting myself back, and only because my family has been fighting for me for the last year. I owe it to them to stand up for myself, and I promised you I'd fight for us. If you just pay the money, it'll be like I didn't do it for myself. Does that make sense?"

He sighed and rested his head back in defeat. "I guess. Will you at least tell me when you're planning to go home? I want to be with you. In fact, maybe you should have one of my attorneys with you."

"Grant! No!" I huffed.

"No to the attorney or me coming home with you?" He was in business mode now. I already knew I wasn't going to win this.

"No to both. You cannot come to my divorce settlement with our attorneys, and no, you are not hiring me another attorney."

"I would like to go and meet your family and Holly, though." He made his big play going for the family card. If I said no, I'd hurt his feelings. If I said yes, he would probably sit outside the door of my meeting. If he could get away with it, we would conduct the mediation with me on his lap, and he would have the final say in the proceedings. Not happening.

"How about you and I fly down to Georgia one day when my divorce isn't on the agenda?"

He buried his face in my neck and spoke quietly into my ear. "I want to be wherever you are. You know that. I'll move heaven and earth to make that happen."

I felt myself melt into him when butterflies erupted in my belly. Who knew a man like Grant Mitchell had such a sensitive side? "I know," I whispered back to him, "and I love you for it, but I don't want my past and present to mingle. I think it sets a bad precedent for the future."

"Future," he said thoughtfully before his phone started buzzing. "Dad?" he answered. I could hear his dad's voice coming from the phone, but I couldn't make out what he was saying. Grant responded, "Not happening. I already told Mom no to all her brilliant ideas. You two really shouldn't push me on this. I did finish the deal with Williams and sent the contracts over to Susan…"

He continued talking as the vibrations in his chest from his voice lulled me to sleep. I wasn't asleep that long, but when I stirred, Grant was off the phone and had his iPad in one hand and the other arm holding me.

"What are you doing?" I asked when I saw his iPad was watching the stock ticker and there was an article beneath it.

"Watching the market. Reading up on some companies I'm interested in acquiring. Watching you sleep." He kissed my hair.

"Sorry I fell asleep. I didn't get enough rest last night."

"That's why I didn't wake you after I got off the phone with my dad. Scott brought us lunch out here when he brought my iPad up."

I sat up and he lifted the top off a tray of fruit and sandwiches. I grabbed a turkey sandwich and took a bite. It was really good. I was starting to like having Scott around for many reasons, the least of which was he also despised Iris.

"This is good. Too bad we don't have any sweet tea." I winked at him.

"You and your damn sweet tea. I'll have gallons of it shipped here for you. Just say the word."

I placed my hand over my heart dramatically as I pretended to fan away tears. "That's the sweetest thing you've ever said to me."

He laughed and kissed my neck. "You're nuts, peach." I smiled back at him, enjoying the moment. After all the drama, these were the moments that made everything worth it.

"You'll understand once you meet the fam."

"Yeah?" I nodded with a wry grin. He laughed then asked, "What would you be doing if you were at home right now?"

"I'd probably be with my family because Fitz's birthday is Sunday."

"Who's Fitz?"

I set down my sandwich and picked my phone up to show him my nephew. "Fitz, the twins Ava and Campbell, and then baby Elle. My nieces and nephews."

"Show me more."

I flipped through my pictures and showed him my parents, sister and John, Holly and Matt, me with the kids, me holding Elle right after she was born, our Easter picture, and then I accidently flipped to a picture of me last Labor Day standing with the twins, looking positively gaunt in a bikini at the lake. I was so skinny my bikini was hanging off of me, and my ribs were showing on my normally curvy body. I stopped there and tried to put my phone away.

Grant noticed. "Show me that last one again."

"No," I snapped.

"Why not?"

"It's a picture for me to remember."

His tone became worried. "Baby, why were you so skinny?"

I closed my eyes, so I wouldn't have to see the look that matched his tone. "Because I wasn't eating. Stomach pain is some kind of somatization of my anxiety and stress that was all brought on when things started to get unbearable in my marriage. The stomach pain makes me sick, so I don't eat when I feel stressed or upset. When that picture was taken I had just moved out and hadn't really started getting myself together yet. Seeing myself in those photos was really the kicker. My sister took several of them, so I would see how bad I looked."

"How long were you not eating?"

"Months. Let's talk about something else. I'm fine now. Sorry I showed it to you."

"I'm not." He put his sandwich down and turned so he was facing me. "I want to know everything about you, the good and the bad."

I looked up at his greenish-bluish-brownish eyes and let out the breath I hadn't realized I was holding. "I wasn't ready for all this. It's a good thing you were so persistent or else I would have never known what this feels like."

"Yes, I think you should listen to me more often. I'm very wise."

I smiled flirtatiously. "One of your many qualities."

"Oh? What are my others?"

I climbed over so I was straddling him. "You're very handsome." I kissed his neck. "And kind," another kiss slightly higher, "and loyal," kiss, "and generous," kiss, "caring," kiss, "and very sexy." This time I kissed his mouth. "Now about this morning…"

"Yes, I owe you, don't I?" His hands slid under my dress. "I really like dresses. I'll make sure to thank Leila for the dresses."

"Don't talk about another woman when you're touching me, not even one who gave you the access."

"Jealous, baby?" he asked and shifted his hand slightly.

I unbuttoned his pants and touched him as I spoke quietly into his neck, "I must thank Maddox for his talk last night. He really—"

Grant flipped me over onto my back, interrupting me. He was lying on top, pinning me to the lounger. "Point made, Eve," he growled. His hands crawled back up my thighs and found my panties. I guess he didn't want me to get up to pull them off because he tore the delicate lace and threw them to the side.

I giggled like a schoolgirl. "I guess it's a good thing you bought those. You can do whatever you want to the panties you buy."

"I can do whatever I want, whenever I want. Remember, we decided you were listening to me, the wise one from now on."

"Oh, right. Well wise one, what do you think

about finding your way inside me now?"

"I think that is the best idea you've had all day."

After some rooftop hanky panky, Grant had to work for a while, so I hung out and watched a movie in his media room. Just after The Rock lets Vin Diesel and Paul Walker go on the bridge in Fast Five, Grant walked into the room. "Hey baby, you need to go pack a bag."

"What? Why?" I sat up confused.

He came over and sat down on the large sectional before pulling me into his lap. "I have some business down in San Francisco, and I'm taking you with me. My meeting will take an hour or two early tomorrow morning, and then it is just the two of us all weekend. We're going to fly down tonight and stay at the Fairmont."

"Then I need to go home."

"You have everything you need here. Go look in the bathroom drawers. I had Lana get you everything that you have at your place."

"I saw that. Thank you, and thank you for the clothes, but if I'm going somewhere I have never been, I want my camera. I also want a book to read on the plane, because knowing you, you'll be working on the flight over."

"Actually, I had other plans while we are in the air. We're taking one of the company jets."

"Ugh. Rich people and their modes of transportation." I rolled my eyes.

"Hey! I think you'll love flying privately." He tickled me on my sides.

I squealed and squirmed. "Stop it, Grant! I'm serious!"

"Me too. Very serious." He stopped tickling me and found himself between my legs. He pressed his hips against me and I could feel just how serious he was. "Unfortunately, we need to get packed and get on the road. Wheels up at eighteen hundred."

"I still want to go by my apartment. You didn't make me forget with your antics." I tapped his nose as he climbed off of me and pulled me up off the couch.

"Fine," he groaned. "I have to pack, so you can pack here or at your place. Either way, we need to leave for the airport in a little over an hour," he said as he dragged me to his closet where he pulled out two tweed weekend bags. "Bring a dress for tomorrow night. I'm taking my girl to dinner," he said with a slap to my bum.

An hour and a half later we boarded the Mitchell family's company jet only to be greeted by a pilot, a co-pilot, and a beautiful Asian-American flight attendant. "Lucy?" Grant said when he saw her.

The flight attendant looked surprised and then smiled brightly. Great…another one. "Grant! I didn't know it was you flying with us tonight. I was expecting your father."

"Where's Otto?" he asked, obviously uncomfortable.

"He took on some commercial flights now that you aren't traveling as much. He's stuck in bad weather in New York, I think, so he called me to cover. Is that all right?" she asked with uncertainty.

Grant cleared his throat. "Yes. I guess it will have to be. Lucy, this is my girlfriend, Eve Bryant. Give her anything she wants. I need to make a call."

He walked to the back of the plane and closed a door behind him.

"Welcome aboard, Miss Bryant. Please come have a seat anywhere you want," Lucy said. "How about I bring you a cocktail?"

I chose one of the four cream leather captain's chairs that surrounded a small round wooden table. "Just water, please."

"Still or sparkling?"

Water! I don't care. "Whatever you have on hand is fine," I replied as politely as I could while I wondered where Grant went.

She brought me a bottle of each and a cup with some ice and set it all in front of me. I poured some of the still water with Grant's company label on it into my cup. They were ready for takeoff and Grant was still on the phone, so I went back to the room Grant closed himself in and knocked lightly before opening the door.

When he saw me, he put one finger in the air. "No, Dad, this is unacceptable. You take care of this before my return flight on Sunday. No more discussion" He hung up the phone and looked at me. "Sorry, baby. Did Lucy get you a drink?"

I just stood there with my arms crossed and eyebrows raised.

"We aren't going to talk about it here. Let's get you buckled into your seat. Safety first, Georgia girl." He smiled at me, but it wasn't his usual easygoing, happy smile. It was forced. I didn't smile back.

Whatever his connection with Lucy was, it ruined his good mood and his plans for the plane ride, considering he gave me his iPad so I could read one of the e-books he let me download onto it. He pulled out his laptop and started working. All of this drama and uncertainty just reminded me it had only been a short time since I met Grant. There was still so much I didn't know about him.

About an hour into the two-hour flight, Grant hadn't said a word and Lucy hadn't appeared again. I put his iPad down and stared at him until he acknowledged me. "What do you need, baby?"

"This was not how this trip was supposed to go. You were in such a good mood until we boarded the plane, so tell me what ruffled your feathers."

"Eve."

"Grant." We went through our usual avoiding the topic routine.

He ground his teeth angrily. "I told you, not here."

"Fine," I snapped and picked his iPad back up. I folded my legs into the chair with me, so I was in a tight little ball.

"Don't be like that, Eve." He sighed and ran a hand through his hair.

I turned back to him and looked him in his brownish-colored eyes. I made sure to speak quietly, so the pretty little flight attendant in her hooker heels wouldn't hear. "You know, it irritates you when I don't tell you something right when you want to know it, but you do the same thing. I think I can get a little peeved when whatever you don't want to tell me has ruined the unexpected trip I gave up my weekend to take with you."

He took the iPad out of my hands and set it on

the table next to his laptop. He reached under the blanket covering my legs and unbuckled my seatbelt, and then pulled me onto his lap into our favorite "can't be naked" talking position. "I love you. You know that, right?" He opened.

"Yes, and I love you. Now talk."

"I used to travel a lot more several years ago. Lucy and Otto were the regular flight attendants."

"And you're a member of the mile high club. I get it, but what about seeing her made you so upset?"

"We slept together for a while, just when I was flying." Okay, that kind of hurt. First I found out that morning he has had girl after girl in the penthouse. Then I discovered his plans to create mile high memories with me were actually a recreation of experiences with the floozy flight attendant.

"And?" I prompted.

"And when I didn't want a relationship with her, she went after my dad. She had an affair with him, and I figured it out one day when Dad and I took a flight together."

"Holy shit." I almost laughed because that was not what I was expecting. She slept with Grant and Harrison. Gross!

"Yeah. She was after money, looking to be a trophy wife. Supposedly Dad let her go after she tried to blackmail him, so you can imagine my surprise when she was on this flight instead of Otto."

"Hmm," I responded.

"Say something," he said, and then pressed his

lips to my head.

"I don't know what you want me to say, Grant. I'm sorry about how girls went after your money, but you didn't exactly let anyone believe you were worth more than what is in your bank account. That being said, you screwing your flight attendant doesn't bother me in isolation, because I know you didn't feel about her the way you feel about me, but the girls are starting to add up."

"Babe—"

I held my palm up to stop him from placating me. "I'm not jealous. I knew you had a past, but it's one thing to know it exists. It's another to have names and faces to put with the places. None of this is ours." Grant was the only man to have been in my bed in Seattle, and the only man besides Nolan to be in my apartment. That meant something to me. I wasn't saying Grant needed to do anything about it or even that he could do something about it, but his past was being thrown in my face every day, especially with his mother on the warpath.

"Eve—"

"Just don't." I climbed off his lap. "Don't say all the right things and make me forget. Just let me be for a minute. I'm not upset. I'm processing."

He leaned over and kissed me gently, but Lucy clearing her throat ruined the moment. I sat up but refrained from looking directly at her.

I did see that she at least had the decency to look contrite. "I'm sorry to interrupt, but the captain has asked that you buckle your seatbelt in preparation for landing."

"Thanks, Lucy," Grant said. He reached over to

buckle my seatbelt, but I batted his hands away and did it myself while he watched me with his lips pressed into a firm line.

By the time we checked into the Fairmont, it was late. A bellboy led us to the expensive suite I suspected would impress most people, but I just saw it as a colossal waste of money. Grant caught me grimacing at the sight of the extravagance and laughed. "Sorry. Old habits. We can downgrade if you want, but they already delivered room service. I figured you'd prefer this to eating on the plane." No. He originally had other plans for the plane ride, but they were foiled the minute he saw the floozy flight attendant.

Grant passed the bellboy a few crisp bills and closed the door after him. He then led me to a dining table with two covered dinner plates, champagne, and chocolate covered strawberries. We ate in almost complete silence until the strawberries. He took the platter and champagne over to a luxurious sofa and then led me to it. He poured me a glass of champagne and then one for him. When he handed it to me, he looked at me with greenish-bluish-brownish eyes.

Grant gently tucked my hair behind my ear. "You're wrong, you know." I tilted my head and looked at him confused. "You said none of this is ours. To me, it is all ours, because it's all new to me. You're the first girl I have ever wanted around for more than…well, for more. I want you with me all the time for everything. That makes you the first girl who has traveled with me, the first girl I have actually invited to spend the night at the penthouse, the first girl who has gotten me to sleep at her place. You're a lot of firsts for me. Most importantly, you're the first girl I have ever fallen in love with. We both have to face the choices the other has made before we met. I wish that weren't the case, but I can't change that. If I had known I was waiting on you, then I would have done a better job of actually waiting."

I felt the tears stinging my eyes at his wonderful words. His words mixed with my emotions of the day were just too much, and a tear leaked out of my eye. He wiped it away with his thumb and kissed me gently.

It occurred to me while he was speaking that there were some firsts I wouldn't be able to share with him. The biggest one was if we ever were to decide to get married, he wouldn't be my first husband, and that made me more than a little sad. He should have been. I should have been so lucky to be this in love with my first husband, but as they say, you live, you learn.

I set my glass down and climbed on top of him. With my body pressed to his and our arms tightly holding on to one another, I whispered, "I'm sorry that I keep letting my emotions take over. Didn't anyone ever tell you women are crazy?" I let out a laugh before turning serious again. "I'm heartbreakingly in love with you, and it scares the living daylights out of me."

"I know, baby. Me too."

We continued to talk and eat strawberries and drink champagne. I told him what was going on in my crazy head, and he told me the whole divorce thing was still hard for him. I tried to make him feel better by explaining I chose to marry someone I wasn't in love with because he was familiar. It was the first time neither one of us held back. I learned he had slept with every one of those girls from his high school at the party, including Kitty, but most of them only had one night with him and it was years ago. We both really struggled through that discussion, but his last little tidbit of information made me feel a lot better. Before me, he hadn't been with anyone in over eight months. He said he thought he was making room in his life for me before he even knew me. I told him I was probably doing the same thing in my life.

When we were all talked out, and our demons of the past were exorcised, we went to bed. We carefully undressed each other, and slowly made love that night. It was a wonderful night, a turning point, and I finally felt like I wasn't holding on with just my fingernails. I had put my feet firmly on the ground in Grant's life, and he, in turn, was grounded in mine.

Chapter 19

The weekend was so amazing that work on Monday was hell. Grant made sure the rest of the weekend was romantic. He went to his meeting early Saturday morning and was back in the room before I was finished getting dressed. He took me sightseeing—okay, Alcatraz wasn't exactly romantic, but I wasn't going to pass up the chance to see it—and out to a romantic dinner. There was no more arguing or even discussing. We were just two people who were very much in love. You know, hand holding, public kissing, whispered 'I love you's every chance we had, the whole nine yards.

I almost started crying when Otto welcomed us back to Seattle because I knew we would be facing reality when we stepped off the plane. Our bubble burst right away when Grant said he needed to go back to his place to work a little. I asked him to take me to my apartment, but he just looked at me like I had said I wanted to walk back to Georgia.

He drove me to work the next morning and

dropped me off with a long goodbye. Tara noticed my new dress courtesy of my very rich boyfriend—hello dramatic eye roll—as soon as I walked in the door. Fortunately we didn't have time for girl talk because we had the anniversary party to prepare. I had to get a minute-by-minute schedule and get the speakers confirmed. We had to go by the florist and meet with the caterer to make final choices on food and flowers.

We did have time to catch up over lunch. I told her about my weekend, filling her in about Iris and San Francisco and the closet, which I think she was most excited about. She, in turn, told me about her weekend with Daniel in explicit detail. Yowzers.

While everything was perfectly successful and pleasant, I was missing Grant and our quiet weekend all day. His text messages didn't help. They started five minutes after he dropped me off and continued throughout the day after that. The all-day conversation gave me butterflies in my belly and a smile on my face.

Grant: You look beautiful in red. Missing your red lips already.

Me: You miss my lipstick? I can get you some of your own.

Grant: Not the same. I want it on your lips and your lips on me.

Me: I want that too. I hate Mondays. :(

Grant: I hate that you work away from me.

Me: Absence makes the heart grow fonder?

Grant: I'm already fond of you. I don't need any help.

Me: Not for that problem anyway ;)

Grant: What are you saying gorgeous?

Me: You might be crazy.

Grant: Crazy in love.

Me: I knew you secretly loved Beyonce.

Grant: I secretly love you.

Me: That is no secret.

Grant: How did you figure it out?

Me: It could have been the closet or San Francisco.

Me: It was probably the way you tell me all the time.

Me: It was definitely the way you make me feel.

Grant: And how do I make you feel?

Me: Like I'm the only person in your world that matters.

Grant: You are. I wish you were here, baby.

Me: Me too.

Me: Are you picking me up today? I can walk, but it is raining. :(

Grant: You are not walking anywhere alone in this city!

Me: I'll be fine. No one wants to kidnap me. I'd drive them crazy!

Grant: I said no. Pick you up around 5:30.

Me: I'll be waiting with bated breath.

Grant: About to go into a meeting now, but I will see you at 5:29.

Me: Have fun. Love you! Xoxo

Grant: Love you, my gorgeous Georgia peach.

At four o'clock Tara and I were back in our respective offices finishing up for the day, and that was when my phone went off and my day really went to shit.

"Evie, it's Martin. How are you?"

I stood and closed my office door for some

privacy. "I'm doing well, Martin. How are you?"

"Good. Good. Listen, I spoke with Mark's attorney. We scheduled the mediation for the sixteenth. Can you get into town for that?"

"It shouldn't be a problem." Except for the fact that my overprotective boyfriend wants to come with me. I jumped online and started looking up flights.

"Good. I'm going to need to get a written statement about the things we discussed on Friday. I'll need the rest of the information on both of your finances included. I also need to get another statement from your parents about how things have been since the order of protections took effect."

"What's that now?" I was sure I misheard him. "What order?"

"Your parents didn't tell you?" he asked disbelievingly.

"No! What is an order of protection?" I didn't recognize my high-pitched voice.

"You should call your dad. He should be the one to tell you."

"I have to go. I'll call you tomorrow. Don't worry about the statements. I'll get you whatever you need."

"Thank you, Evie. Talk to you tomorrow."

As soon as I was off the phone with Martin, I was calling my dad. "Evie?" he answered.

"Dad, why do you have an order of protection against Mark? What did he do?" I asked in a rush.

"Shit…" he uttered. "Martin spilled the beans, huh?"

"Daddy!"

"All right, all right. Mark kept coming around the house. It started when you first moved in, and I would never let him in or tell him where you were. He had been seen following you around, and after you left for Seattle, he forced his way into the house in one of his drunken rampages."

"What?" I screeched. "Why didn't you tell me about this?"

"Evie, you were in such bad shape when you finally decided to leave that sack of shit. We just wanted him to stay away from you. His behavior was one of the reasons we encouraged you to move all the way across the country. We needed you to be safe. The restraining order is simply a way to make sure he goes away for a long time if he tries anything else."

"Has he been bothering you since?" I was upset and worried now. How did I not know anything? Was I really that out of it?

"No, but you might want to talk to Holly and Jane. When you first moved away he tried to get information from them about where you went. The girls didn't tell him anything, but he was pretty awful to both of them." He sounded regretful when he spoke about my best friend and my sister.

"Dad, anything else I need to know?"

"No, Evie. That's pretty much it. I'm sorry we didn't tell you, but we were just trying to keep you safe and make sure you got better."

"I know, Dad. I love you."

"I love you, peanut."

My head was whirling and tears were pooling in my eyes. It seemed Mark was way worse than I imagined. I knew he was drinking more after I left and filed for divorce, but he couldn't really expect me to stay after how bad things had gotten.

I picked my phone back up and dialed Holly.

"Hey, Evie. Ready to tell me all about San Fran?" Holly said by way of greeting me.

"Maybe later. Right now I need you to tell me about Mark. Martin told me my parents had a restraining order, and then my dad told me about Mark breaking into their house and following me. He also said you've had some trouble."

"Evie…" She sighed.

"Tell me. I have been blissfully in the dark long enough while people I love are getting hurt. This is not okay, Holly. It's all my fault," I sobbed.

Hearing me upset always riled Holly up, and she climbed right up on her soapbox. "No, it isn't, Evie. It's Mark's fault. He's the asshole. He's the one who can't control his drinking. He's the one who verbally abused you to the point where you thought you weren't worth anything. It's him who's the problem, not you!"

"Holly, what did he do to you?" I asked.

"Evie."

"Holly! Tell me," I snapped.

"He came by my work a couple of days after you left. I had to work late, and no one was there. When I wouldn't tell him anything, he kind of roughed me up a bit."

"What do you mean roughed you up?" I asked slowly.

"I mean he may have backhanded me across the face and then held me down on the hood of my car.

The bank security guard pulled in and he got in his truck and drove away. I was okay, Evie. Matt has been keeping an eye on me, and the bank manager walks me to my car every day. It isn't so bad. I have a really good relationship with my boss now. I didn't press charges or anything because I didn't want the bastard to rot in jail. His mama would be devastated if she had to visit him in jail. He'd be someone's bitch for sure."

"Oh, Holly, don't make light of this." She had been hurt and she was trying to make it easier on me. For the millionth time this week it seemed tears filled my eyes. My tear ducts were going to eventually run out of liquid, or at least I was hoping this sobbing mess I had become would eventually stop.

"I'm sorry, Evie," she whispered.

"Me too, Hols." We were silent on the phone for a moment. "I have to go. Grant is about to be here to pick me up. I need you to do me a favor, though."

"Anything," she said.

"I need you to write a statement saying what happened, so I can give it to my lawyer. It's just in case he tries to fight me on the settlement after the mediation. We'll have to go to court, and I'll need everything I can to get the judge to give me a more permanent restraining order."

"Of course. I think the judge would give you half the assets too if you asked for that. After this, a judge might be willing to give you everything except the debt."

"Thanks for the support, Hols, but I would prefer to be prepared."

"Sure thing. I'll take a copy to Martin."

"Thank you."

I hung up with her and laid my head down on my desk just as Tara knocked. "Yeah?" I said.

She peeked in the door. "I'm out. Whoa! You've been crying. What's wrong?" She came in and sat in her seat in my office.

"Everything's fine. I just got some bad news from my lawyer, and my dad, and Holly. Everything's fine, though. Everything will be just fine." I couldn't think past what they had all just told me. I replayed each conversation in my head. I slammed my hands down on the desk.

Tara stood up and came up to the other side of my desk. "Slow down, Eve, before you throw something. What happened?"

"He was following me, and he hurt Holly and broke into my parents' house," I practically screamed.

"Who?" she asked confused.

"Mark!"

"Oh. Okay. Okay." She started pacing while I worked to get control over my breathing. "I take it you didn't know he was following you?"

"No!"

"Does he know you're in Seattle?" she asked.

"No. I don't think so. I don't know. I didn't intentionally hide it specifically from him. My parents, Jane, and Holly did, though." Jane! "I need to call my sister." I looked at my watch. "Five-fifteen. Shit. Grant will be here soon. I need to get myself together."

"Here." Tara pulled a mirror out of her bag. I

pulled out my little makeup bag and touched up my powder and reapplied my lipstick. I wiped the mascara from under my eyes. Tara let me use her hairbrush, and we did our best to minimize the damage.

By the time Grant arrived, it looked like Tara and I had just been chatting in my office. He appeared in the doorway looking striking as always in his three-piece suit. "Hey, baby. You ready to go?"

"Yeah. Let me just…" I threw my stuff into my bag.

"You all right?" he asked.

"Yeah, I just…" I couldn't think of anything to say.

Tara saved me. "We had a rough day. We've been all over town, and Eve has been on the phone non-stop."

I could see he wasn't satisfied with Tara's answer, but he let it go for now and reached out his hand to me. "I see. Let's go, gorgeous."

"Yeah." I took his hand, and we followed Tara out to the parking deck.

I told Tara I would see her tomorrow, and I didn't miss the worried look on her face. I knew she had never seen me this upset. Hell, I don't think I had ever been this upset. The son of a bitch hurt my best friend. It was one thing to call me names and tell me how fat and disgusting I was. He could even give me daily reminders of how worthless I was. What he couldn't do was mess with my parents or hurt Holly, and who knew what he did to Jane. I hadn't had a chance to talk to her yet. My mind was all over the place. I was officially freaking out.

"Eve?" Grant said.

"Yeah."

"Did you hear me?"

"What? No. I'm sorry. What did you say?"

Grant's brow furrowed. "I asked if you wanted to go to my place, so I could work, and Scott could make us dinner."

"Oh," I responded and still didn't answer his question.

"Well?" he asked. Grant reached over and grabbed my hand. "Baby, what's going on?"

"Nothing. Sorry. I'm tired." I stared straight ahead. "Will you just take me home? I need to call my mom and do some laundry."

"Do you want to get something to eat first?"

"No."

Grant frowned and sighed. "Eve, you're eating dinner, and while we're eating, you're going to tell me what has you so distracted. You were perfectly happy this morning. Now I can hardly get a word out of you."

"Sorry," I said, then turned to face out the window. It was raining now, and the drops were slowly chasing each other down the tinted windows of the Range Rover. "I talked to Martin this afternoon."

"Who's Martin?"

"My attorney."

Grant pulled into a parking lot and put the car in park. He turned toward me in his seat. "And?"

"And nothing." I shrugged. "He just shared some information I should have known a long time ago.

I'm still processing everything."

"Then let me help you."

"I will when I'm ready," I tell him, trying to appease him more than anything.

"Then let me feed you."

I really did not want to try and shove food down my throat. The thought alone made me queasy. Stress and food did not mix well for me. "I want to get home. My mom goes to bed early, and it's already almost nine o'clock there."

Grant sighed with annoyance. "Fine, I'll take you home and order take out. While we wait, you can call your mom and I'll take care of some things on my computer. When the food arrives, you eat and then start talking, so I can start fixing. This is not up for discussion."

I didn't even have the energy to be annoyed with his bossiness and his impatience. Grant put the car in drive and drove us the rest of the way to my apartment. I called my mom from my bedroom while Grant ordered food, but she didn't tell me anything I didn't already know. She did apologize and said she and Dad would both write statements. I called Jane, but she couldn't talk. The kids were around her, but she told me to call her in the morning, and we would talk. There was one other phone call I was tempted to make, but there was no way I could make that one with Grant around.

I changed into some shorts and one of Grant's t-shirts he had left at my place. Once my hair was tied up in a bun on top of my head, I came out of my bedroom to find Grant sitting on my sofa with his shirt unbuttoned at the top and bare feet on a pillow on the coffee table and his laptop on his lap. His jacket, tie, and vest were hanging on one of my bar stools, and his shoes and socks sat on the floor next to it. I loved that he was so comfortable in my apartment.

"I ordered Thai. I hope that's okay." I nodded, and he added, "You look good in my shirt, babe."

I sat down on the sofa and curled into his side. "What are you doing?" I asked.

"Reading over a contract and sending emails." He kissed my temple. "Did you talk to your mom?" I nodded. "Ready to talk to me?" I snuggled closer to him, and he understood. Grant set his laptop on the table, pulled me into his lap, and held me close with his arms wrapped tightly around me.

"Just hold me for a minute, then I'll tell you everything."

He spoke quietly with his chin resting on my head. "You never have to ask for that, Eve. I'm always here to hold you."

I closed my eyes and listened to the rumble in his chest as he spoke. When he was silent, I nuzzled my head into his shoulder. "I love you."

"I love you too."

We sat in silence for a moment before I was finally able to start talking. "Martin told me my parents took out a restraining order on Mark. I called my dad to find out what he was talking about, and he confirmed it."

I could feel him tense up. "Why?"

I sat up and looked at him. "Here's where I need you to stay calm and not freak out on me, okay?"

"Okay…" He was very suspicious now.

"Apparently, Mark was following me. When he was drunk one night, right after I moved here, he approached my parents when I wasn't home. He forced his way into their house looking for me. I guess he was following me when I was so out of it all the time I wouldn't have even noticed. When I moved out of his house, I had already hired Martin, a friend of the family, and filed for divorce, but…well, you saw the picture."

Grant's body was tense all over, and he was gripping me tightly. "What else?" he asked.

I snuggled back into him, and I felt him soften. "I never knew he was following me, and they never told me about the restraining order. My dad said they encouraged me to come here because they were worried about my safety. He didn't know where I was, but he knew I left, so he grabbed Holly one night and hit her." I felt the tears again. "He hit my friend because she was protecting me."

"Did she tell him where you are?" His voice was like ice.

"No. A security guard showed up. Mark has a drinking problem. It's gotten worse over the years. I know he wouldn't do this if he were sober, but I—"

Grant lifted me off of him and set me on the couch. "Don't do that. Don't make excuses for him. He hurt you, and now he has hurt your family and friends. He wouldn't do that if he weren't an asshole. It has nothing to do with his drinking."

Just then the buzzer went off, letting us know the food was there. Grant pulled out his wallet. "Stay put. I'll be right back." Grant went downstairs to get the food, and I curled up into a ball and thought about what I was going to have to do.

I tried to settle the divorce peacefully, but it looked like Mark was so far past peaceful he couldn't even find the breadcrumbs to make his way back. I guess I wouldn't just be petitioning for a divorce, but I would also be looking to get a permanent restraining order for my family, Holly, and me. How did things get so messed up? How could I have brought this horrible man into their lives? I knew he wasn't good. I knew it in my bones, and I still kept him around.

"What do you want to drink, babe?" Grant called from the kitchen. I didn't even hear him come back.

"Water." I needed some water. My throat felt all gravelly from trying not to cry. I was trying to keep it together, really I was, but every time I thought about Mark hitting Holly, I literally felt the burning in my eyes and the bile rising in my throat.

Grant brought the food and bottled water over to the table. We ate in silence. Well, he distractedly shoved food into his mouth, and I pushed my pad thai around on my plate.

"Eat." Grant nodded toward my plate.

I complied. I ate a few bites slowly. "I'm sorry. I just can't. I promise I'll eat breakfast, but I just can't eat right now."

He sighed and nodded. "Okay, but so help me, if you don't eat breakfast, I'll make you spend all day Saturday alone with my mother." He was serious.

"That won't help me eat, I assure you."

He kissed my neck. "Now tell me the rest of what you found out."

"Really? Because you handled the last part so

well." I rolled my eyes.

Grant lowered his eyebrows and narrowed his eyes. "Hey, watch that tone, peach. No need to be difficult."

My eyes widened in mock offense. "Same could be said to you, bull in china shop."

"Point made." He tapped my nose. "Talk."

I told him everything else I knew except for two key points. I didn't tell him when my mediation was scheduled, and I didn't tell him I planned to call Mark's mother tomorrow to get information from her.

It was after eight when we finished talking about my disastrous divorce, and I was exhausted. "I thought you had to work?"

"I passed some of it off to Rachel, and the rest of it I can do here."

"You made Rachel work this late? You're a terrible boss."

"She's paid a lot of money to work when I need her to work. Plus, she doesn't mind. She loves working for me. I'm awesome," he said proudly, making my lips almost lift in a smile.

"Yeah. I bet she loves working for you," I teased. "I bet she tells all her friends about what a great boss you are. She probably tells them about how good-looking you are, and demanding you are, and how she wants to peel off your sexy suits and do dirty things to you."

"Then it's a really good thing I'm not interested. Besides, I already have you doing dirty things to me whenever I want." Just like that, Grant turned my night around.

Even though he was able to take my mind off of things for a little while, it haunted me in the silence of the night. I listened to Grant's even breathing and tried to match its rhythm, but it didn't help. I tried counting down from one hundred, but I kept getting distracted. When I resigned myself to a sleepless night, I watched the clock count the minutes until I could get up and call my sister. I knew she was in her car at seven in the morning because we used to talk everyday on my way to work. That meant I just had to make it until four in the morning Seattle time. Tick tock.

I must have fallen asleep for a few moments because I was dreaming. I was back at home, not my parents' house, but my house, the one I built and shared with Mark. Mark. As soon as he appeared in my dream, I shot up in the bed. I was breathing heavily and shaky. I noticed the clock said three fifty-eight, and I realized I could call my sister.

Grant woke up when I tried to get up. "What are you doing?"

I kissed his cheek and whispered, "Go back to sleep. I'm just going to get some water."

"Have you slept at all, babe?" he asked when he rolled over and scrubbed his face with his hand.

"Yes. Go back to sleep." I kissed him one more time before I climbed out of bed, grabbing my phone on the way to the kitchen.

I was going to have to be quiet. The apartment was small, but there was no way I could unlock both deadbolts and the chain without Grant waking up again. Instead, I grabbed a bottle of water and sat down on my kitchen floor and called Jane.

"Evie?" she answered. "Isn't it like four in the morning on your coast?"

"Yeah. I couldn't sleep. Mom and Dad told me about the restraining order yesterday, and Holly told me how he attacked her. I wanted to know if he messed with you at all."

"Oh, Evie. Why are you doing this? It isn't going to make what you're going through any easier."

"Jane, I'm not a little girl. I made the choice to marry Mark, and I made the choice to divorce him. I cannot make decisions if I only know half the information. I couldn't figure out why he wouldn't sign the papers no matter how much I gave him."

I could practically hear her grinding her teeth. Dr. Chadwick, our family dentist, would be really annoyed with her. After a silent minute she said, "John and I took an order of protection out on him at the same time Mom and Dad did. We were out that first Saturday night you were in Seattle. Mom and Dad had the kids, and Mark showed up at their house and walked in the front door like he lived there. He pushed Dad out of the way, causing Dad to fall and hurt his back. Mark ran all over the house yelling and looking for you. He knocked stuff over and broke some things. It really scared the kids."

"Then what happened?" I whispered.

"He showed up at the restaurant where John and I were eating and happened to catch us on the way to the car." She stopped talking.

"Jane?"

"Yeah, I'm here." She was crying now. I could hear her voice crack and a sob escape.

"Oh, Janie! What happened?" Tears dripped

down my cheeks. I hated hearing my sister hurt. She was the strong one. She had a good head on her shoulders, was always rational and practical. I think I had seen her cry maybe five times in my whole life.

"Mark grabbed me, and I couldn't get away. He was yelling all kinds of bullshit. John made a move to get him off me, and Mark twisted me, so he was holding me with his arm around my neck. I couldn't breathe. He kept asking John how he would feel if he didn't know where his wife was."

"Oh my god," I whispered. "I'm so sorry. I'm so, so sorry, Janie." They came out as sobs.

"It isn't your fault, peanut. You know that. Don't worry. I'm okay. John's okay. Everyone is fine. He hasn't bothered any of us since the judge agreed to the restraining order. John had it taken care of that Monday."

"That's good at least. Don't worry, Janie. I'll make sure he's out of our lives as soon as possible. I promise."

"You do what you need to do, Evie. I love you, and I don't blame you for anything, okay?"

"Yeah," I sobbed.

"I have to go. I need to get myself together before I walk in the office and everyone thinks I'm pregnant again."

I laughed through my tears. "Love you, Janie. Thank you for telling me everything."

"Of course, peanut. Love you too."

After I hung up the phone and set it on the tile floor, I curled myself even tighter into a ball and willed the tears to stop. I felt Grant come in the room and sink down to the floor. He pulled me into his lap and let me cry. I didn't know if he heard me on the phone or woke up to an empty bed, but he was holding me. He didn't say anything. No questions asked. He was just there for me because he loved me.

After my sobbing subsided, he gently lifted me from the floor and took me back to bed. He climbed into bed keeping me in his arms. "You need to get some sleep, baby."

"I know, but I can't turn my brain off." I snuggled as close to him as I could. "Sorry for waking you."

He spoke in a whisper as if there was someone else to wake up in the apartment. "I heard you crying. What did Jane say?"

"Basically the same thing. He attacked her in a parking lot and said some really awful things to John. The kids were at my parents' house when he went tearing through their house looking for me after I left."

"Hmmm…" That was all he said. He didn't tense up and get angry and start pacing again. He was just holding me. Even if I could hear the wheels in his head turning, he was giving me what I needed in that moment.

"Thank you."

"For what?"

"For not flipping out again."

I felt him smile against my hair. "Sure thing, gorgeous."

"Gorgeous? Disaster is more like it."

"My gorgeous disaster," he said with a kiss to the top of my head.

Chapter 20

Grant left shortly after our morning chat to go workout and get dressed for work. I felt bad he ended up with such little sleep. His routine went uninterrupted, though—workout, shower, dress, work, etc. The only difference was he brought me breakfast this morning. He usually only does that if he thinks I'm mad at him, but today I knew he was checking up on me.

"Babe! I brought you a bagel and a coffee. You ready?" he called from the kitchen.

I came out of my room dressed in black ankle pants, flats, and a black and white striped shirt. It wasn't the dressiest work outfit, but I was not exactly on top of my game. Besides, I would just be in my office all day stuffing menus into vellum sleeves and folding place cards. Who cared what I looked like? Considering my eyes looked like something had been nesting under them, and my brain felt like scrambled eggs, I was pleased to at least have clothes on.

"Thank you," I told him when I took the coffee

and the bacon and egg bagel he brought me.

"You know I love you, right?" Grant said after I gave him a quick kiss.

"Yeah?" I asked suspiciously, noting he was trying to hide his amusement.

"Then you know it is with love when I tell you that you may want to change your shoes." I looked down and saw that I was wearing one pink and one red shoe. I had forgotten I didn't pick which one I wanted to wear.

"Fuck!" I huffed and slammed my breakfast down on the counter and then stormed back into the bedroom. In my closet I stood there staring at my shoes, and I couldn't decide which ones I liked better. It was then that the tears started threatening again. I might have been a little tired and touchy.

Grant came up behind me and wrapped his arms around my waist. "Go with the red, baby." I nodded and traded my one pink shoe for the other red one.

I turned in his arms. "I'm sorry. This is the kind of crazy you don't want to see until way, way later."

He smiled sweetly. "I like all your crazy. I know you didn't sleep last night, and now I know what happens. From now on, we'll be making sure my gorgeous girl gets her eight hours."

"Yes, please," I pouted.

"Why don't you just take a personal day? I could work from home, and you could come and relax at the penthouse. Scott will cook for you, and I could run you a nice bath…maybe join you in it," he added suggestively with a wiggling of his eyebrows.

I frowned. "I can't. I have only worked there for less than two months for one thing, but we have the anniversary party on Saturday. There is still so much to do. Whoever thought planning this for the week after the fourth was a good idea deserves to be kicked in the face."

"You can thank Iris Mitchell for that, and please make sure I'm there when you decide to kick her in the face. I would like to film it and watch it over and over."

"Grant!" I slapped his arm lightly. "That's your mother, your deviously manipulative, yet lovely and chic mother."

"Aww, baby. Don't make her sound so good. You know she isn't nearly as pleasant as you described."

I giggled. "Thank you for making me laugh. We better go if we're going to make it to work on time."

He kissed me goodbye in the parking lot, and I knew I wouldn't see him until late. He had a business dinner, and I planned to go home and go to bed after making a couple more phone calls. I couldn't wait for this day to be over.

After stuffing menus all morning on the floor of my office, I was struggling to stay awake, let alone get off the floor. That was the moment Nolan and Tara decided to show up.

"Well, hello there, jet setter. What happened to lunch Saturday?"

I roll my eyes. "You know what happened. I was actually visiting Alcatraz while you two were eating salads and wishing they were bread."

Nolan fisted his hands on his hips. "Visiting a prison on your romantic weekend? I need to have a talk with your charming boyfriend."

"My idea, Nolan. I wanted to see it since I have never been out there before. I'm from Georgia, remember? East coast. He did the romance thing that night and the next morning." I winked.

He changed his tune after my wink. "Sounds like I need to talk to my charming boyfriend then."

"Trouble in paradise?" Tara asked.

"No." Nolan smiled sadly. "Let's lunch and complain about our boyfriends over food. You get to go first, T. Misery loves company."

Over sandwiches, Tara told us about Daniel's busy life. That paired with Tara's busy life resulted in a slow-moving relationship. Nolan had a slightly different problem. He and Maddox were always out together without being together. Maddox had been dragging Nolan along to more and more events where his father was, without actually telling his father the truth. Tara thought it was because Maddox was hoping his dad would figure it out, so he wouldn't have to tell him.

"Eve, you're up," Nolan said.

"I don't have any problems with Grant. He's very attentive both in public and at home. Does complaining about his mother count?" I asked.

"No." Tara shook her head. "This is where we all find out that Grant is actually a normal guy and not the perfect catch we all think he is."

"Sorry. This conversation is all a little depressing for me, and I don't need additional depressing shit in my life. Can we please move on to a new topic?"

"Okay." Nolan leaned in like he was about to go in for the kill. "Why did your boyfriend call me and tell me to make sure you actually ate your lunch?"

"He did what?" I snapped.

He pointed to my plate where I had torn my sandwich apart without actually eating much of it. "What's going on, E?"

"I might be under a bit of stress, and my stomach constantly feels queasy when I have stuff going on. I have a hard time keeping it down. I can think of few things that are worse than vomiting, so I don't risk it. It's no big deal. I mean, do you two want me to upchuck in front of you?"

"If it isn't a big deal, why is Grant calling me to check up on you?"

Tara frowned. "When did you last eat? And is this about yesterday?"

Nolan's brow furrowed. "What happened yesterday?"

"Eve found out some information about her ex yesterday before we left work," Tara told him.

"Tara!"

"What?" She looked surprised at my annoyance. "You would have told him eventually. Now, when was your last meal, and I mean actual meal? Did you eat breakfast? I mean protein, carbs, and all the things that go into a well-balanced meal."

I threw my napkin down. "Look, I appreciate your concern and all, but I don't need this right now. Nolan, tell Grant that if he wants to check up on me then he should do it himself. You know what? Don't tell him that, because I don't need anyone else to communicate for me." I threw some cash on the table and stood up. "I have some work to finish."

As I walked away I heard Tara slap Nolan. "Nice

going, dumbass."

I called Grant on my walk back to my office, and he answered on the third ring. "Hey, baby. You all right?"

"Getting Nolan to check up on me? What? Too busy to make sure your crazy girlfriend was eating?"

"Eve." His voice was a warning.

"Do you know what lunch was just like? They had a million questions and were looking at me like I need to go straight to the psych ward."

"Can we talk about this later?"

"No need, Grant. Did it occur to you that adding to the stress doesn't help? If you're going to be part of the problem, then please leave me alone until I get the last problem dealt with." I hung up the phone and threw it in my purse. As expected, it started ringing right away, but the only reason I pulled it out of my purse was to turn it off.

I finished the rest of my work in the conference room so I could ignore my ringing office phone. Thankfully the student worker didn't work on Tuesdays, and Tara was in meetings and then running over to the building where the party was being held on Saturday, so no one was there to ruin my peaceful afternoon. Once I had taken care of everything I could, I left right at five. I drove home as quickly as I could and changed into comfortable clothes, leaving my work clothes on the floor.

I grabbed a pillow and blanket then headed out to my comfortable grey couch. I settled in and picked up my phone to make the phone call I had been waiting all day to make. When I turned on my phone, I ignored the voicemails and text messages from Grant, Nolan, and Tara. Instead, I found the Florida number I was looking for and hit send.

A sweet older woman's voice answered the phone. "Hello?"

"Mrs. Stevens. It's Eve."

"Oh! Hello, dear. How are you?" Mark's mom was the kind of lady who made you cookies and lemonade when you walked in her door. She was almost too kind to visitors, but her relationship with Mark was a whole other ballgame. He was a mama's boy, and if anyone could whip him into shape, it was Mary Ann Stevens. It really was too bad that she moved to Florida when she retired. Mark would have probably been better off had his Mama been there to tell him what to do.

"I'm not doing great, to be honest. Listen, I don't know how much Mark has told you, but things weren't going well for us. I filed for divorce eleven months ago."

"What? Evie, I had no idea. Mark acts like you are always busy when I call. I thought you were upset with me, especially when Mark cancelled your trip over Christmas. I tried to call your cell, but your number was disconnected, and then a Hispanic man answered a couple of months later."

"I'm so sorry that I didn't call. Things were…bad. I wasn't exactly communicating with anyone. When I finally had myself together again, I figured Mark had convinced you that I was to blame, and I just couldn't take that."

"Oh, honey, no. I know how Mark can be, and a mother can always tell when her boy is lying. I knew he wasn't being truthful, but I had no idea this is what he was keeping from me. Is he still drinking?"

"Yes, ma'am, and from what my parents and sister have told me, it's gotten really bad."

"Evie, don't you worry. I'll take care of him. I'll be on the phone with him first thing in the morning. No use calling him now. I'm sure he's already three sheets to the wind." No one could say this mother didn't know her son.

After that phone conversation, I felt relieved. I knew she would get the truth out of him, and by the time I was back in Georgia, Mark should be more agreeable. If he gave his mama any trouble, I would be willing to bet Mary Ann Stevens would be present at the mediation with our attorneys.

I heated up some leftover Thai and watched a few minutes of a movie before falling asleep on the couch. I was woken up hours later when I was lifted off the couch. "Grant?"

"Yeah, baby. It's me," he told me as he kissed my forehead.

"Why are you here?" I asked as I nuzzled my face against his neck, smelling his cologne and him.

"I'm putting you to bed." He gently placed me on my bed, but stayed close to me. I wrapped my arms around his neck and pulled him close.

"Are you staying?"

"Do you want me to stay?"

I sighed against him. "Yeah. I want you to stay."

"Good. I missed you today. I hated knowing you were upset, and I couldn't get to you." He kissed my lips and stood up to undress. I climbed out of bed and went into the bathroom to brush my teeth. Grant followed me. "We had investors in the office from New York for just today, so I couldn't leave the negotiation without compromising everything. When Maddox told me Nolan was going to be eating lunch with you, I figured I would call Nolan to check on you for me. I didn't think about how he would handle my request to take care of you when I couldn't be there."

I spit into the sink before turning and looking up to his unreadable expression. "There are some things no one needs to know about. It only makes it harder."

"I know, babe." He sighed unhappily. "After seeing that picture of you, I swore to myself you would never hurt like that again. Yesterday was so hard for you, and you wouldn't eat dinner, then this morning was no better. I was worried about you and felt helpless, and that feeling doesn't sit well with me. I thought if I could just get you to eat, if I could get you to do that one thing, I would feel like I was doing something for you."

"You did help me. You were here for me." I wrapped my arms around his middle. "You will also be happy to know I ate leftovers for dinner and slept for a few hours."

He frowned. "So, all it took was for me not to be around you for you to feel like you could eat?"

"No. I called Mark's mother. She made me feel better. I bet by next week, I'll be officially divorced in the eyes of Georgia law," I said proudly.

He smiled and pressed his lips to mine. "Let's hope so, baby. Now, you ready to go to bed?"

I smiled flirtatiously up at him. "It depends on what you want to do when we get there."

He smiled brightly at me. "There's my gorgeous girl. I was missing you."

Chapter 21

My life in numbers:

40. The number of days I have lived in Seattle.
30. The number of minutes in my shower before the water gets cold.
29. The number of days I have known Grant.
20. The number of dresses I tried on for the anniversary party.
19. The number of days Grant and I have been officially together.
18. The number of days it has rained since I moved to Seattle.
17. The number of minutes it took to tell Grant goodbye in the parking lot this morning.
16. The number of times I told myself not to tell Grant when I fly home.
15. The number of times I have considered telling Grant when I fly home.
12. The number of red roses in the bouquet on my desk this morning.

11. The number of minutes it took me to drive to work since I was running late.

10. The number of hours I slept last night including my nap.

9. The number of times I have been to the gym since I moved to Seattle.

8. The number of messages I received yesterday from Nolan and Tara.

7. The number of times my mother has called since Monday.

6. The number of days until my mediation is scheduled.

5. The number of purple hyacinths in the bouquet this morning.

4. The number of outfits I went through before I was finally dressed.

3. The number of giant pancakes Grant brought me in bed this morning.

2. The number of times I "thanked" him for the pancakes this morning.

1. The number of people on my mind this very minute...Grant.

0. The number of times I have actually told Grant when I fly to Georgia.

Needless to say, Wednesday morning was a much better morning for me. I'd had my coffee and breakfast, my morning orgasms, plenty of rest...I was floating on cloud nine while ignoring the darker parts of my life. I truly believed it would all be taken care of this morning after my phone call to his sweet mama, but God himself couldn't have predicted how the rest of my day would go.

Tara came in with a mocha for me and an apology. I had already forgiven her and Nolan for their interrogation yesterday, so it was completely unnecessary but still appreciated. Moving on with our day, we tested bows for the chair sashes, and quickly agreed to a silver chiavari chair with a white cushion and a black double wrap sash with a center tie knot. With one task accomplished, we went our separate ways for a little while to finish a few tasks. I ran to the venue to make sure they set up the lighting properly then headed over to the rental company to give them the final numbers and double check that they had the correct china, chairs, sashes, table cloths, and dance floor pulled.

I was feeling beyond accomplished when I brought lunch back for us, but walking into Tara's office erased all good feelings I had built up throughout the day. She looked devastated and disheveled.

"What's wrong?" I asked as I set the bags on the conference table over by the window.

She shook her head and her eyes filled with tears. "I have some bad news. It's really bad news, and I would rather do anything than have to tell you this news, especially this week of all weeks."

I sat down on the edge of the chair facing her desk. "What's going on? You're scaring me."

She took a deep breath and then said, "Human Resources called me. Apparently they reevaluated the budget at the end of June. Someone was supposed to contact me last week, but the paperwork became lost in the campus mail. At the end of the next pay period—" She stopped and pressed her lips together.

"What?"

"Your job's been eliminated." She spoke very quickly, like she was spitting the words out of her mouth. "I feel terrible because I convinced you to move out here and now there's no job for you. They want me to cut back on events and share the planning of them with the departments. The lecture this Wednesday will be the last one my department manages. I'll only be handling special events and fundraisers…alone."

Okay…okay…I can handle this. They say things come in threes. First Mark and now this, what's next? "It's fine, Tara. Don't worry. I'll figure something out. When's my last day?"

"Next Friday." The words barely came out as a whisper.

Feeling deceptively calm, I had the need to comfort her, as if she was the one losing her income. "I'm flying home Monday night anyway. Why don't we just say I'm finished after the party on Saturday? I can always apply for teaching jobs or something."

Tara came around her desk and hugged me. "I'm so sorry. I'll do anything I can to help you get a job here. If you want a teaching job, I know a few people I can contact for you."

"Sure. That sounds good." I stood and walked to the door. "I need to go pick up the desserts for tonight. Do you mind if I go on home, so I can make Dr. Clarke some red velvet cookies? I don't want him to go without if it's our last lecture together."

"Of course. Go. Do what you need to do. We start setting up tomorrow for the party anyway, and we have the lecture tonight. I'll start emailing people now to see if we can get you something set up before your last paycheck."

"Thanks, Tara. I appreciate everything you've done for me."

"I really am sorry, Eve."

I smiled sadly. "It isn't your fault. Everything will be fine. It'll all work itself out. You'll see." With that, I walked out the door, only stopping by my office to grab my purse.

Back in my apartment, I changed clothes and started the red velvet cookies. Once they were on their cooling racks, I picked up my phone to call Grant and tell him my news, but the phone started ringing in my hand. I recognized the number immediately, but it wasn't someone who should have my number. I resigned myself that this week was only going to continue to get worse, so I went ahead and answered the call.

"Mark." I answered with absolutely no emotion in my voice. Keep it together, Eve, I mentally reminded myself.

"You called my mother! I always knew you were a bitch, but I didn't think you would involve my mother." He wasn't nearly as calm. "I told you, I'm not signing the fucking papers. You're my wife. End of story."

This was typical Mark, drunk and a pain in my ass. Actually, this was relatively composed for him. "Is that why you called? To call me names and remind me how uncooperative you are? I already knew that, hence the phone call to your mother, who knew nothing about the divorce, by the way. Stop being so difficult."

"Listen to me, you fucking cunt." Ahh…this was more like it. "You push me in that bullshit meeting you set up with our attorneys, I'll make you regret it for the rest of your life. When you come back into town next week, you should just come to your senses and come home. This bullshit separation should be over. You understand me? You made your vows, and now it's time to stop dicking around and honor them. If you come peacefully, I'll think about forgiving you. If not, I'll make sure you come home another way, and I promise you won't like it."

"Quit threatening me, Mark," I snapped at him. "I'm not the same scared girl who left you almost a year ago. I've moved on, and it's time you do the same."

He laughed, an evil, mischievous laugh. "You're big and bad in Seattle, but wait until you come home. Just wait, Evie. Wait until I get my hands on you."

How does he know where I am? I knew Holly and Jane kept their mouths shut, but I didn't know who else knew. "Who told you where I am?" My voice shook a little when I asked, but it was nothing to how my hands were reacting to this conversation.

"Does that worry you, Evie? It should. Maybe I should just fly out there to get you," he taunted further.

"How did you find out, Mark?" I screamed.

"I still have friends who are friends with your friends. You didn't think I'd be faithful to you while you were gallivanting all over the country, did you? It doesn't matter if I'm single or married. The sluts love getting a piece of this…like you used to, Evie. Remember that? When you used to like having my dick in your mouth, or when I used to bend you over the kitchen table and fuck you so hard you were sore for the next few days. Remember that, Evie?"

My voice came out stronger than I felt in that moment. "And I regret every second of it. Fuck off, Mark. Don't call me again." I hung up the phone. Tears were running down my face, and I was suddenly very grateful I left my lunch in Tara's office. I wasn't sure why I didn't just hang up before he had the chance to walk me down nightmare lane. Better yet, I didn't know why I even answered. I guess the buildup of events finally made me angry enough to fight back. Turns out that was something I was about to regret.

After I calmed down, which took longer than it should have, I iced the cookies with cream cheese icing. I packed the cookies into boxes, and then I dressed for the lecture in a black skirt and a yellow and black floral cardigan. I threw on a thin black belt at my waist and black Mary Jane heels. Once I was ready with my hair pinned up and my red lips, I started on my way back to campus for my final lecture. Feeling down? Dress up.

The text messages started while I was setting out the desserts. I didn't enter his number into my contacts, but I knew it was Mark. He'd had that number since high school. One message after another came through with insults and crude messages. Some were personal, some were creative, but all of them were meant to hurt me. I saved every last one of them for the meeting on Tuesday. Keep it up, Mark. Those papers were as good as signed.

Dr. Clarke approached me as soon as he arrived at the lecture. "Eve! Lovely to see you. What surprises did you bring for me this week?"

I opened a box for him. "Red velvet cookies. Try one."

He took one from the box and took a generous bite. "Now, this is my favorite. I love soft cookies, and these are wonderful."

"Thank you. I think the cookies might be my favorite as well. Good, I may have a small box set aside just for you." I winked at him knowing he would be thrilled with the gesture.

"Excellent! Thank you so much. I can't wait to see what you have for me next week." The reminder hit me like a ton of bricks.

"I won't be here next week," I told him. "The event on Saturday will be my last. Apparently Human Resources cut the position as a way of saving the college some money."

"What? That's ridiculous. Do you know how much money this college brings in? And that's because of the work that your department does keeping alumni connected, which keeps them donating. This isn't right." Dr. Clarke was not a happy camper.

"I know, but what can I do? I'm sort of stuck."

Dr. Clarke pushed his glasses up on his nose. "Aren't you dating the grandson of the founders? Can't he help?"

I grimaced. "I haven't exactly told him yet. He has this thing about taking care of me, and I have a thing about wanting to do things on my own. It's something we're working on."

He laughed. "I see. Well, if I can do anything for you, please let me know. I wish you all the best of luck."

"I appreciate that, Dr. Clarke. It has been wonderful getting to know you over the last several weeks."

He smiled kindly. "Yes, I'll miss our conversations as well as your desserts." He held up a second cookie to emphasize his point then headed into the lecture as I set out the final desserts. I walked into the lecture just as he was introducing the guest speaker. I spent the entire lecture thinking about how much to tell Grant. The secrets were starting to pile up, and I didn't like the way that felt either.

Grant came and met me at the reception and enjoyed a few red velvet cookies himself. As Dr. Clarke was leaving, he came over and gave me a hug and wished me luck. He then turned and shook Grant's hand and said, "Take care of our girl. She's one of a kind."

Grant's eyebrow quirked. "Yes, sir."

After Dr. Clarke left along with everyone else, I cleaned up the rest of the desserts. Grant came over and helped out by eating another cookie. "What was that all about?"

I didn't look up because I knew my face would give me away. Pretending to not know what Grant was talking about, I asked, "What was what all about?"

"With Dr. Clarke," he said as he took another cookie.

This time I had to turn my back. I couldn't lie as easily as I could pretend. "I don't know. He's just a nice guy."

"Hmm…yeah. Ready to go to dinner?" He was dropping it? I looked up and found him passively waiting for my answer.

"Yeah, let's go," I said, trying not to be suspicious or worry he would get the story out of me another way. I wasn't even sure why I didn't want to tell him. I had planned to tell him this afternoon before Mark called, but now it seemed important to deal with it myself. After thinking about it more, I only came to one conclusion—my stomach hurt.

Chapter 22

The rest of the week was relatively uneventful, and before I knew it, it was Saturday—my last day of work. I still hadn't told Grant anything, even though the text messages continued and my job was ending tonight.

Last night was the perfect distraction as we went for pizza and gave half of a supreme pizza to Frank, Grant's favorite homeless man. I didn't know if it was the look on Grant's face or Frank's face that made me happier when Grant gave him the pizza. Either way, that simple gesture made me fall more in love with Grant. This time it led to a little guilt for the lies and a whole lot of lovemaking, ending in Grant's version of the perfect wake-up call this morning.

I was in Grant's bed with one very sexy Grant trailing kisses all over my naked body that had been uncovered from the covers at some point. "Good morning, baby."

"G'morning." I rolled over onto my back, revealing my very naked front to my very dressed boyfriend. "You're dressed."

The trail of kisses continued on the other side of my body. "I am. Scott prefers me to walk around in clothes, and he's busy making you an elaborate breakfast to help you get ready for your very busy day."

"That was very thoughtful of Scott. I guess I should get dressed, so I can go eat this fancy breakfast he made me. Although, I'm sure Scott wouldn't mind if I ate in my current attire."

Grant growled and crawled over me to take my face between his hands. "Scott might not mind, but I will. This body is for my eyes only," kiss, "and my lips only," kiss, "right, Eve?"

"Yes," I whispered and wrapped my hands around his neck and slid my fingers into his hair. I pulled his mouth to mine and he nipped my lips before sliding his tongue in my mouth. I tasted the coffee on his tongue and a hint of the mint from him brushing his teeth this morning. As I slid my hands up his shirt feeling his hard stomach and chest, I asked, "Why are you still dressed?"

He ran his nose down the side of my face and whispered. "My gorgeous girl is a little frisky this morning, isn't she? Let's see if we can't do something about that."

***

Grant drove me to work after taking me by my apartment to get everything I needed to get dressed for the party later. Tara was already there tying bows on chairs when I arrived at noon. The room looked amazing. Black and white fabric was draped from the ceiling, creating four triangles that met in the middle. A huge chandelier hung in the middle of the room and other spotlights illuminated the dance floor. Each table was covered with a white tablecloth that draped to the floor and then a smaller black square tablecloth on top. White bone china dishes were being placed at each seat with crystal glasses and silverware. On top of each place setting I placed a white menu wrapped in black vellum. I set candles and crystal vases of all different sizes with bright white flowers atop them on each table. The only color in the whole room by the time we were finished was the greenery from the flower arrangements. Even the dance floor was solid black and lit with the Mitchell College logo in white light. It was stunning.

Most partygoers had arrived for cocktail hour, but there was still no sign of Grant. I was standing by the windows of the ballroom watching as limo after limo pulled up and let out people dressed in elegant gowns and tuxedos. In fact, none of the Mitchells were there. Dr. Clarke was, though, and he was headed my way.

"Eve. You look ravishing as always," Dr. Clarke said as he hugged me gently. "This is my wife, Deborah. Deb, this is the baker of the delicious red treats I told you about." He was so cheerful tonight, and I couldn't help but smile at his zest.

"Nice to meet you, Mrs. Clarke. I'm so sorry, but I didn't bring any red velvet treats tonight. I didn't have anything to do with the food here."

Deborah smiled kindly. "I must say it is nice to

finally meet you. I have been hearing about those darn cupcakes all summer. You'll have to join us for dinner one night so you can show me how to make them."

"I would love that."

Deborah saw someone she knew and stepped away as Dr. Clarke pulled me away from the crowd and closer to the window. "Listen, I've been meaning to call you. I called Human Resources on your behalf. I figured if they couldn't keep you employed then I might be able to give you a grant-funded position. Unfortunately, I don't think it will matter. I asked my friend over in HR what happened with the budget. He didn't know what I was talking about but was willing to look into it. I was about to call Miss Tanner and talk to her when my friend called me back. It seems Harrison Mitchell called HR and eliminated the position, giving the reason of budgetary restraints. If they eliminate the position altogether, they don't have to pay severance or unemployment."

Neurons suddenly started misfiring in my brain. Harrison? He seemed so nice to me, but Maddox's words came flooding back to me. Harrison cares about the money and their reputation as much as Iris. He just handles it more privately. He can be duplicitous. Don't underestimate Harrison. "Wait...I don't think I'm understanding you correctly."

"I'm saying your boyfriend's father, who also happens to be the founders' son, called to get your position eliminated. Why would he do that?"

I blankly stared in front of me as my mind was

sufficiently blown. "They're trying to get rid of me."

"It appears that way. You might want to talk to your boyfriend. It looks like your chance will come sooner rather than later." He nodded toward the window.

I looked out the window only to find a perfect-looking Grant dressed in his Armani tux climb out of the limo. He straightened his jacket and turned when a hand reached out for him from the car. Expecting to see Daphne, I watched as he held out his hand. A thin, bare leg from a high slit in a dress stepped out first. I noticed the killer heels and thought that was strange of Daphne to wear such tall shoes. Then her head appeared. It was blonde and beautiful and definitely not Daphne. It was Katherine…Kitty.

Grant held out his hand for her, and she smiled widely as she placed her dainty hand in his big paw. Jealousy sunk like rocks in my gut, and I felt my lunch churning in my stomach. Katherine's arm slid into the crook of his, and I watched as she smiled up at him like they were the picture-perfect couple. Harrison and Iris followed them out of the limo, and I knew right then they had made this happen. None of this was Grant, but that didn't make it hurt any less. They would do anything to get rid of me, just like Mark would do almost anything to keep me. Suddenly I felt my lunch trying to make its reappearance, and I knew I didn't have much time to find some privacy.

"You all right, Eve?" I had forgotten that Dr. Clarke was still standing there with me. He had been watching the scene unfold as well. "You look a little pale."

"No. I'm…I need to go. Thank you for helping me." I patted his shoulder quickly and ran upstairs to the dressing room before I emptied the contents of my stomach over and over into the toilet.

By the time I was finished throwing up, my body was covered in sweat. I looked in the mirror and saw my brown eyes were red, with mascara all around them. I was glistening with sweat, and pale just as Dr. Clarke said. My whole body was still shaking from vomiting. I couldn't go back down there. Heck, I didn't want to go back down there. Knowing there were people who were actively trying to get rid of me made me want to run. Up until that moment I was sure Grant was worth the fight, and really, he still was. I was the one who wasn't worth it, not when I was such a mess.

I slipped off my dress and left it on the floor, not caring what happened to it. I threw my jeans and t-shirt on from earlier over my black corset and lace panties I had worn for Grant. After I slid into my chucks and threw the rest of my stuff in my bag, I snuck out the back door and practically ran the few blocks home. My phone was off because the text messages kept coming several times a day from Mark, so I wouldn't have known if Grant or Tara called me. Honestly, right then I didn't care.

Back at my apartment, I sat on my bed for a minute. I needed a break from Tara, from Grant, from Iris, from Kitty, from Harrison. I needed my family. With that one thought, my decision was made. I packed a bag and called a cab. In the car on the way to the airport, I called Delta. With the excuse that I had a family emergency, I was able to change my flight from Monday night to tonight. It boarded in an hour. I had to hurry through security, but with only a carry-on slowing me down, I was able to get to the terminal in hardly any time at all. Ignoring the missed call and text from Grant that popped up, I texted my sister telling her I was on my way and would be landing before six the next morning. She replied letting me know she would be there to pick me up. No questions asked.

Finally, on the plane I settled into the middle seat I ended up with from scheduling a last minute flight. I didn't mind. Both of my neighbors fell asleep as I sat there and allowed my thoughts to torture me. When had Grant noticed I was gone? Was it when Tara went up to get her stuff and saw my dress? Did he and Kitty dance the night away? Did Iris make sure his and Kitty's place cards were next to each other? Or did he panic when he couldn't find me? Did he leave and go to my apartment? I knew he didn't leave right away. He would have made it there before I left. There were so many people there, and they all would have greeted him. He probably didn't notice I wasn't around until everyone sat down to dinner. I knew how upset he was the first time he couldn't find me. This time would be worse since he wouldn't be able to track me while my phone was off.

Then it occurred to me it had been off all day. Maybe he tried to call me all day and warn me. Maybe he tried to call me all day to end things with me. Maybe Harrison finally gave him the ultimatum he had been waiting to deliver. Harrison made sure I didn't have a job, so I was sure he had something in store for Grant once I was out of the picture. Maybe he was hoping I would look like a gold digger, because if I stayed, I wouldn't be able to pay rent unless I somehow found a job in the next week or two. He was wrong about me asking Grant for help, but right about not being able to pay my rent. Mark made sure of that. I had no back up money. I had spent almost everything I had saved from living with my parents by starting this new life that was practically over. What a waste.

The flight attendant stopped by to ask if I needed anything. I asked for water, and she brought me a cup with ice and water, and some tissues. I hadn't even realized that tears were dripping from my eyes. I thanked her, and she smiled sadly at me like she knew what I was going through. I wasn't even sure I knew what I was going through. I couldn't seem to wrap my head around everything that had happened in the last week. I was so happy that first week I was here, like I was finally free, like I could finally breathe again. On that flight it was like my breath had been stolen from me all over again, so I did the same thing I had done last time I felt like this. I went home to my parents.

I must have nodded off at some point because I woke with a jolt when the plane landed. I waited until almost everyone was off the plane before grabbing my bag and going to the place my sister and I always met outside baggage claim. Her giant SUV was parked just where I expected it, and she was in the driver's seat in her pajamas. I threw my bag in the back seat on the floor and climbed in the passenger's seat.

"Hey, peanut."

"Hey, big sister. Thanks for coming to get me. Thanks for coming alone."

"Of course." She smiled and grabbed my hand. "I thought you might need to talk, or sleep by the looks of it." She started driving out of the airport and onto the interstate.

"Yeah. I slept a little on the plane, but my mind has been going like the Energizer bunny running on a hamster wheel, and I can't keep up. This whole thing with Mark is out of control. Wait until I show you his text messages. Then I have all of this stuff going on with Grant's mother, not to mention I have been lying to Grant about everything with Mark. Grant's dad made sure I lost my job, so I don't know how I can afford to live there, but I can't afford to move back here either. I don't know how my life reached this point, but I want a do-over."

She ran her hands through my hair like she did when we were kids. It was still pinned up, but it felt comforting to have my sister do her normal big sister routine. "I'm sorry, Evie. I know that this is hard, but we're all here for you. Don't worry about the money stuff. That's easily fixable. The other stuff...I need more information, but we'll figure everything out together. Let's get you home and in bed first."

She took me to my parents' house where both of my parents were awake and expecting me. With big hugs from both of them and few words, I headed up to my old bedroom and went to bed. I was so tired that as soon as my head hit the pillow, everything was forgotten and I was out for the count.

A sweet voice was saying my name when I woke up. "Evie, I think you need to wake up. You need to eat something." It was my mom.

"Mom?"

"Yeah, peanut. It's Mom. Wake up. I made your favorite." She was unpinning my hair and running her hands through the knotted curls.

"You made me pancakes?" I asked.

"Covered in butter with powdered sugar and strawberry preserves." She kissed my forehead.

"Thank you."

"You're welcome. Now come before they get cold." I rolled out of bed and changed clothes into a pair of pajama pants and a cami. Downstairs in the kitchen I found my dad, sister, and my mom waiting for me at the kitchen table. It was just like I was a kid again. Mom used to make pancakes for dinner for Janie and me. Dad would get eggs and bacon, and Mom would eat an egg sandwich. This was what I wished for. They were giving me a do-over, even if it was just for one night.

I went back up to bed early, and I decided it was time to face the music. I turned my phone on and found thirty-four text messages and twelve voicemails when it finally loaded. I clicked the first voicemail. It was Grant. "Baby, I have been walking around this party now for an hour, and I still haven't seen you. I know you're upset, but it isn't what you think. I'm sure you don't have your phone on you, but if you happen to check it, please come and find me. Love you."

At least I know he was looking for me. I skipped the rest and clicked the last voicemail. Grant's voice came through the phone again, except this time it was strained. The message was from this morning.

"Eve, I'm still at your apartment, and you aren't here. I don't know if something has happened to you or where you are. We tried tracking your phone, but it's off. I need to know you're okay. Please call me, text me, anything." His voice cracked. "Please baby. I love you."

That one hurt. He thought something happened to me. He didn't know I left. I hated that I made him worry because I was weak and needed to get away, so I took the easy way out and sent him a text.

Me: I'm safe. Call you when I can. I'm sorry about everything.

I immediately turned my phone off, knowing he would message back or track it, and I just couldn't handle either.

Chapter 23

I slept soundly that night, having taken steps to move forward in life. I didn't even remember dreaming. I woke up to the sun in my face—the warm Georgia sun—and I stretched every limb as far as I could. It was early for me, but I decided to go for a quick run anyway. I threw on some old running gear, and although the shorts felt a little short, everything still fit.

Mom was waiting downstairs drinking her morning coffee. "Good morning," I said cheerfully as I walked into the kitchen and sat on one of the stools at the big island. My parents' kitchen was white with grey granite called "jet mist." It was really beautiful, and I loved sitting in my spot while my dad read the paper in the morning, and my mom stood in her spot drinking her coffee. "Where's Dad?" I asked when I realized his usual morning seat was already cleaned up.

She poured me a glass of orange juice and gave me a bagel with cream cheese. "He went to a build site today, but he'll be home for lunch. Going running?"

I nodded because my mouth was full. When I swallowed, I said, "I need to move. I slept too much yesterday."

She ran her hands through my ponytail. "You needed it, peanut. It looked like you hadn't slept in weeks. You still look tired and a little pale, but a run couldn't hurt. Just be careful. You aren't used to running in this heat."

I finished my bagel and told her I would be back later. I ran around my parents' neighborhood twice, which was about a mile, before I was so sweaty I couldn't take it anymore. It wasn't just hot. It was humid as well, and that was a painful combination. I walked the rest of the way to my parents' house and went inside to take a shower. I let my hair air dry in a mess of curls that hung down to the middle of my back and dressed in short cutoff jean shorts and a tank top. I felt like a teenager again.

I brought my laptop to the kitchen to work on job applications while my mom sat there balancing her checkbook the old fashioned way as she wrote checks for bills. Jane and I both had tried to get them to do that online, but they just liked doing things the way they always had. We drank freshly squeezed lemonade and snacked on cheese and crackers and grapes.

Our peaceful day ended abruptly when an unexpected knock came at the front door. My mom looked at me. "You expecting someone?"

"No one knows I'm here except for people who have a key to the house. I didn't even tell Holly." She looked nervous, and I felt it. We were both thinking the same thing. Mark.

We went to the door together where my mom looked through the peephole as I peeked out the curtain in the dining room. In the driveway I saw a sleek Mercedes Benz convertible—definitely not Mark. When I turned toward the door there was no mistaking who it was standing there. "Mom, open the door."

"Who is he?" she whispered as she turned the knob.

"Grant." I placed my hand over hers and pulled the door.

Light filled the entry hall, and there stood a beautiful man, looking like a worn-out CEO in charcoal slacks and a blue button-down with his sleeves rolled up. He took me in as I pushed the glass door open for him. I didn't even have words, so we stood there silent for a moment while I stared into his tired eyes that were a disconcerting shade of brown.

"How did you…" I started to ask.

"Tara. Dr. Clarke. Maddox," he said without taking his eyes off of me.

My mom chimed in, trying to break the tension with true southern hospitality. "Hello, Grant. I'm Evie's mother, Ellen. Won't you please come in?"

He looked up like he just noticed her and gave her his polite million-dollar smile. "Ellen," he took her hand. "It's nice to finally meet you. I've heard so much about you from Eve and Tara."

"Oh heavens! I'm sure those girls only tell lies." You have no idea, Mom. She laughed, and he smiled. Mom just had a way with people. "Would you like lemonade, sweet tea, water?"

He sat down on one of the wooden chairs at our round kitchen table. "I would love to try this sweet tea Eve has been raving about. She can't find it anywhere in Seattle and says hers is not nearly as good as yours."

I moved my computer to the side and saved the page of the application I was working on, so I wouldn't have to start over. "It's the water, Mom. Their water isn't made for sweet tea like it is down here."

She tweaked my ear like I was still a little kid as she put down his drink. I didn't mind. "Sure, peanut. That's the problem."

"Peanut?" Grant said.

My mom smiled. "That's her name in this house. Jane was five when I was pregnant with Evie. When we told Jane that we were pregnant, Jane asked how big the baby was because I wasn't showing yet. Their dad said the baby was the size of a peanut, and it stuck. She's been our peanut ever since."

"That's a good memory. Tell me more about peanut." He took a sip of his sweet tea. "This is delicious."

"Of course it is. You're in the Deep South now, my friend. Everything is fried, sweetened, or dipped in butter. In some cases all three." She smiled warmly like a mom should.

She sat down at the table with her freshly poured lemonade. "So, you want to hear about Evie, huh? Let's see…She was a tough little soccer player growing up. She quit in middle school because she discovered dresses and the curling iron. She loved singing and dancing. I think we have some videos of her playing Ado Annie in Oklahoma and Rizzo in Grease. She was incredible." Oh jeez, could this get any more embarrassing? "Boys drooled over her and called the house at all hours of the day and night." Turns out, yes. Yes, it can get worse. "I thought her dad was going to have a heart attack before she graduated high school. She was our good girl, though. I never had to worry about her while she was growing up. Jane, on the other hand, she was the one who made their dad's hair turn grey."

I stopped my mom. "Enough walking down memory lane, Mom. I'm sure Grant didn't fly all this way to watch videos of me singing off-tune in my high school musicals." I gave her a pointed look.

He laughed. "Actually, I would be happy to see these videos."

"No," I snapped. He laughed.

My mom realized Grant and I probably needed alone time, so she made her excuses. "I have some laundry to take care of. This summer heat has been a nightmare, and the kids go through three outfits each on Saturdays. I hope you can stay for lunch and meet Bill, and dinner to meet Jane and John and the kids."

"I would love to stay. Thank you, Ellen."

She smiled and headed up the back staircase.

He turned to me and there was no trace of a smile anymore. He brushed hair from my face and then ran his hand down my cheek. "Hi."

"Hi," I replied nervously.

"I think I died on Saturday night. My heart

stopped beating, and I couldn't breathe." He leaned forward and pressed a kiss to my forehead, my cheeks, and my lips. "What the hell were you thinking leaving like that?"

I pulled away from him. "There's a lot I didn't tell you, and when I saw you get out of the car with her—"

He quickly interrupted. "You know my parents did that. I was just being polite walking her in. As soon as I passed the crowd at the door, I was searching every face for you."

"I know it was your parents, but they aren't going to stop until I'm gone. Your dad called the college and had me fired. That night was my last night, and that was their way of twisting the knife."

"Dr. Clarke and Tara filled me in. Tara found your dress, so I knew you chose to leave, but I didn't know why until Dr. Clarke told me to leave you alone. That little old man is very protective of you."

I smiled at his truth. "He's protective of his baked goods. Dr. Clarke and Tara didn't know I left. How did you know where to find me?"

"I called Maddox and had him track you. We couldn't find your phone. Finally, yesterday afternoon, he found your name on a passenger manifest. I knew you came home. I just didn't know why you wouldn't have told me. You know I would've flown with you out here." He looked so tired, probably because he hadn't slept since he got up on Saturday morning.

"I didn't want you to follow me. There's more going on than I have told you, and I was drowning.

I am drowning. The last straw was watching you hold out your hand for her and then escort her in. She looked so happy. At first I just went home to my apartment, and then I realized I needed my family, so I came home. I had to be here anyway this week for the mediation, which I also didn't tell you about because I was afraid you would interfere."

He was angry. His jaw was so tight that it looked like it would break. He leaned forward and rested his elbows on his knees then said, "Why…" He paused, and I watched as he physically got control over his temper. "Why couldn't you just talk to me?"

"I need to deal with some of this on my own. I wasn't ready for you in my life. We've been together like five minutes, and I wasn't ready for any of it. I wasn't ready for a relationship or to feel this way about you. I fell in love with you. God, do I love you. You are so strong and caring, and I'm such a fucking mess. I have only brought drama and problems into your life, and I'm so tired of being the weak one who needs help all the time. It isn't who I am, so I was trying to finish this divorce bullshit on my own. I thought if I could get that out of the way then maybe I could deal with all the other bullshit, like finding a job if I want to stay in Seattle."

"Let's not worry about the job thing right now, and you're staying in Seattle with me," he said matter-of-factly, then kissed my hands that he was now holding. "You're not weak, Eve. I want to help you. So much of what you're going through is out of your hands, and I happen to have the power to handle some of this for you. It's what we do for people we love. You would help me if I needed it."

"Grant, you have your parents to deal with. You don't need my problems on top of that. If we're going to be together, we have to find a way for your parents to accept us, and Kitty to stay out of the way. If not, then I already know how this is going to go, and I'm afraid you wasted a trip."

"What are you saying, Eve?"

"I'm saying what I have been saying all along. I will not come between you and your parents. They're your family, Grant. If I know anything, it's that you never come between someone and their family. Family comes first in my world."

"So that's it?" he snapped without raising his voice. "You'd give up that easily? You would just have me marry Kitty to make my parents happy? You know that's the only thing that will make my mother happy."

"What happens the next time my life goes to shit?" My voice was shaking, but I willed myself not to cry. Not this time. "What happens when you decide that you are done with my drama and with me? You'll have given up your family for some crazy girl who became a huge regret?"

Grant leaned forward, so we were nose-to-nose. "I don't know what that asshole did to you, but I hate that you talk about yourself like that, because it isn't true. You are worth so much more than he led you to believe. You are not some crazy girl, and if you think I can just give up on you, on us, you've got another thing coming. I have enough fight for the both of us, and I can only hope that you get on board because I don't plan on spending another night without you. The last two were hell, and I will not go through that again. For the first time in my life, I was terrified. I felt what you feel when you worry. That terror, it was unbearable."

I leaned into him and pressed my lips to his. My arms went around his neck into his messy brown hair. He pulled me into his lap. "You promised you would stop running. You have to start letting me in without making me chase you."

I burrowed my face into his neck. "I know, but I'm terrified of letting you handle everything and losing myself again in the process. I just put some of the pieces back together, and I can't afford for them to fall apart again."

"I know," he whispered in my ear with his face buried in my neck. "We will fix all of this together. You don't have to do any of this on your own. I fell in love with the feisty beauty who thought I was going to murder her when I tried to ask her out. I've been chasing you this whole time. Slow down and let me catch you, Eve. I will. I promise."

"Well, well, well, what do we have here?" My dad's booming voice filled the room. When I looked up, he had his arms crossed and resting on his big belly. My dad wasn't a tall man, but he was a big man. He had a bowling ball head with brown hair that was combed into the same style he'd worn since high school, just a little shorter. Right now he was wearing his angry eyes, but it almost made me laugh, because even angry, Dad looked like the nicest guy in the world.

My mom came rushing down the stairs. "Bill, I need your help upstairs. Right now." She was trying to keep him from interrupting the private talk Grant and I were having in the kitchen, which was sweet, but I think he and I said all we needed to for the time being. I was sure there were a million more things we needed to work out, but right then I wanted him to get to know my family and the girl they raised, the stronger, brighter, and funnier girl than the mess who moved to Seattle.

"It's okay, Mom," I said. "Dad, this is Grant. Grant, this is my dad, Bill Bryant."

Grant lifted me off of his lap, so he could politely stand and shake my dad's hand. "Nice to meet you, sir."

"So this is the man I have heard so much about? Apparently you're quite a catch, son. The women in my family have been talking about you nonstop."

"Daddy!"

"I'm just teasing him, peanut," he said to appease me, but we all saw him shake his head to tell Grant he wasn't kidding.

Grant smiled. "It's all right. Eve has been the topic of conversation among my family members as well."

My mom looked displeased. "Yes, we've heard."

"Mom," I warned, then turned back to Grant. "By the way, nothing in my family is a secret…ever."

"And that's how it should be, Evie," Mom said. "Grant, we're pleased to have you as a guest in our home. Do you enjoy chicken salad?"

"I pretty much eat anything you put in front of

me." He smiled.

"It's true," I told them. "He has been eating a pizza he doesn't like because he gives the leftovers to a homeless man."

My mom smiled and Dad nodded and said, "That is nice of you. Tell us more about you, Grant."

Grant rested his hand on my thigh. I could tell he was nervous and needed me for support. I put my hand on his as he started talking. "Well, there isn't much to tell, truthfully. I grew up in Seattle and went to Harvard business school with my best friend, Maddox. Both of our fathers are alumni, but Maddox and I didn't care for the elitist atmosphere that can come with Harvard, so we decided to get jobs off campus. I worked at a pizza place, which is where I found out how much homeless people like pizza.

"After business school and giving up tossing pizzas, I moved to New York where I interned at my dad's company under a different executive. I planned to stay there and build my own life, but my parents had other plans. It wasn't long before I was back in Seattle and taking over the company with my father that my grandfather had left us. Then I met Eve." He squeezed my thigh.

I looked up at him with a smile after he summed up his life in less than a minute. "Just the highlights, huh?"

"Why didn't you go to Mitchell College?" my mom asked as she set down chicken salad sandwiches, a bowl of potato salad, a bowl of fruit, and a pitcher of sweet tea. We all helped ourselves, and I served Grant as he spoke.

"Both of my sisters did, but it was written long ago in my life plan that I would follow in my dad's footsteps and go to Harvard. I didn't mind leaving Seattle. I had the chance to meet new people who didn't know my parents, and I was able to go and see the world while I was away. We grew up fairly sheltered, so it was my first experience in the real world."

My dad swallowed his bite of chicken salad. "It's good for you to get out there. Both my girls went away to college, but they were only a couple of hours away. Until Evie left for Seattle, they haven't seen much outside of the southeast."

"That's not true, Dad. My sorority sisters and I went with Jane and her friends down to that resort in Mexico one Spring Break." I smiled widely knowing what was coming.

"Getting drunk and laying out at the pool for a week does not count as seeing the world. I still can't believe you let them go on that trip, Ellen. They could have been murdered!"

"Oh Bill, hush. You just had to bring that up didn't you, Evie? Just for that I might change my mind about making you barbecue chicken for dinner," my mom threatened.

"I was just teasing, Dad. You know Ricardo and Juan took great care of us." I winked at my Dad, who groaned and rolled his eyes.

My mom pointed her fork. "One more word about that trip, young lady, and I change my mind about making peach cobbler for dessert as well."

I pressed my lips together in an effort not to laugh.

Grant watched my face as I took a sip of my tea. "I'm sorry to ask, but what happened on the trip?"

I burst out laughing, and my mom threw her fork down on the plate. Dad just groaned. I turned to Grant. "My sister ended up getting really sick our first night there. We thought it was from her drinking too much, but it ended up being food poisoning. Mom and Dad flew down a couple of days later to either bring her medicine from here or take her home, but by the time they arrived, she felt better. Instead of being normal parents and going to bed at nine, they came out and partied with us that night. Dad was protective of the girls because the men in Mexico tend to stare. After a few drinks, though, he was dancing up a storm with our sorority sisters and ended up with a hellacious hangover the next day. Mom, on the other hand, was quite the rock star with her karaoke and dancing. She really enjoyed dancing with that pole, didn't she, Dad?"

Grant was smiling, and I was in a fit of giggles when my mom said, "That's enough. He gets the idea."

Dad was laughing now too. "I don't think he does, Ellen. Why don't you demonstrate?" I laughed even harder and looked over and saw Grant laughing too.

"I hate you two." She got up and walked over to the counter to bring over the plate of brownies she had made.

"You love us!" I called after her. "Come on, Mom. It was really funny. I think we have pictures."

She was back at the table with the brownies. "Since these two are so rude, would you care for a brownie, Grant?" That just made my dad and me laugh harder.

"Sure, thank you." He took a brownie from her plate and took a big bite of chocolaty goodness. "These are delicious. Now I know where Eve learned to bake."

I reached for one, and she slapped my hand. "You don't deserve one, you little brat, but you can have one because I don't want to save all of these for the kids."

"And because you love me." She smirked. I tried to sweetly say, "Thanks, Mom," but I was still trying not to laugh as I pictured my mother gyrating around a pole in Mexico.

After lunch my dad left for the build site, and my mom ran to the grocery store, leaving Grant and me alone in the house. I showed him around the main floor and down into the basement where I walked him out into the backyard. My parents had built a little oasis out there with a large swimming pool surrounded by rock walls and plant life. The water feature was running, so it was very relaxing out there.

"This is beautiful," Grant said. "It's hot as hell, but it's really nice out here."

"I like it. This is where I spent most of my free time after college. Do you want to go change into something cooler? The less clothes the better in the south." I gestured to my cutoffs and tank top.

He pulled me against his body, and I swear the temperature went up even more. "I like this little outfit, but I really hope you don't dress like this in public."

"Lord, no. My dad would kill me. He was probably annoyed that I was dressed like this in front of you, but they feel sorry for me, so I can get away with anything right now."

"Anything?" he asked with a raised eyebrow.

"What did you have in mind, handsome?"

"Show me the rest of the house." His green eyes sparkled, making me smile. I took his hand and guided him on the last leg of the tour, the third floor.

My bedroom was a pretty decent size with an iron queen-sized canopy bed. White bedding and sheer white curtains hung decoratively from the corners, giving the bed an ethereal quality. My windows overlooked the pool, and I had my own en suite bathroom because Jane was already living in her own apartment when my parents built the house. I was just a freshman in college.

"Are you going to stay here with us, or did you get a hotel?" I asked him as I started unbuttoning his shirt, revealing a white t-shirt underneath. Grant kept his arms wrapped around me.

"I have reservations at a place called Chateau Elan, but I'll do whatever you want to do. I was planning on taking you back to the hotel with me, but I assume you'd rather stay here."

"Chateau Elan is nice, but I'd much rather stay here. I miss my parents. I'm used to them being down the road or sharing the same house with them. It's strange not being able to see them whenever I want to."

"Then we'll stay here. I'm going to be wherever you are. Not another night, remember?" he said as he kissed me, tasting of chocolate from the brownies. "Plus, your parents are really great. You have the kind of parents Maddox and I used to wish for when we were kids. This is what we thought was normal life."

"This was my normal life, and now you're a part of it. Let's get your stuff. Did you bring a bathing suit?"

"I doubt it, but Lana packed for me, so I don't know." We walked downstairs and out to his car to get his bags.

"Why did Lana pack for you?"

"I was still at your apartment when Maddox found you, so I called her on my way home. I grabbed my bag and my briefcase and drove to the airport where the plane was waiting. It took me longer to pick up the rental car here in Atlanta and drive all the way up here from the airport than it took me to get the plane ready to fly in Seattle."

"What about your work? I don't know when I was planning to fly back. Originally it was tomorrow night because I was just flying down for the day, but I don't have a job to get back to now." Back in my bedroom, he took off his now wrinkled dress pants and his wrinkled blue shirt and threw on a pair of shorts and a t-shirt. He sat down on my bed with his back against the headboard, and I climbed up and went to curl up next to him, but that wasn't close enough for Grant. He pulled me onto his lap, so we were in our favorite talking position.

Once settled he said, "You'll fly back with me whenever you are ready to go home. I can work from anywhere right now, and my dad isn't going to challenge me on that."

"What happened with your parents on Saturday?" I asked, not sure I really wanted to know.

"My mother called after I dropped you off and told me Daphne and I were going to ride with her and Dad to the party. Ian was supposedly going to be late, and Grace and Harvey were going to meet us there. I didn't have time to check with Daphne because I got caught up in some calls after I worked out. My parents' limo picked me up at the penthouse. I thought we were going to pick up Daphne, but sure enough, it was Katherine who joined us.

"When we arrived at the party, I climbed out of the car and started to walk in to find you, but Katherine called my name and asked for my help, saying she was afraid to fall. I helped her out of the car, and next thing I knew her arm was linked through mine. I didn't want to make a scene, so we walked into the crowd of people who greeted us immediately.

"As soon as I was through the crowd, I was looking for you. Tara hadn't seen you since she opened the doors. Dr. Clarke was watching me, though, and I caught his eye. That was when he warned me off. I knew something was wrong, because he had always been friendly to me. I started looking everywhere for you. Daphne was there, and she was helping me. That's when Tara found me and told me she found your dress. I was on the phone with Maddox telling him to come get me when Dr. Clarke found me again. I asked him what happened, and he must have known how panicked I was, because he told me about you losing your job and what he found out from HR."

"Yeah, your dad had my position eliminated in a way that they wouldn't pay unemployment or a severance, not that I had been there long enough for that anyway."

He nodded. "While I waited for Maddox, I confronted my dad. He blew it off like it was no big deal, like you were no big deal. I may have gotten in his face and threatened him a bit. He let me go without another word. My mother tried to stop me from getting into Maddox's car, but I told her if she ever came near you again or put me in a situation that could hurt you again, I would take the company to the ground, effectively depleting her entire source of income, including her properties."

"Can you do that?" I asked, surprised by his willingness to destroy the business that his family built.

"Yes. My dad found himself in a little trouble a few years back, which is why he isn't the CEO. The company almost went under, but because of my contacts and negotiations, we were able to get back on track with one major change. I'm now the majority shareholder. I own sixty percent of the company, and Dad and Daphne each own twenty. He has no control. This was part of the deal. The reason he was going under was because of his ineffective business practices after my grandfather died. My mother doesn't know this, but she doesn't know a lot about my dad's activities."

"You were willing to give up all of that for me?

We have only known each other a month or so." I mean, sure, we spent almost every day of that month together, but it was still only a month. Can you know in a month that you are meant to be with someone?

"Have you been listening to anything I have said to you? I would move mountains to be with you, to make you happy. Baby, I felt you that first time I met you. I felt you from across the room. There is no doubt in my mind you were made for me. You make me feel for the first time ever. I lose my breath when you walk in a room. When you opened the door downstairs, I literally couldn't breathe after not seeing you for two days. You make me laugh, and you make me crazy. There is no one else in the world who does what you do to me, and I know a lot of women."

"Grant!"

"I'm just kidding about the other women."

"No you aren't," I pouted.

He took my bottom lip between his teeth. "No woman has ever made my heart beat as fast as you do. I had never felt butterflies until I met you. I don't know what else to do to prove I am totally, without a doubt, head over heels in love with you." He kissed me again. "I'm out of words, Eve. I've told you over and over how I feel. I have chased you all over Seattle, and now across the country. What else can I do?"

I ran my finger across the worry lines on his forehead and looked into his worried eyes that were his usual mix of colors. "There isn't anything else you could do to show me that you love me. I never doubted our feelings for each other. When it is just the two of us like this, I forget about everything else in my life. This is happiness right here, but unfortunately, we can't spend all day, every day like this. The outside world has a way of creeping in, and for whatever reason, I'm still so weak. Knowing what you were willing to risk for me makes me want to try harder, though. Knowing you think I'm worth all of that makes me kind of believe it too. You are a wonderful man, and I'm just the lucky one who happens to own the heart that was meant to connect with yours."

He smiled before his lips found mine. He rolled me onto my back and kissed me with everything he had. I felt his love pouring into me, and I could only hope he felt mine. I had been such a fool to think I could do anything without him by my side. When I put back the pieces of myself, I knew I was missing a few. I always thought Mark was holding onto the missing pieces, because he was the one who tore me apart, but he never had the piece that mattered. I had never given my heart away, but I did right there on my bed in my parents' house. I finally gave my heart away to someone who I trusted to take good care of it.

Chapter 24

Lana turned out to be an excellent bag packer. She happened to throw in a little of everything into Grant's bag. He told her he didn't know how long he'd be gone, so she planned for everything. Because of Lana's expert packing and my mother interrupting our love fest, we were in the pool when my sister arrived.

I was lounging on a float Grant was pushing around the pool, discussing my mediation I had to face in the morning, when we heard the three little monsters come running through the house. I was about to warn him when all three kids jumped in the pool without any regard for anyone they were splashing. Grant and I both laughed, but my sister came out and yelled at them, then introduced herself to Grant. The kids wisely hid behind the float.

Once Jane had stepped inside because Elle needed to be fed, the kids started crawling all over me like they always did.

"Aunt Evie! We missed you," Ava told me as she beat her brothers to the top of the float. Being the smallest had its perks.

"I missed you too. I want you to meet someone. Ava, Fitz, and Campbell, this is Grant. Grant, this is Ava the beauty, Fitz the hero, and that is Campbell, the best swimmer in the southeast."

"Hi, guys," Grant said. "I've heard a lot about you."

"Like what?" Campbell asked suspiciously.

Grant laughed. "Like you and Ava can jump off the diving board, but I can't remember who your Aunt Evie said was better."

"Me!" they both shouted in unison.

"I think you'll have to show me," Grant said. They started swimming over to the ladder. "Fitz, I heard you're quite the soccer player. You get that from beating up the other kids?" he asked, pointing to his broken arm in its blue waterproof cast.

"No, I fell." Fitz was a pretty honest kid. He was also the quietest of the bunch. He must get that from John, because there wasn't a quiet Bryant known to man.

"Watch us!" Ava yelled as they each took turns showing us who the best diver was.

"Who's the best?" Campbell asked.

"I don't know," Grant said. "Show me again." We went through this several times before we called it a tie. Grant and I had to get ready for dinner, so when my sister was finished feeding Elle, we went inside.

Grant didn't want to be disrespectful and shower with me in my parents' house, but I was able to convince him it was absolutely necessary. It didn't take much to convince him. In fact, it became too hard to deny me. Wink, wink, nudge, nudge.

"I like seeing you like this," he told me as he kissed my neck after I finished my hair.

"Like what?"

"Carefree. Happy. I don't think I have seen you smile or laugh as much as you have since I've been here with you."

I smiled brightly into the mirror where our eyes met. I could see the difference in me too. I could feel it. "They make me happy, like I'm safe and connected. The only other time I feel like that is when you and I are perfectly alone, usually in bed, with no other distractions."

"Then I'll make sure that happens more often."

I turned and wrapped my arms around his neck, careful not to mess up his perfect hair. He hugged me to him and lifted me up, so I could wrap my legs around him as well. "Good, because it would be really expensive to fly them all out there all of the time just to make me feel grounded."

"I would if that's what you needed," he said very seriously.

"I know you would, but it isn't what I need."

"What do you need, baby?"

"You. Us. Everything that allows us to be us. I need for my damn divorce to be final, and I need for your family to accept us, because it really tears me up inside that they don't let you make your own choices and support you like my parents. So many people think you're so lucky because you grew up rich, but I know I was the lucky one in that regard. It kills me, because despite the kind of people who raised you, you turned out to be an amazing man."

This time it was Grant who smiled sadly while I looked into greenish-bluish-brownish eyes. "Parents like yours are the one thing I always wanted and could never have. I love my parents, but all I ever wanted was what you've had all along." Money couldn't buy everything, unfortunately.

"Come on." I smiled and unwrapped my legs from his body. "There's a whole group of people downstairs hoping to find out you are everything I told them you were. Let's go prove them right." With a quick kiss to his lips, I led Grant down to meet John, the remaining member of my family.

I introduced Grant and John, and they started talking like they were old friends instead of new acquaintances. I left them alone in favor of going to chat with Jane and take over baby holding duties. "Come here, Ellie girl," I said as I held out my hands to her. She smiled happily and fell forward from her mother's arms to mine.

"Umm…can we discuss how hot your boyfriend is?" Jane said as she put the burp cloth on my shoulder.

"Sure. Where should we start? The eyes that change colors? The perfect hair? His beautiful face?"

"How about that ass? Or his perfectly shaped body. He even has nice legs, and I don't think I have ever said that about a man."

"Yeah, Grant hit the gene pool lottery, but he also works hard for that body."

Jane nodded appreciatively. "I can tell." Just then, Grant caught us staring at him and gave me a confused look. "Don't worry, Grant. We were just appraising your gene pool."

I elbowed my sister just as John grumbled, "Jane, come on. I'm standing right here."

"Honey, you know I think you are the sexiest man on the planet. The evidence is running around here somewhere and right here in Evie's arms. It's just nice to get some new eye candy up in here once in a while."

Grant looked surprised. "Me?" He pointed to himself. "I'm the eye candy?" he asked incredulously.

I laughed. "Don't act like you don't know what effect you have on women. He has gaggles of women hitting on him everywhere we go. They don't even have the decency to wait until I'm not around. They would hump his leg if he would let them, but he doesn't like that." I winked at him. "I've tried."

"Evie," my dad shouted. Everyone started laughing except my dad. Whoops! I guess he heard that. "Dinner's ready. No more talk of humping." He gave me the evil eye, and I hid behind Jane to laugh. "The kids will be at the table."

Jane and John led the way to the table. Grant came up behind me and pinched my sides. "If you're going to get me in trouble with your dad, let's make it for something good."

"My dad is just trying to act tough in front of you. He probably thinks I'm hilarious like everyone else."

Grant smacked my rear just before we walked out onto the covered porch with powerful ceiling fans. We all sat down at the table. I kept Elle in my lap, and Ava sat on my right, in between Mom and me. Grant sat next to me and to the right of my dad. Fitz and Campbell sat on the other side of the table, in between Jane and John because they needed more supervision, supposedly. I think the adults were more of a problem than the kids, though. Maybe the kids were there to supervise us.

We all started to dig in when Ava panicked. "Campbell's eating beans, Mom! He's not supposed to eat beans."

"Why can't Campbell eat beans?" I stupidly asked.

"They make him fart," Fitz, the little truth-teller said without looking up from his plate.

"Oh. I see," I said, trying not to laugh. I couldn't hold it in once my dad started, though, and Grant and John followed suit.

"Now, come on, y'all. It's no big deal." My mom tried to calm everyone down, which only made us laugh harder. "Stop it! You'll embarrass him."

I gathered myself...sort of, and said, "Sorry Camp, but that's pretty funny. Is it all beans, or just baked beans?"

"All beans," Campbell said like he didn't care. "They give me gas, and Ava says it stinks. I don't smell it, but I hear it." Dad was laughing so hard he had tears, which made John and Grant laugh even harder. Now even Jane was laughing.

Mom finally rolled her eyes. "New topic. How long are you and Grant staying, peanut?"

"I don't know, Mom. I guess we'll wait and see when the beans hit Campbell. We may be leaving sooner rather than later."

She smacked me on the back of the head. "Didn't you turn thirty this year? Good heavens, you'd think you turned six. Fitz is more mature than you."

Jane laughed. "Look at Dad, Mom. He's the one crying like a baby. Where do you think Evie gets it?"

Dad and I reached in front of Grant to give each other a high five. "You know it. Peanut's my kid."

When Campbell and Fitz started arguing over a corn muffin, Grant leaned over and whispered, "You really can get away with anything, can't you?"

I smiled and nodded. "This is why I'm the fun aunt. John's sister has nothing on me."

Elle was reaching for Grant, so he actually volunteered to take her. He was pretending to grab her nose, making her giggle over and over. All three of us women watched in adoration. That was something Mark would never have done, and Grant was doing it on his first day with my family.

"Aunt Evie, is Grant your boyfriend?" Fitz asked.

I looked at Grant, and he was looking at me, waiting for my response. "I guess you could call him that, but he's really more of a man, Fitz."

"So, he's your man-friend?" Fitz clarified.

"Yes. That is precisely what Grant is to me." I smiled at Grant, who was chuckling behind Elle. She was happily standing on his legs with his help.

"Then what happened to Uncle Mark?" And the table went silent. Jane started to talk, and I shook my head, telling her I could explain.

Fitz was seven, so I had to be concrete without vilifying Mark. He already scared them enough when he broke into my parents' house. "Well, Fitz, Uncle Mark and I decided we didn't want to be friends with each other anymore, so he isn't going to come around from now on."

"Is that why he was so angry?"

Everyone's eyes bounced back and forth between Fitz and me.

"Yes. He was angry I moved away without telling him, but I didn't tell him because we had already decided we weren't going to be friends anymore."

"Is he still my uncle?"

"He'll always be Uncle Mark to you, but no, buddy, he isn't your uncle anymore."

"That's not what he said."

"What do you mean?"

"When I saw him at camp, he told me that he was still my favorite uncle." Everyone's head whipped in Fitz's direction, but he just kept talking like he didn't notice. "He's not, though. I don't even really like Uncle Mark because he was so mean to Grandpa."

"When was this, buddy?" I asked cautiously, trying not to worry anyone at the table, including Fitz. My stomach was in my throat. I gripped Grant's hand tightly while he held Elle in the other.

"Last week when Jeremy's mom picked him up from camp. Uncle Mark was with her, and he said he was still my uncle and he'd be seeing me soon. I thought we'd see him today when Mommy said you were here. That's why I didn't want to come. It wasn't because of you."

I nodded at Fitz, unable to speak. Everyone else was looking at each other, but I was just focusing on one specific fact. He saw him last week. He approached Fitz last week. Mark broke the restraining order.

John broke the silence that was confusing Fitz. "Buddy, are you sure you saw him at camp last week?"

"Yeah, Dad. It was the last day of camp."

"And Uncle Mark talked to you, or did you talk to him first?" John was getting the details to press charges.

"He came up to me. I didn't even see him until he grabbed the ball from me. He gave it back, though."

"He was just playing around with you," I told Fitz. "Fitz, what's Jeremy's last name?"

Jane answered, "I think it's Sanders. Why, Evie?"

"Shit." I stood up from the table and headed inside.

I didn't get away before my mom yelled, "Language!"

"Not now, Mom," I said as I ran in the house to get my phone. It was up in my room, and I was grateful for the privacy for this phone call.

Of course Grant followed me after passing off Elle to find out what was going on. My phone was already calling, so I held one finger up, telling him to wait.

"Hey, girl!" Holly answered.

"Hey, Holly. When's the last time you saw Ashley Sanders?"

"Saturday night, why?"

"Have you ever mentioned to her that I moved to Seattle?" I asked, trying to keep the anger out of my voice.

"Probably. We hang out a lot. She used to like the drummer in Matt's band, which is gross because I swear that guy never showers. Why?"

"Doesn't she have a kid?"

"Yeah, Jeremy, but he goes back and forth between her and her ex, so I've only met him a few times."

"Holly, Ashley has been hanging out with Mark. Jeremy goes to camp with Fitz, and Mark was with her one day when Ashley picked up Jeremy."

"What?"

"Mark called me last week and told me he knew where I was, and that he would make sure I came home to him. She told him where I was. I don't even know how he got my number. His mom could have given it to him, but I don't think she'd do that." I looked up to see the shocked expression on Grant's face turn to anger. I didn't know if he was angry at the threat or at me for not telling him.

"Oh shit, Evie. I had no idea. I swear I didn't."

"It's fine. The mediation is tomorrow, and I'm going to have Martin file for another order of protection restricting his contact with my family for a longer period of time. I have probably a hundred crude text messages from him that they can use to support my claim. Mark is really a dumbass."

"You're in town?"

"Yeah. I'm here. I'll call you after the mediation like we planned, but I have a surprise for you."

"You brought Grant!"

"He's here. Right now he looks like he could breathe fire because it was his first time hearing about the phone call and texts, so I need to let you go."

"Oh my. I bet he's hot when he's ticked. Talk to you tomorrow. Good luck."

"Thanks. I'll need it."

I hung up and faced Grant. "Don't be mad. I told you there was other stuff that I hadn't told you yet, and I planned on telling you. We had other things to talk about first."

Grant's face was so tense that he had a vein popping out of his temple. "Of course I'm mad that you didn't tell me, particularly because he threatened you. What if something happened to you, Eve?"

"Nothing did. If I promise to show you everything, can we go back down to my family now and pretend everything is hunky dory? I probably upset Fitz, and I need to make it better."

"Fine, but this discussion isn't over."

"I know. I love you."

He grabbed me and pulled me tightly to him. "I love you too. No more keeping things from me."

"That was the last thing, I promise."

After a quick kiss and another ass slap, we were back downstairs with the family. The kids were playing in the yard when we came back outside. Elle was in my mother's arms with a bottle, and everyone was watching us come back to the table.

"Well, Holly told Ashley Sanders, Jeremy's mom, about me moving to Seattle, which is how Mark knew where I was. I'm going to apply for a Family Protection Order like Martin and I had discussed. Then I'm going to force him to give up the house. He'll have no choice but to either find a friend, which won't last, or go live with his mother. I'm banking on that one since I called her last week."

"You called his mother? Ha! That's awesome." John laughed. Everyone knew what a mama's boy Mark was.

"New topic," I said and clapped my hands together. "This episode of Eve's pathetic, drama-filled life is getting boring."

"Now seriously, Evie and Grant," Mom said, "How long are you staying? I know Holly would like to see you, and we have the barbecue at the Morris' this weekend if you want to come and introduce Grant to everyone you grew up with." Well, that sounds like a nightmare for Grant.

Grant looked over to me, and I looked at him. "It is completely up to you," he said like the good man-friend that he was.

"I'm gonna pass on the barbecue for Grant's sake. He'll fly back to Seattle without me just so he can get away from those crazy women. I think either tomorrow night or Wednesday morning. He actually has a job and a life he needs to get back to."

"Eve," Grant said quietly in warning.

"I know, Grant, but you really should get back. I need to start applying to schools anyway."

"You're going to go back to teaching?" Jane asked.

"Already back on me? All right then." I was tired of talking about me, even though I had come home to get help. They seemed more helpful over pancakes last night when no one was talking.

"Teaching is the only thing I'm actually qualified to do. Plus, it isn't like I stopped teaching because I didn't like it. I figured I'd apply and see what's out there. Come the end of August, I'll be homeless if I don't have a job, and Grant will be feeding both me and Frank on Fridays at the pizza place."

"Why don't you come work for my company?" Grant suggested. "Rachel usually handles planning all of our charity dinners and events, but it makes more sense to have someone else do it as their primary responsibility. She's better suited for other tasks anyway."

"No and no. Event planning was just something Tara brought me into. I'm not coming to work for your company. Your father already had one job taken away from me. I don't want to give him the chance to take another."

"He doesn't really have a say in it, now does he?" Grant said, pointedly reminding me of the conversation we had earlier.

"That could be your back-up, peanut. You could go work for Grant if you can't find a teaching position you want." Jane was always the practical one in the family. That's why she was in finance. She had back-up plans for her back-up plans.

"Would you ever work for John?" I asked her.

"Oh god no!" she exclaimed. I held my hands up

as to say point proven. She shook her head at me. "Not the same and you know why." She wore the pants in her family, that's why, but John didn't like to be emasculated, so we weren't supposed to talk about it.

"Can we talk about someone else for a little while?" I asked, trying not to whine but was unsuccessful.

"Sure, peanut," Dad said. "I went over to the build site today…" Everyone immediately groaned, except Grant who looked confused. "What?"

"Dad, no one wants to hear about roofing shingles or plumbing," Jane told him like she had a thousand other times.

"Well, I'm sorry if my life isn't as interesting as Evie's, but that's what happens when you get old. You get boring too."

"Speak for yourself," Mom said.

"Really, Ellen, how's book club?" Dad said.

Jane and I immediately jumped up from our chairs. "Is that Ava crying?" Jane asked.

"It has to be. I'll come help. It sounds terrible," I said and started walking out to the yard with her.

"I don't hear anything," Mom said.

"That's because you're old!" my sister shouted back as I turned to wink at Grant, who was obviously confused by the whole thing.

Moments later, John and Grant walked up to us at the playground my dad had built for the kids. "You two are so mean. Grant had no idea why you were running away, and he was going to ask until I thankfully stopped him," John scolded us.

I climbed off the swing and wrapped my arms

around Grant. "Sorry, handsome, but you do not want to get my mother started on her book club. She reads erotic romances, and there are some words that should never come out of a mother's mouth in front of her children."

Grant laughed out loud. "Not what I was expecting, but I understand."

John grabbed the twins. "Dessert is ready, so we should all go inside. We need to go soon, so we can get these smelly kids in the bath."

We all walked back in the house where Mom had served her peach cobbler with vanilla ice cream for all of us.

"This is really good. I've never had peach cobbler," Grant told my mom.

"Then I'm glad you like it. It's Evie's favorite summer dessert. I'm sure you don't have peaches in Seattle like we do down here, but you could always use canned ones instead of sweetening your own."

I wrinkled my nose and Jane looked shocked. "Canned ones?" Jane asked. "When is the last time you used canned peaches for something?"

"Your grandmother's funeral, but don't tell anyone. I didn't have time to cut and peel twenty peaches for a dessert that size."

I laughed at my mom whispering her big secret. If that's the biggest secret she's had to keep lately, then I couldn't wait to get old and boring.

Chapter 25

Later that night, Grant and I were curled up in my bed. I showed him all the text messages I hadn't read until now, and I couldn't even get through them. I stopped about ten messages in. They varied from threats of what he was going to force me to do if I gave him a hard time tomorrow to reminders of all the things he had planned for my body, which were actually a little more horrifying to read. My peach cobbler revisited after the tenth message, and Grant had the opportunity to see how my body reacts to stress. It was a turning point for us.

The tenth message said something about him getting me home and tying me up, so he could fuck me like an animal. Alone it wouldn't have been too bad, but paired with the nine others we had already read, and the fact that Grant was reading these as well, my stomach couldn't take it. I ran to the bathroom but couldn't get the door shut before my face was in the toilet. Grant was right behind me pulling my hair away.

"Can you not watch this?" I said as I flushed the

toilet.

"Baby, I'm not watching you throw up. I'm taking care of you." He pulled my hair into a ponytail and then filled a glass with water for me.

I took a sip of water and spit it back in the toilet before sitting down and leaning against the wall. My body was clammy, and I could only imagine what I looked like. Usually I was pale with watery eyes and a layer of sweat on my skin. "Welcome to my world, Grant. Isn't it colorful?" I said sarcastically.

He slid down the other wall. "I told you I want to know the good and the bad. Does this happen often?"

I tilted my head from side-to-side. "No. It started a couple of years ago. Before that my stomach bothered me when I felt stressed or anxious, but I didn't feel the need to throw up. Now, it's like I can't keep it in. It isn't every time I get stressed. It seems Mark makes me sick more than anything." I smirked.

"You know everything will be okay. I'll make sure of it."

I smiled appreciatively at him. "I know you would if you could, but you have to let me handle this tomorrow. Mark's not a bad guy. He's just a little lost, and I don't know why. I'll make sure he signs the papers tomorrow, but I also want him to get help. I don't want him to go to jail, even after all of this. That's what has me so tied up in knots. I can't make sense of the contradiction of the old Mark and new Mark in my head, and it's making me physically ill. I feel like it won't go away unless

I can come up with the best possible solution for everyone."

"And what's that?"

I shrugged. "I don't know yet. I want the divorce, and I want Mark away from my family and me, but I also want him to get help. That would be ideal, I think."

He grabbed me and pulled me over so I was sitting in between his legs against his chest. "If I could make that happen, would you allow me to help you?"

I looked up at him in disbelief. "How can you make all of that happen?"

"You said his mother lives in Florida, right?" I nod. "What if I agree to pay off his debts, and you agree to giving him half the assets, or whatever you want to give him if he permanently moves to Florida? I can have my attorney draw up a contract tonight. It's only six-thirty in Seattle."

"Absolutely not. I don't want you paying to fix my mistakes. He doesn't get to take the easy way out, not this time."

He groaned and shifted. "I understand what you're saying, but my guess is he'd be willing to go away quietly with a little bit of cash."

"You know my answer." I used the door to pull myself off the floor so I could brush my teeth.

I climbed into bed exhausted from the exciting day and the less than glamorous cookie toss, or cobbler toss as it was. Grant climbed in with me. "Do you mind if I work here? I can go downstairs if my laptop bothers you."

"No, I like having you here. Work away."

He kissed my forehead. "Love you, baby."

"I love you, and so does my family. Thank you for coming here and for chasing me...and for catching me."

His eyes were a bright green and told me all I needed to know, but just in case I had forgotten, he said, "I told you, wherever you are."

"Thank goodness." He pulled out his laptop and passed me his iPad. I smiled and curled up next to him and downloaded another book onto the Kindle app he put on there for me.

It wasn't long before I couldn't keep my eyes open and I felt the iPad slip from my hands. "Night, peach." With those words, the world disappeared.

I woke up the next morning with the sun. I watched Grant sleep peacefully for a few moments. He had to be exhausted, and it was only four in the morning his time. I snuck out of bed and went down to my dad's office to print the rest of the documents I needed to take with me to my meeting with Martin. Once everything was organized, I went into the kitchen where I found my mom in her spot.

"Morning, Mom," I said as I went to the fridge to get some juice.

"Morning, peanut. No coffee?"

"No. I have enough nervous energy running through my body." I sat down in my seat with my juice.

"You sure you don't want one of us to go with you? I hate that you have to face this on your own."

"I'm sure. Thank you, though. This is something I need to do on my own. Hopefully after today, everything will be okay. I just keep thinking about how pleasant dinner will be tonight. If I just focus on dinner, I don't feel nearly as sick to my stomach."

I watched as my mom grimaced and then turned toward the coffeemaker to hide it. "Have you been eating in Seattle?"

"Yes, Mom. I've been eating. Grant knows about it too, and he has been on my case enough for the both of you."

She exhaled a breath in annoyance. "Don't take that tone with me. You know why I worry. Do we need to go through last summer's photo album to remind you?"

I winced. "No."

"All right then. What do you want for breakfast?"

"Mom…"

"Pancakes? How about waffles this time?"

"Waffles are fine." She wasn't going to let up if I didn't eat, and I didn't need any additional stress today.

Mom nodded and started getting out the ingredients and talking about who knows what. I sat there pretending to listen while I silently wondered what I would be facing in the meeting today. It wasn't like I had been to one of these before. I had no idea how this would go, which was why I was meeting with Martin an hour early to prepare. That helped me relax slightly.

Grant walked in the kitchen wearing a dark grey t-shirt and khaki shorts. He smiled when he saw me and came around the island to give me a kiss good morning.

"Good morning, handsome. Did you sleep okay?"

"Yes," he said aloud and then leaned in to whisper in my ear, "until I woke up alone." I smiled, and he kissed my ear.

"You hungry, Grant?" my mom asked.

"Sure. Can I help you do anything?" My man was so thoughtful and polite.

I got up and made his coffee just how he likes it, as my mom said, "No way. I don't put guests to work in my house. You just sit down and relax. Entertain Evie. I think her mind is probably running away with her."

"Mom," I groaned. She just waved me off, so I rolled my eyes and turned back to Grant. "Did you get a lot of work done last night?"

"More than I expected. Where's your meeting?" He tangled his hands into my ponytail, the same one that he pulled my hair into last night while my head was in the toilet.

"My lawyer's office, which is about fifteen minutes away. At least that's familiar." I offered him a forced smile.

He pulled me close to him, and I snuggled into his shoulder. "It will all be fine, gorgeous. Afterwards we'll go to dinner with Holly, and then we'll fly home to Seattle and stay in your tiny apartment. In just a few hours, it'll all be over."

"Here you two go. Waffles and fruit." She set down our plates and went back to standing in her spot eating a waffle and drinking her coffee. "Evie, did you print an extra copy of everyone's statement?"

"Yes, and I filled out the forms that Martin asked for. I should be good to go with the paperwork. I also printed out screenshots of all his messages. Now we just have to get him on board. Hopefully his lawyer isn't a complete moron, but we shall see."

My mom watched me the entire time I ate, so there was no way I was getting away with shoving my food around this time. I should have been hungry, but my stomach was so tied up in knots, I was pretty sure there wasn't room for waffles. I shoved them down anyway. I think me eating my breakfast made both my mom and Grant feel better. Too bad it made me feel worse.

After waffles, I showered and dressed in a conservative black sheath dress. I looked like I was going to a funeral, but in a way I kind of was. I wore minimal makeup because looking pretty wasn't my goal. Grant distracted me in the shower and stayed with me as I dressed and pinned up my hair. He gave me a supportive pep talk in my room before I went downstairs to leave for my meeting. He wanted to drive me, but I wanted to have a car there so I could have a few minutes to myself when it was over.

With a kiss goodbye from Grant and hugs from my parents, I took my mother's car to face the music. Martin's office was in an old house near the square of another historical town in our area. When you walked in the front door, it smelled like old houses do, but they had office furniture set up instead of what you might find in a home. Marilyn, Martin's secretary and niece, greeted me when I walked in. My family had known Martin's a long time, so her warm smile was comforting right then.

"He knows you're here, Eve. How ya doing?"

I gave her a tight smile. "Hangin' in there today, Marilyn. How are you?"

Her smile was warm and friendly. "Doing well. The kids are all busy with sports and their friends this summer, so it has been nice and quiet around the house. You know Tim is driving now?" She showed me a picture of her teenage son and his Mustang convertible.

"Wow. I didn't realize he was already sixteen. He'll be in college soon."

"Don't remind me. He's my first one to leave the nest, and he wants to go to FSU. So far away."

"You'll be able to drive back and forth, though." She nodded.

"Evie!" Martin's old man voice echoed through the foyer of the old house. He held his arms open for a hug, and I openly embraced him. "How you doin' today?"

"Little stressed, little nervous. I guess it's all expected though."

He shook his head. "With Mark, nothing is expected. Come on back. We'll go ahead and get set up in the conference room."

In the conference room, which was a mini law library with a table that comfortably seated ten people, Martin and I went through each document carefully to make sure we were fully prepared. He explained what to expect when Mark and his lawyer showed up, and I filled him in on what I wanted for a restraining order, which would have to be granted by a judge. By the time we had gone through everything, they were supposed to be there, and I was a nervous wreck.

Mark's attorney, Larry Smith, arrived first. Where Martin was the quintessential old man attorney, Larry was the salesman kind of attorney. No surprise there. Mark probably hired him off a television ad. He walked in wearing a cheap black suit made for his height, not his thin build. His hair was probably combed at some point, but it needed a little touch up. He wore wire-rimmed glasses, and bless his heart, his ears stuck out like Dumbo. Who takes this man seriously in a courtroom?

After introductions, Larry said to Martin, "My client should be here any minute." Martin just nodded and gave me a reassuring smile.

Ten minutes later and fifteen minutes late for the meeting, Marilyn brought Mark into the room. I was in terrible shape when I last saw him, so I didn't really have room to talk, but he looked awful compared to how he was a year ago. Mark had dirty-blond hair that was getting darker with age. He was a big guy like you would expect from a football player, but he used to always workout and stay in shape. Now he just looked like a big guy. He hadn't shaved and his hair was a mess. He at least put on khakis and a polo shirt, which was honestly more than I expected.

He came in and shook hands with Larry and Martin and pretty much ignored me, which was fine. Once everyone was seated, Martin went over the last petition, which said I get my inheritance back, and he keeps everything else. Larry said no to the money because his client didn't have a steady job and was unable to pay it. The sale of the house was suggested, but that was also denied for the same reason. What everything boiled down to was Mark didn't have a job and couldn't afford to move or pay anything. With my willingness to give up the house, Larry said that money was part of the house, and I had already conceded to that.

Mark and I didn't say a word during that entire discussion. We just let the lawyers basically have the same conversation they had been having for us since I moved to Seattle. But Martin wasn't finished yet. "My client is prepared to go to court, and with her petition claiming habitual intoxication as well as cruel treatment, she will be filing another request for an Order of Protection, which will be the third request in two months. With that being said, we not only have statements from my client's family members regarding her safety, but we also have evidence of threats he has been sending over the course of the previous week." Martin passed the copies of the statements and screenshots that I brought him this morning across the table.

Larry looked really irritated now. "Can I have a moment with my client?"

"Sure," Martin said. "Just let Marilyn know when you're ready." Martin gestured for me to stand, and I grabbed my purse and followed him out. He closed the door behind him and said, "We'll see."

Marilyn came clip-clopping up to us when she heard Martin's voice. "Martin, you have someone in your office who needs your urgent attention."

Martin looked confused but said to me, "Why don't you go get yourself some coffee? I'll be out in just a moment."

I went to the kitchen of the old house where Marilyn always had fresh coffee and treats. I grabbed a bottle of water from the fridge because I still didn't need the caffeine. Seeing him again had my body on high alert as it was. I sat down at the table and pulled out my phone to text Grant.

Me: Should be finished soon. :)

After I sent the same text to Jane, Holly, and my parents and received messages back from each of them, I sat at their little kitchen table waiting for Martin. I was in there for a good half hour and Grant never messaged me back. I wondered where he was. I couldn't picture him sitting out at the pool or taking a nap. It was possible he was working, but he would have his phone on him. I thought he would have been waiting anxiously on news from me.

I didn't have too much time to worry, though, because Marilyn came and told me they were ready for me. I threw my empty bottle of water in the recycling bin and headed back into the conference room. Martin was standing at the door. He looked nervous now, which made me uncomfortable. "There's been a change of plans, Evie."

"What? What do you mean?"

"I'll let them explain." He led me back into the room where the table was now full. My eyes shot wide as I took in the scene. Everyone except a defeated Mark stood when I walked in. Standing in front of the chair next to the one that was meant for me was Grant. Well, that explains the lack of communication. Next to Grant sat a man I didn't know, but at the head of the table was my father. To his left was Jennifer Dyer, my dad's real estate agent. John stood in between Jennifer and Mark, who still had his face down, refusing to look at me.

"What the fuck?" I asked out loud. It was unintentional, but what the fuck!

"Evie," my dad scolded. I widened my eyes at him. Really, Dad? Now is not the time to worry about my potty mouth.

"Ms. Bryant, please sit down," said the man who I didn't recognize. Martin escorted me by my elbow over to my seat.

Mark groaned and finally lifted his head. "Her name is Mrs. Stevens, not Miss Bryant."

"Sit down, Eve," Grant said through a clenched jaw. He was in his executive mode with his work pants and dress shirt and perfect hair. This was another one of his stampedes, and this time he brought all of his friends to run over me with him. I looked at him for a moment before I turned my disappointed eyes away. He just couldn't let this be.

"Someone better start talking," I said angrily.

"Evie," my dad said. "It's time for this to be over. Mark needs help, and we need to make sure you're safe and healthy. You told Grant exactly what you wanted last night, and Owen," he nodded to the man seated next to him, "drafted the agreement to make it happen."

"Eve," the stranger said. "My name is Owen

Graybill. I went to law school with John. With video evidence and statements provided by your father, John, and Holly Benton, we are prepared to press charges against Mark for the assault of Holly Benton and your sister. Here." He turned a laptop around and pressed play on a parking lot security feed.

It was Mark attacking Holly in the parking lot. You can't see their faces, but I could pick Mark out of anywhere. I knew his walk and how he moved. I had been watching him for years. Another video started, and this time the parking lot was crowded. This video was grainier than the last. A couple was walking to their car until someone interfered and grabbed the smaller person. That was when I could tell the other figure was John.

"Turn it off." I had tears running down my face. "Where did you get those?"

Grant spoke up. "Maddox was able to get them, Eve, along with some additional incriminating evidence."

"Mark, I didn't know about this." I sobbed horrifically. "I didn't want any of this. I just wanted a divorce and my inheritance back. I was willing to give you everything if you would just sign the fucking papers." I stood abruptly and looked down at Grant. "I asked you specifically not to do this. You wondered why I didn't tell you anything? Now you know why." My eyes went to my dad. "You of all people should have known better, Dad." With that I darted from my chair and out of the room. I heard the men's voices calling my name, but I was in the car and racing out of the parking lot before anyone caught up to me.

I drove straight home and ran in the house. "Mom! Mom! Where are you?" I was running around the house looking for her.

"I'm right here. What's wrong?"

"Did you know?" I sobbed.

"Know what, honey?"

"What Dad, Grant, and John had planned for today?"

"No…I…What are you talking about?"

I started crying even harder, and she wrapped her arms around me. "They are threatening him with jail time. I told them I'd handle it. I wanted to handle one thing on my own. It was a done deal. Mark was about to give in, but they just couldn't let it be." My stomach rolled. I quickly got up to run to the bathroom, but I didn't make it and threw up all over the wood floors in the hallway. "Oh my god. I'm so sorry, Mom."

"It's okay, peanut. Go into the bathroom. I'll clean this up. It isn't the first time I have cleaned up your vomit."

My stomach rolled again, and I just kept heaving and crying. It was miserable, and I had no control over it. My mom came in and rubbed my back until I stopped heaving. I lay down on the floor, and she put a towel under my head and cleaned up the bathroom. "Sorry, Mom."

"It's all right, honey. I'm going to call your Dad and find out what's going on. You stay here just in case you feel sick again." I nodded and she left the room.

I must have fallen asleep, because when I woke

up, my sister was in the bathroom with me, stroking my hair like she always did. All the pins were out and on the floor in front of me. "Janie?"

"Yeah, peanut. It's me. How you feeling?"

"Like shit."

"Yeah. Mom said you threw up waffles all over her hardwoods." She laughed and I did too.

"Did you know what they were up to?"

"No. John didn't tell me, but he and Grant had been talking since last week when we told you about the restraining order."

I sighed and sat up. "Why couldn't they just believe that I would have handled it? It was a done deal."

"They interfered because no one wants you to go through anything like that. I have never known anyone to go through a dark time like you did, and I'd do anything for you not to ever feel so helpless again. When you moved out of that house, you were terrified. We thought you were going to hurt yourself Eve, and Mom, Dad, John, and I have never been so scared or worried. Grant caught a glimpse of that last week and called Dad. We're lucky we have men in our lives who would drop everything to make sure we're safe, you know that?"

"I'm not helpless," I said again, even though it felt like no one believed me.

"We know that, but they can't sit back and watch you hurt. Our guys are fixers. Remember that time the neighbor kid pulled the chain off your bike? Dad went over there and made him come apologize to you, then he taught the kid how to fix your bike.

It's what they like to do. Mark wasn't like that. He only brought you down. Grant, on the other hand, is like Dad and wants to protect you."

"Then why do I feel so terrible?"

"You have never been good with surprises, for one thing. Mom and I would have told them that if they had asked us. For another thing, even though Mark has been really awful to all of us, you probably didn't want to be the one to cause him any more pain."

"Close the door." She leaned over and pushed it shut. "I feel like this is all my fault, like Mark would have never been this way had I done something. I only made it worse by divorcing him. He wasn't like this in high school. His dad had just died, and he was the nicest guy. When we met back up, he was just kind of a mess. I always thought the old Mark would come back, but he never did. I thought that if I handled this without making it worse for him, then maybe I could redeem myself. I need Mark to forgive me."

"I just don't think he's going to forgive you, because there is nothing to forgive. He needs help, Evie, and Dad and the boys are going to make sure that happens."

"What do you mean?" I asked.

"I think it's time you leave the bathroom and go talk to Grant. He's been wearing a hole in the family room since I got here. Dad even opened a bottle of scotch."

"Everyone is pretty upset with me, huh?"

"No one is upset with you. They just want to explain. Remember, they're on the outside looking in, so they don't have the emotional ties you feel to Mark." I hadn't thought about that before. What would I have done if I had watched Jane or Holly go through what I did? I can't even imagine what that was like for my parents.

"I'm ready." I stood up and looked in the mirror. "Holy shit, I look like the bride of Chucky." I washed my face and rinsed my mouth out again. My sister tried to comb out my hair with her fingers and pulled it into a braid. My sister gave me some clothes that my mom left for me, so I changed into jeans and an old sorority shirt and looked in the mirror. "Not a total Betty but a vast improvement."

"Well, we did our best," Jane said, finishing the quote from *Clueless*.

"We gotta book it if we're going to make it to P.E." We laughed as we walked into the living room to find my dad was indeed drinking scotch and Grant was sitting on the edge of the sofa with his elbows on his knees and his hands together like he was praying. John had a beer and the remote in his hand.

"Gentlemen, she's all yours," Jane announced happily as we walked in the room.

Grant looked up and was in front of me in two strides. He took my face between his hands and made me look up into his worried brownish eyes. "You okay?"

I nodded, and he led me over to the couch. I sat on the middle cushion between Grant and John and pulled my knees up to my chest. John turned the television off, and Mom and Jane came in from the kitchen and sat in the matching light grey tufted club chairs after Jane handed me a bottle of water. I waited for someone to talk, but no one said anything.

I spoke first. "Someone talk."

Grant started to speak, and Dad interrupted. "It's all right, Grant. I got us into this mess. Peanut, Grant called me after you told him what we talked about last week. He told me how upset you were, so I got in touch with Martin. He told me what the hang up was on your divorce. I understood what that money meant to you, but Mark's problem was never with the money. He wouldn't have signed the papers if you gave him your left kidney, and he was banking on you wanting to stay out of court."

"Dad, he was about to agree. We had just told him that we were going to court, and he and his lawyer were discussing it."

"We were already there at that point, and Martin went into speak with them. Mark was about to make another big ol' mess for you."

"He was just trying to hurt you, Evie," Mom said.

"It doesn't matter," Grant cut in angrily. "There was no way I was giving him the chance to hurt you anymore. We made him an offer he couldn't refuse. He could fight the divorce and go to jail where a judge would still grant you the divorce, or he could sign the no-contest papers now."

"And?" Everyone looked at me except Grant.

"And what?" my dad asked.

I turned to Grant. "I know you better than that. You're an expert negotiator. It wasn't simply sign the papers, was it? It was sign the papers and something else. There was some other stipulation, wasn't there?"

Grant ran his hands through his messy hair. "Does it matter?"

"Yes," I said simply.

"What was it, Grant?" my sister said. When he didn't answer she tried the other two. "Dad? John? What were the other stipulations?"

"Sorry, man," John said to Grant. "She wears the pants in my house. Mark had to agree to enter a ninety-day treatment program, sell the house, and give you half of what was left prior to his credit card debt being paid."

"That doesn't sound so bad," my mom said, but I knew better. They weren't finished. Grant hadn't looked up since he last spoke.

"Tell me the rest."

"Jennifer is selling the house for you," Dad added. That explained her presence at the meeting.

"Keep going."

John was sipping his beer, ignoring my death glare. Dad found something interesting in the kitchen that he was staring at, and Grant hadn't looked up from his hands.

Grant finally spilled his guts. "I'm paying for his treatment program and for him to move to Florida with his mother. I purchased him a condo near her that he will be able to live in, because he signed an agreement never to contact you or your family again. If he contacts you he loses everything. The condo will not be transferred into his name for five years, so he can't sell it. If he chooses to move, he does so without financial support."

"You bought him a condo?" Jane screeched, and I sat dumbfounded.

"Yes, it's nothing extravagant, but it'll keep him out of Georgia and near his mother. The treatment center is only an hour away from her, so she will be able to visit. When he decides to move on or if he ever wants to buy it from me, I'll likely make money on the condo. It's in an up and coming area, and Mitchell Corp owns the company that owns the building anyway."

"I don't know what to say to that," my mom said more to herself than anything.

"Your dad also lined up a job for him with a construction crew. That will help him stay sober and give him some money," Grant added and nodded to my dad.

It was all too much to take in. Jane and Holly could have pressed charges, but they didn't because they knew that would upset me. I had put everyone in danger while I lived my five minutes of bliss with Grant in Seattle, and they had done all of this because of me. With the help of John and my dad, Grant made sure that my family was safe and Mark was taken care of and getting help.

The room stayed silent for a moment until my sister said, "Evie, say something."

I looked around the room with tears in my eyes, happy tears. I had never felt so loved as I did right then. They did everything to make sure what I wanted, happened. Grant made my wish from last night come true. I looked at him last. "Thank you," I said before I crawled in his lap to hug him.

I surprised him, but he automatically pulled me

to him and wrapped his arms around me. "You aren't mad?"

"No. You made everything I wanted actually happen. I wanted to be free and for my family to be safe, and I wanted Mark to get help and stay out of trouble. You guys made it happen, so thank you." I hugged him tightly.

"I told you I'd move mountains for you," he whispered in my ear.

"And you did. Thank you."

Just then the front door burst open and Holly's voice shouted, "I'm ready to celebrate." We all looked over at her in surprise, and her face dropped when her eyes met mine. "What happened? Why do you look like shit?"

I climbed off Grant and went to give her a hug. "Thanks, Holly. Nice to see you too."

"Why are you crying?" She looked at Jane and my mom. "Why are you two crying?"

Jane laughed. "These are good tears. We just had a moment. Everything's good."

Holly looked relieved. "Oh good! I brought champagne."

In that moment the tension broke, and I introduced Holly and Matt, her very apologetic fiancé, to Grant. As they chatted, I went over and hugged my dad and thanked him and did the same with John. My sister was right; I was lucky to have them.

"Dinner's ready," my mom called out, and we all piled in the dining room to eat a celebratory dinner, complete with a toast from my dad that had me teary-eyed and then laughing happily. That was my dad in a nutshell.

While Holly was busy grilling an amused Grant about what his intentions with me were, I noticed it was a little quiet for our usual dinners. "Where are the kids?" I asked, feeling bad it took me this long to realize they were missing.

"They are staying with John's parents tonight. John called them last night when he and Grant decided…well, you know."

I smiled to myself. "Yeah. I know." I slid my hand into Grant's, and he winked at me while he continued to pay attention to Holly's asinine questions.

After dinner, everyone was around the house talking. Grant and John were hanging out at the table with my dad. Holly, Matt, and Jane were talking in the kitchen with my mom, and I took the opportunity to sneak away for a minute.

"I'll be right back," I told Grant before I grabbed my purse and ran up to my room. I closed the door and pulled out my cell phone. The ringing on the other end made me nervous, but I knew I had to make the call.

"Hello."

"Mark?"

"What do you want, Evie?"

"I wanted to apologize. I didn't know they were going to do that, and I really do wish you all the best."

He let out a loud sigh. "You know what's crazy? I loved you. You were everything to me, and I wanted to be married to you forever, you know that?"

"I'm sorry," I whispered, still feeling guilty.

"You never felt that way about me. The way you looked at me in high school, I used to dream about it. It was like I was the best thing to happen to you. One day that look was gone…prom." The first time we had sex. "You never looked at me that way again, but you agreed to marry me, to spend your life with me, and now look."

"I know. I'm sorry."

"No, I'm sorry. If I had just waited, I would have gotten to see that look for the rest of my life. Now that guy who's sending me to rehab and putting me up in a condo near my Ma is going to see that look, and I get what?"

"You get a free condo and the help you need. I know it isn't what you want, but maybe with this fresh start, you can get everything you want. It just won't be with me."

"Maybe. I'm sorry about Jane and Holly and the texts. I don't know what got into me."

"I know that wasn't you. Deep down you're a good man, Mark. You just need to find that man again."

"Yeah. We'll see."

"Look, I have to go, but good luck in Florida."

"Good luck to you too." He paused. "Bye, Evie." He said the last two words in a whisper.

"Goodbye, Mark."

I hung up the phone and went back downstairs. Everyone was eating dessert and sitting where I left them. My mom gave me a bowl of strawberry shortcake, and I went over to sit next to Holly to spend time with her before I had to fly back to

Seattle to face the rest of my problems. For now, I just absorbed being around all the people who loved me the most.

Chapter 26

That night I took a long, hot shower—alone—and crawled into bed where Grant was waiting on me in just a pair of blue boxers. "Hey, baby."

I crawled right on top of him, so my forearms were resting on his chest. "Hey, handsome."

"You tired?"

"Nope. I took a nap on the bathroom floor." I smirked.

"Not funny." He smacked my butt.

I laughed. "My mom didn't think so either."

"You aren't upset with me, are you?" he asked as he ran his hands through my wet hair and down my back.

"How could I be? I wish you had included me, because I may have handled it a little differently, but you made everything I wanted happen. It wasn't perfect, but you did it for me, and for that I'm grateful."

"Grateful…hmmm…I didn't expect that."

"I need to tell you something."

His green eyes glittered in the light of my

bedside lamp. "You love me?"

"That too, but I have something else to tell you. Something you might not like," I warned him.

"Spill it, peach."

"I called Mark."

I could actually see his eyes darken as he tried to keep that maddeningly passive expression. "Why?"

"Because I felt bad about the way things were handled today. I don't agree with what he's done to hurt everyone, but I didn't like that we ganged up on him. I desperately needed him to let me go, and we forced his hand. It worked out for the best, but I would have never known had I not called him."

"As much as I hated you running out of the room, it was probably for the best. Things were not as simple as we made them sound, but maybe after he had some time to think about it, he felt more agreeable."

"I don't know. I think he knew he needed help, but he didn't know what to do. His friends are probably trying to fix it with getting him drunk and laid."

"Let's see if the second part of that works." He wiggled his eyebrows.

I slapped him and laughed. "Stop it. I'm being serious. This is hard. It's hard to not care about him, no matter how horrible he's been. I've known him since kindergarten."

"I know, babe, but you have to think the guy who was sitting in that room wasn't the kid you knew in school. You both have changed and need different things now. He knew he couldn't hold on to you, so he tried to take away your self-worth, so you wouldn't see how undeserving he is of you."

"You may be a little biased," I said with a small smile.

"Maybe, but it doesn't make it any less true. Here's what I need to know. Between finalizing your divorce and your phone call to Mark, did you get what you need to move on?"

I smiled widely at him. "I think so. Had I not talked to Mark tonight, I wouldn't have felt good about it, but he let me go. He said some things I needed to hear, and I reminded him I really only want good things for him. It was a good talk."

"Good." He splayed his hands flat on my back under my shirt. He seemed nervous. "What about us?"

"What about us? I told you I wasn't mad at you."

"I'm sure this is terrible timing, but I have to know if you think we have a future together now that you can move on from this."

"Until I got off that bathroom floor, today was as far into the future that I could see."

"And now?"

"I don't know. I know how I feel about you, but I'm not sure if I'm ready to look ahead yet." Grant nodded his agreement, but I could see the disappointment all over his face. "It doesn't mean there isn't a future, but I just can't make any plans yet. I'm still wrapping my head around today. Remember we've only been together a month. My life was on pause until I met you, and you like it on fast-forward. I'm not there yet. Let's just take it one day at a time, okay?"

"Whatever you need, baby." I knew it wasn't

what he wanted to hear, but I didn't have anything to offer yet. A part of me felt like it was unfair of him to even bring up our future on the same day I finalized my divorce, which was the reason I didn't want him here for that. Had he not been there, though, who knows what would have happened? I needed a change of topic before my brain ran away with my reason.

I started pressing kisses to Grant's chest. "What about what you need? Today has been all about me. How about we make tonight about you?" I started trailing kisses lower and lower.

"I like the way you think, gorgeous." By the time I lowered his boxers to continue my trail of kisses, he was hard and perfect. He pressed his hips up as I continued to tease him. "Baby," he groaned.

"What do you need, Grant? You never told me."

"Mouth. Now," he demanded.

"Your wish is my command, Prince Charming."

***

Grant woke me up the next morning by running his fingers up and down my back. I found myself using his chest as a pillow and our legs entwined. "Good morning," I said without lifting my head.

"Good morning, peach. You ready to go home?"

"Ugh!" I groaned and rolled over. "Go back to Seattle and face reality? No. Let's stay here. I hired you a cook and a housekeeper and a builder."

He climbed on top of me. "Let's see what your cook and builder think when I make you scream my name like you have a tendency of doing when I'm inside of you."

"Hey! I've been quiet since we've been here," I reminded him.

"Because I covered your mouth with mine. I can't do that if it's my mouth making you scream, now can I?" He started kissing his way down my body. I squirmed with need.

"Okay, okay," I squealed and squirmed away. "Let's go home."

He pulled me back to him and looked down at me, smiling sweetly.

"What?" I asked.

"You called Seattle 'home.'"

"It's where I live, silly."

"That's all?"

"It is also where my charming boyfriend lives, and I couldn't stand to not be where he is."

"Better."

We both climbed out of bed and helped each other shower before we repacked and headed downstairs for breakfast. My mom was in her spot, and Dad was actually still in his seat reading the paper. He set it down when we walked in the room.

"How ya feelin' today, peanut?"

I walked over and gave him a hug and a kiss on his cheek. "Like a million pounds has been lifted off my shoulders. Thank you again for what you did."

"No problem, kiddo. You guys flying out today?"

"Yes, Grant has a private jet on call." I rolled my eyes and scoffed. "Rich people." Grant pinched my side, making me squirm away.

"Must be nice," Dad said. "I'm not even allowed

to buy a boat. Women just don't get it, do they, Grant?"

Grant laughed and tapped me on the nose. "No sir, they don't."

"Oh jeez. Not the boat thing again," Mom chimed in.

As my parents argued about a boat, Grant and I happily ate the bacon, eggs, and toast my mom made us. Dad kept trying to get Grant on his side, but he was smart enough to say he wasn't getting in the middle. Wise man.

After a long goodbye where both parents told me how much they loved Grant—yet another thing no one ever did with Mark—Grant and I were on our way to the airport. Grant talked about how much he loved my family on the drive down there and asked questions about everyone as if he hadn't learned enough about them. It felt really nice to have everyone connected like that, and I sighed happily as we held hands and talked.

We came back to my apartment where everything was just how I left it. It felt nice, homey. I unpacked while Grant made phone calls letting people know he was back in town and would be back in the office tomorrow. I would be filling out online applications tomorrow for a new job. I hadn't had much time to think about what I would do if I didn't find one, but tomorrow I would have to deal with it. Right then I just wanted to enjoy the time with my man who promised he would spend the afternoon with me and more.

Epilogue

"Why do I still work for you, Eve?" Scott asked as he gave me a plate of saltines and a glass of ginger ale.

"Because I love you and your risotto," I told him. Tonight was a huge New Year's Eve ball Mitchell Corp was hosting, and I was a nervous wreck. My stomach had been a mess for the last few days, and I was starting to wonder if I would ever keep any food down. My family was in town, and my mom insisted I try crackers and ginger ale because I hadn't kept anything down in two days. I felt fine most of the day, but the second I was around food, I was running to the bathroom.

"Then quit throwing everything up."

"Sorry. I'll try to control it better." I smirked as I took a bite of another cracker and then laid my head back down on the island in our beautiful new kitchen. Grant surprised me one night with a wonderful date and an even better house, large enough for us to grow into and have my family visit. It was ridiculously extravagant and homey, a perfect combination of Grant and me. That was the night I finally admitted I saw no other future than one that included Grant. We had lived in the giant French-style estate for a little over two months since then, and I couldn't have been more excited to spend my first Seattle Christmas here. He flew my whole family out to surprise me, and my mom and Jane had been helping me prepare for tonight's party ever since.

Grant came into the kitchen and found me with my face on the cold granite. "Not feeling well again, baby?" he asked as he kissed my upturned cheek and rubbed my back.

I didn't even lift my head off the counter when I spoke. "Just peachy. I can't wait for tonight to be over with."

"You know everything will go perfectly."

"No, I know this is the first event I have planned for your mother. She just started actually trusting me. I don't want to go back to her bad side because I ruined her biggest event of the year."

"Won't happen. She adores you. Besides, tonight you will be there as my date, not to work. You hired Michelle to make sure the event runs smoothly, remember?"

"Doesn't mean I'm not worried about it."

"Good morning," my mother said cheerfully as she entered the room. She looked fresh as a daisy, which just made me feel worse. "Peanut, I need your help with something. I can't decide which dress to wear."

"Mom, we already picked the ice blue one. Quit changing your mind."

"Could you just come and look one more time, please?"

"Fine," I grumbled as I climbed off my stool.

Grant pulled me back to him. "Be nice," he reminded me before he kissed my neck. "I love you."

I turned around and hugged him. I needed to go back to bed and spend the day alone with him. He had been getting up early to take care of some things in his office before anyone woke up, so he could hang out with everyone during the day. I missed my mornings with him.

When he let me go, I followed my mom to the guest suite upstairs where they were staying. Jane was already in the room waiting on us. She was dressed too. What was with people getting up and dressed so early?

I collapsed on the bed. "Morning, peanut. Feeling better?"

"Nope. The crackers won't kick in for another five or so minutes. Little bastards. The Pepto didn't help either. I just threw that up."

"I think I have something that might help you," Jane said and handed me a plastic bag from a pharmacy.

"What is it?"

"Open it," my mom encouraged.

"You want me to take a pregnancy test? I'm not pregnant. I'm on birth control for one thing. For another, I can't get prego, remember?"

"You were on antibiotics last month. Those negate the helpful effects of birth control. That's how you came into existence," my mom helpfully informed me.

"Humor us," Jane said as she pulled me off the bed and guided me to the bathroom.

I did my business and set the tests on the counter while I washed my hands. I hated taking these things because it was so depressing when it read "not pregnant" after the two minutes or however long. I didn't even look at them. I opened the door and went back to my spot on the bed. I may have also been a little tired and cranky.

My mom went in and picked up the test. "Hmmm…just as I suspected."

"What?" I asked.

Jane was smiling and suddenly bouncing around clapping her hands. "You're pregnant!"

"What?" Then I followed up with a very confused, "How?"

Jane smiled. "Well, when a man and a woman love each other very much…"

"Shut up. You know what I mean."

"Maybe you and Grant are just a better fit. Oh my god. You have to go tell him. He'll be thrilled. This goes right along with your warp speed relationship."

I ignored my sister's comment while I let the results settle in my brain. "Oh my god, I'm going to have a baby!" Nausea was forgotten and excitement took over in my belly.

We celebrated for a few minutes more before we calmed down and joined the boys. Dad, John, Grant, and Scott were playing with the kids in the basement when we joined them, but I needed some time alone with Grant. I had been missing him, and for the first time in days my stomach didn't hurt.

I excused us and dragged him up to our little private oasis in our bedroom. "Baby, what's going on?"

"Nothing. I just miss you. We haven't had very much alone time since my family came into town, and I wanted an hour with my man before I spend the rest of the day preparing for a night with hundreds of people."

He wrapped his arms around me. "Why didn't you just say so? What did you have in mind?"

"Whatever you want. I just wanted you, now you get what you want." I ran my hands down his body before stopping to unbutton his jeans.

"I take it you're feeling better?"

"Much better."

"I'm glad to hear that, my gorgeous Georgia peach, because I have been missing you too." He lifted me up, and I wrapped my legs around his waist while he carried me over to our huge bed. The next hour before I had to get ready to go up to the venue was well spent in that huge bed.

At the venue I made sure everything was set and ready to go before I rushed home to get dressed. I refused the help of a glam team Grant always offered because I still didn't like the idea of wasting money on something so frivolous. Rihanna was singing about wanting him to stay, and I was stepping into my shoes, dressed in my black strapless bra, matching panties, and my garter belt with my thigh highs on when Grant walked in to check on me.

He stopped dead in his tracks and stared at me

after he closed the door to the bedroom. Yeah, that made me feel good. "Damn, baby, forget the party. We'll stay here since you dressed up just for me." He was dressed in his Burberry tux with a light pink bowtie. My black dress also had a pink sash to match his bowtie. The pink was in support of breast cancer research, which was the theme of the night since we had just found out Iris had been diagnosed with it after they found a lump in a routine mammogram last month. She was handling it like only Iris could, even though she would be undergoing a double mastectomy in just two short weeks. Impressed by her strength, I made sure this night would honor her.

"What is it you need, handsome?"

"I need you to hurry up. Both of our families are here and are waiting to toast to our evening."

I stepped into my fitted black velvet gown and turned so Grant could zip me into it. Once he buttoned the top button, I tied the pink satin sash around my waist into a nice bow. I put on the diamond teardrop earrings and the matching necklace Grant had given me for Christmas. They were on full display with my hair up in a smooth chignon and my lips a dusty rose color.

"Okay. I'm ready."

"You look amazing, baby. I can't wait to walk down that pink carpet with you on my arm." Yes, I really did get a pink carpet instead of a red one. We were supporting breast cancer awareness this New Year's Eve in every way possible.

We walked downstairs together only to be greeted by my entire family including Holly and

Matt, Grant's entire family including a pregnant and now showing Daphne, Maddox and Nolan—yes together, they were telling, or showing rather, his dad tonight—Tara and Daniel, and Scott and Lana, who agreed to watch all seven kids. With Jane's four and Grace's three, all I could say was bless Scott and Lana. I didn't think they knew what they signed up for when they agreed to babysit.

After exchanging greetings and pleasantries with everyone, Harrison tapped the side of his glass. "I'm happy to be here with everyone tonight. This year has been interesting to say the least. We have had some highs, like finally welcoming Eve into our world, and some lows, like finding out my wife has the fight of her life in front of her, but tonight I look around and find myself grateful for every moment. My children couldn't be happier, and that alone makes me the luckiest man in the world. Grant, I believe you wanted to say something?"

Grant smiled and moved from behind me to my side. "I agree with my dad that tonight is a special night. This is the first time everyone most important to Eve and me is here, in the same state, in the same house, in the same room." Grant turned to me. "With that being said, everyone in this room knows how much I love you. I've been waiting my whole life for you, and you have given me just about everything I could have ever wanted." He slid down on one knee and pulled a small box out of his pocket. My hands immediately went to cover the gasp that came out of my mouth while tears flooded my eyes. "Evelyn Elaine Bryant, you are the other half to my soul, and I wouldn't be complete without you. Please say you'll marry me and spend the rest of your life completing mine."

I nodded before I whispered, "Yes." A whisper was all I could manage through the flood of emotions coursing through me. He slid the ring on my finger and stood to hug me.

While he held me, everyone started surrounding us to congratulate us, even the kids. Apparently everyone was in on his proposal, but Grant had always been the go big or go home kind of guy. I hugged every person there before it was time for us to pile into the limos.

In our limo, Holly and Nolan also became best friends, and she told me later she was okay with him as her local replacement. Maddox was a nervous wreck about showing up with Nolan on his arm, so I grabbed and held the hand that wasn't resting on Nolan's knee. He looked at me with grateful eyes and squeezed my hand, because he knew I was telling him that we were right there if he needed us. Grant didn't make a joke like he normally would, because he knew tonight was a big deal for his friend.

I rested my left hand on Grant's knee and watched as my new engagement ring sparkled in the lights. It was a stunning, classic Harry Winston ring with an oval cut diamond and tapered baguettes set in platinum. It must have been around four or five carats because it was huge, but this was Grant we were talking about. He didn't know any other way. Grant's hand covered mine as he thoughtlessly twisted the ring on my finger while he talked to John and Jane. Moments like this where the wonderful from my old life entwined with my new life still made me giddy.

Thinking about it made me tear up a little—damn pregnancy hormones—and of course someone noticed.

"Eve, you okay?" Tara asked.

I smiled. "I'm great." I played the tears off by wiggling my ring finger for her, and Grant wrapped his arm around me and kissed my head. I was deliriously happy in that limo on the way to the party.

The party was perfect. The pink carpet was fun for people, and there were reporters lining the carpet trying to catch the famous people we had invited. Grant and I both made a short statement about the event for the papers, because we wanted people to know how they could donate to the cause.

Once inside, the room looked like a dream. There was white and silver everywhere, except the flowers were light pink. People were dressed in black with some kind of pink somewhere on their body—my idea. People were really creative with hats and shoes and jewelry. It was really fun to see how everyone incorporated their pink into their formalwear.

Before dinner Harrison made a speech, sharing the news of Iris's diagnosis with everyone there. He thanked me for making the event happen and thanked everyone for coming. It was a really nice speech. Dinner was good, but all it took was one whiff of the fish to have me out of the seat and running to the bathroom. Jane followed me, knowing exactly what was going on. I rinsed my mouth and ate a few crackers she had brought with her. After chewing some gum, I was back at the table like nothing happened. Jane sent me a conspiratorial wink when I was finally able to eat my filet mignon.

After dinner, everyone drank and donated money while they danced the night away. Our large group stuck close together because we knew we only had a limited time before half of us were on a plane headed for the other side of the country.

Maddox and Nolan were dancing together because Maddox's dad took the news surprisingly well when he simply said, "About time you admitted it," and shook both guys' hands.

Daphne rested at the table with Iris and Grace while their husbands enjoyed time together.

The rest of us enjoyed the music and the dance floor, trading partners as we went because it is a rare day that we are all together. I was dancing with my dad when Grant came over to tell us midnight was drawing closer. "Mind if I steal her from you?" he asked my dad.

Dad smiled. "No son, she's all yours."

Grant pulled me into his arms to dance to "At Last" by Etta James. "I have barely gotten a chance to dance with my fiancée. She's a popular girl."

"I'm sorry. Are you missing the hordes of women vying for your attention?"

"Not even a little bit." He gave me a quick kiss.

I wanted to share my big news with Grant, and this was our moment. It was right before midnight, and everything was perfect. I wanted him to share this moment with me whether the doctor had confirmed it or not. "You said I gave you just about everything you want when you proposed. What else do you want in our life?"

"One day I want to fill our house with babies and watch you feed them, bathe them, kiss them good night, and love them. I want everything with you, you know that."

"What if one day was sooner than you think? Would that be okay with you?"

"Baby, what are you trying to tell me?"

"I think we need to get married sooner rather than later, because in a few months I'll be showing like Daphne."

"You're—" His shock was apparent.

"I'm pregnant. That's why I've been so sick. My mom and sister figured it out before me and made me take a test this morning."

"We're going to have a baby!" He was smiling wide now.

"We're going to have a baby," I confirmed. He picked me up and twirled me around just as I heard everyone counting down. On the stroke of midnight Grant's lips touched mine, and they didn't stop for the entire duration of "Auld Lang Syne."

New Year.

New life.

All thanks to my CEO.

The End

Acknowledgements

Thank you to the readers for exploring Eve's world. She wouldn't leave me alone until I found her a man worthy of her heart. I can't wait to share more with you in the rest of this series. Kitty is next. She just couldn't let Eve have all the fun.

I don't know what I would do without my Twitter buddy and critique partner, Ryan Ringbloom, who was the first to read the very rough copy of this novel. You are an amazing writer, reader, and friend. Thank you so much for all of your websites, advice, humor, and writing wisdom.

Much love to Sarah Cosey who lets me bounce ideas off of her daily. If I didn't have someone who lets me pretend my imaginary friends were real, I might actually go crazy. Thanks for keeping me sane and giving me writing wisdom along with a better understanding of the strange people that exist only in my head.

I do not write in correct grammar the first five times I go through the story, so my writing would be impossible to share without the help of Karla Reed. Everyone needs a friend like you, but your editing skills, while priceless, are only a small part of why I am thankful to have you in my life. Thank you for everything.

I have recently joined the Limitless family, and I am loving every second of being in this supportive group. Thank you to the Limitless team who turned Whole Life Re-Do into The CEO.

Last but not least, I am so grateful to all the bloggers that help sell my books, but Debra with

The Book Enthusiast Promotions is my go-to girl. She's the one who helps guide me on this journey of self-promoting my books.

About The Author

Shealy James is a Georgia native who teaches math by day and writes romance at night. As an avid reader, expert on romantic comedy films, and lover of realistic characters who could be her best friends if only they really existed, Shealy appreciates when humor mixes with drama to guide her imaginary friends to their happy endings. And there must always be a happy ending. Shealy openly eats enough candy to feed a small nation, drinks sweet tea by the gallon, hopes to hit 10,000 steps each day, and lives every day with her amazing daughter.

Facebook:
https://www.facebook.com/shealyjamesbooks

Twitter:
https://twitter.com/ShealyJames

Google plus:
https://plus.google.com/106403920973921051995/posts

Goodreads:
https://www.goodreads.com/author/show/7280344.Shealy_James

Website:
http://www.shealyjamesbooks.com/find-me-in-manhattan/

www.ingramcontent.com/pod-product-compliance
Lightning Source LLC
Chambersburg PA
CBHW030512120726
47904CB00005B/1434